The Hilo Hustle

by

Tom Bradley Jr.

For the love of beer.

Also by the same author:
THE KONA SHUFFLE

Find out more at **AuthorTomBradley.com**.

Mahalo to:

Faith Williams with The Atwater Group for her invaluable editing and proofreading prowess;

Deborah Bradseth with Tugboat Design for creating yet another colorful, eye-catching cover; and

Lehua Parker, author and beta reader extraordinaire, without whom my characters—and by extension, me—would have mangled that otherwise wonderful, complicated, and endearing local patois known as Hawaiian pidgin.

This is a work of fiction. Any resemblance of characters to actual persons, living, dead, cryogenically frozen, or held in some state of suspended animation, is purely coincidental. And also quite unlikely.

The Hilo Hustle
Copyright © 2014 by Tom Bradley Jr.

Cover design © Tugboat Design

Chapter One:
The Floater

Before dawn on Monday, the body of a barefoot man in a blue tee-shirt and khaki cargo shorts washed ashore on a beach in Hilo, Hawaii.

A triathlete in training who was out for a morning run found the corpse, face down in the sand at Bayfront Park, just a few yards from a row of outrigger canoes. He took out his cell and called the police—after he tweeted a selfie with the stiff to all three hundred forty-six of his followers.

***

Sitting on the dusty ground under a tree on Coconut Island Park, as families and kids cavorted around her, Noelani B. Lee threw occasional glances at a couple standing a couple dozen feet away. The man wore jeans shorts and a red tee-shirt with the sleeves cut off; the woman wore green painters' pants and an orange button-up blouse.

Noelani watched them play grab-ass for the world to see, unclenching only when some children dashed past them. Then the man and woman sat on a bench overlooking the bay. The man lit a cigarette, and then he and the woman chatted.

As they did, Noelani looked up at the cloudless blue Hawaiian sky. She frowned.

Four straight days of uninterrupted sunshine with no end in sight.

Noelani hoped for rain. She needed it.

She then looked through the viewfinder of her Canon with the telephoto lens and squeezed off several shots of the man and woman talking. Which was all they did.

Noelani's hopes for precipitation rose on Wednesday evening when word spread about a storm moving down from the Aleutians; forecasters predicted it would drench the Big Island's windward side, perhaps nonstop, for several days.

Hearing this welcome news, Noelani selected a spot in her front yard where she could sit and meditate amid the refreshing and mind-clearing raindrops.

All this aridity was out of place in Hilo, where rainfalls exceed well more than one hundred inches in a normal a year. I might as well be back in Vegas.

But the sun rose bright on Monday morning. The huge Alaskan storm had changed course and was bearing down on Northern California.

She watched the man toss the cigarette aside and rub his hand on the woman's right thigh. She leaned in close, nibbling his earlobe.

Noelani raised her camera and focused. "Come on," she whispered. "Give her a smooch. Pretty please?"

The man and woman pressed their foreheads together.

"With lots of tongue."

The couple locked lips. Noelani fired off dozens of shots as the woman's hands fumbled around under his muscle shirt and the man unbuttoned her blouse. Noelani kept the shutter squeezed until she caught a glimpse of braless boobs, at which point she lowered the camera, closed her eyes, and shook her head.

Hoping to avoid further retinal damage and figuring she had all the evidence she needed for her client, Noelani slipped the camera in her canvas tote bag. She got up, dusted herself off, and walked toward the footbridge that connected the little island with a parking lot on Kelipio Place.

As she did, she took out her cell phone. "Hello, Mrs. Medeiros? Noelani Lee… Yes, it sure is a beautiful day… I was wondering, do you have time to meet today?… Well, I have something—"

A quarter of the way across the span, a uniformed police officer and a plainclothes detective in a lime green, short-sleeved shirt and khakis, with a badge clipped to his belt, blocked her path.

"Um, Mrs. Medeiros, I need to call you back." She disconnected the call.

"Miss Lee," said the plainclothes cop.

"You're Detective Ahuna," she said. "I remember you. You used to work over in Kona, right?"

"I transferred to South Hilo a few months back. My father, it's—well, his memory's going downhill in a hurry. Figured I'd better be closer to him so he doesn't forget his grandkids."

Noelani blinked at the uniformed cop, who stared at her but said nothing more. "I'm so sorry."

"Miss Lee," Detective Ahuna said, "I'm wondering what you can tell me about a gentleman named Milton Nihoa. He's a licensed private investigator, like you, correct?"

"Like me?" Noelani laughed. "In name only, and he's not a gentleman. If you want the truth, Milt gives all of us PIs a bad name."

"How so?"

"Because he's a client-poaching, lazy, lying, slimy, cowardly weasel."

"Hmm." Detective Ahuna said, "Strong words."

Noelani held up her hands. "I know, you cops think we're all of those things and then some. Trust me, I've heard it all."

"Well, I'm not one to judge, Miss Lee."

"But Milt's the worst of the worst. Ask anyone."

"We will."

"So what did he do now? Take payment for services not rendered? If he did, it wouldn't—"

"Miss Lee, I understand, at a seminar last month on Maui, you and Mr. Nihoa butted heads."

Noelani rolled her eyes. "That's putting it mildly."

"I heard from various sources that during this confrontation, you threatened to rip out his lungs."

"If it would guarantee he'd stop breathing, why not?"

"Uh huh."

After a moment, Noelani said, "Detective, I'd love to chat about the jerk all day if I could, but I'm on my way to meet a client."

The uniformed cop stepped forward and positioned himself next to Noelani. He towered a good foot over her five-foot-eight frame.

"Miss Lee," Detective Ahuna said, "I'm afraid you need to put your business on hold."

Chapter Two:
The Person of Interest

In an interrogation room at the police station on Kapiolani Street, Detective Ahuna removed a photograph from a folder and pushed it across the table.

Noelani Lee studied the picture of Milt Nihoa's shoeless body prone on a beach, just as Detective Ahuna told her he'd been found. He wore tan shorts and a blue tee-shirt with a "7" printed on the back.

The detective produced another photo—Milt on his back, his eyes open and glassy, mouth agape. Except for a bruise above his left eye, Noelani saw no other signs of trauma—no bullet wounds, nothing obvious to indicate he'd been stabbed or strangled. There was no blood on him or his clothing, though she figured if he'd been in the water for a while, any traces would have washed away.

She read white script lettering on his shirt: Wally's Dive Inn.

"The few friends of his we could find told us Mr. Nihoa couldn't swim," Detective Ahuna said. He picked up a pen from the table and clicked it several times.

Noelani ignored the detective's fidgeting. "Oh, so he drowned."

"We haven't officially determined cause of death," he said. "But I wonder if you can help us figure out what a man who can't swim would be doing in Hilo Bay, fully clothed, and without shoes."

"You asked me the same question five minutes ago," she said. "And like I said, I don't know, unless he was drunk and fell in or something."

Detective Ahuna sniffed. "Earlier, you said the last time you saw Mr. Nihoa alive was, what, about a week ago?"

"Yes," Noelani said. "I ran into him when I was grocery shopping."

"At the KTA store on Holomua Street."

"Yes."

"Do you always shop there?"

"I was driving by and remembered I needed a few things."

"Did Mr. Nihoa shop there on a regular basis?"

"I wouldn't know. I only saw him there the one time."

Detective Ahuna clicked the pen once, twice, three times. "When you saw Mr. Nihoa at the KTA store, what did you say to him?"

"Nothing," Noelani said, staring at the pen.

"Nothing? Not even a polite 'hello'?"

"I saw him coming toward me, so I turned around and went down the next aisle."

"Why?"

"To avoid another embarrassing scene in public."

"You mentioned," Detective Ahuna said, "Mr. Nihoa had a drinking problem."

"Milt could put it away, yes," she said. "He didn't like me anyway, but when he was loaded, he was especially nasty."

"When you saw him at the KTA market, could you tell if he'd been drinking?"

"Trust me, I didn't get close enough to get a whiff."

"And you haven't run into him since, by accident or otherwise."

"Detective, I did everything I could to avoid Milt," Noelani said. "I didn't want anything to do with him, and"—she pointed at the photos—"I definitely didn't have anything to do with this."

Detective Ahuna waited a beat. "Where were you last night?"

"I was working."

"In the middle of the night?"

Noelani said, "See, Detective, I hardly ever sleep when I'm working a case. And since Mrs. Medeiros hired me to follow her husband, I've had maybe four hours all week."

"Help me out here, since I don't know how these things work with you people," Detective Ahuna said. "How long does it usually take to prove a husband's messing around?"

"It depends," she said. "With Mr. Medeiros, it was several days and nights. You see, Mrs. Medeiros suspected her husband was seeing his mistress on his way home from work—he's a graveyard shift security guard at a petroleum company down on

Kukila Street."

"Okay, I know where you're talking about."

"She figured it was his only opportunity to fool around, since she was home three days a week and he crashed well until late in the afternoon on those days. So, I started following him home—"

"Wait a minute," Detective Ahuna said. "You told me you were up all night doing computer searches and stuff."

"It depends on the situation," Noelani said. "During my investigation, I observed Mr. Medeiros never visited another woman's house. But last night—well, after seven this morning, when he got off work, he stopped at a house over by the municipal golf course and left a note on the door."

Two pen clicks. "He didn't knock or try to go inside?"

"No. See, he'd written instructions for this woman to meet him today on Coconut Island. I took a picture of the note—it's still on my phone if you need proof—and sent it to Mrs. Medeiros. I knew she was working today, which meant he'd have plenty of time on his hands."

"Hmm."

"Turns out he had other things in his hands."

"You're certain you went nowhere else last night."

"All I did was follow Mr. Medeiros," Noelani said, "then I went home and got my camera and prepared to catch him in the park today."

"You know," Detective Ahuna said, "left unchecked, these odd nocturnal work habits of yours can be unhealthy."

"I just happen to do my best thinking late at night."

"Sometimes when people are sleep deprived, they forget things they've done, or they just do things by rote, almost like they're unconscious of what they're doing." Detective Ahuna sat forward. "They might go on a long walk or go for a drive and not remember anything about it when they wake up. Like it never happened."

"Detective, I think you're confusing sleep deprivation with sleepwalking," Noelani said. "The truth is, when I'm not working a case, I'm out like a light."

"And how often is that?"

She smiled. "Not very."

"So you can swear for a fact you weren't anywhere near Milt Nihoa last night, or before dawn this morning?"

"Well, I don't have anyone who can corroborate my story except my cousin, Wanda," Noelani said. "She came over with Thai take-out around seven thirty and stayed till ten before she went home."

"We've already spoken with Miss Fong, which still leaves plenty of time unaccounted for."

Noelani rubbed her temples in a futile attempt to tame an oncoming headache.

Detective Ahuna asked her to provide details about her encounter with Milt Nihoa on Maui.

She said it happened around noon on the second day of the conference. Milt, reeking of cheap whiskey, accosted her and loudly berated her about a case she'd handed off to him several weeks previously.

"At the time," she said, "I had a full plate and couldn't give it—the case—all the attention it needed."

"What was the case?"

"There was this moke who fell way behind on his child support. Milt was between jobs, so I did the courteous thing and asked him if he wanted to take it. He did, but he bungled it huge and turned around and blamed me."

"Just so I have this straight," Detective Ahuna said. "You passed a paying client along to a man with whom you had a mutual dislike."

"Like I said, I was quite busy, and I was just trying to be nice," Noelani said. "Besides, Milt had moments when he could be human, when he was sober."

"All right. So why did he blame you for messing it up?"

"He told the client, this guy's ex-wife, it was my fault she'd never see any money the baby-daddy owed her, because he couldn't read my handwritten notes." Noelani took a deep breath. "I said I also typed them up, but he claimed they were missing from the file. So I told him if he'd lay off the booze for a change and get off his lazy butt, he could do his job in a professional manner. Then he called me a 'bitch' and a 'titless dyke.'"

Detective Ahuna glanced at her flat chest. "Are you a lesbian, Miss Lee?"

Noelani waited a beat. "No, so don't get your hopes up."

"Just clarifying, in case you turned down Milt's advances somewhere in the past and he took it personally."

"If he even so much as thought of it, I'd have castrated him." She felt a lump in her throat. "What I meant—never mind."

She watched the corners of Detective Ahuna's mouth turn upward. "Tell me what happened next at the conference."

Noelani said, "We started going at it pretty loud with all kinds of name-calling. It was ugly. Next thing I knew, hotel security's breaking us up."

"And they kicked you both out."

"They invited us to leave. But what upset me more than anything was it happened right before I was supposed to give my presentation on new advances in audio surveillance technology."

"Huh." Detective Ahuna rubbed his palms together. "You, uh, happen to have your presentation on disk?"

"I can burn you a copy."

They sat in silence for several seconds. Then Detective Ahuna asked whether she knew if Milt had other enemies.

Noelani said, "Only if you count every other PI in the state and a bunch on the West Coast."

Detective Ahuna clicked his pen twice. "Miss Lee, I'll have a uniform give you a ride to your car."

Noelani hesitated, and then said, "We're done?"

"I also suggest," he said, as he rose from his seat, "you stay away from the Nihoa investigation. We don't need you sticking your nose in it. I'm sure you understand why."

Noelani stood. "I do."

"But if you hear anything out there, I'm the first and only person you call." He handed her a card. "And one more thing, please."

"What?"

"Do the world and yourself a favor and get a decent night's sleep."

As she slid in behind the wheel of her white Nissan Sentra, Noelani noticed she had a voicemail on her cell.

Her cousin, Wanda Fong: "Noe, what's going on? The cops were here asking questions. Are you okay? What's this about the bruddah they found on the beach? Cuz, I'm all worried about you, like big time. Call me."

Noelani arrived at her tiny house on Iwalani Street a few minutes after five o'clock. Wanda greeted her at the door.

"Where you been, Noe?" Wanda held a stack of papers in her hand. Noelani recognized them as overdue bills and unmailed invoices. "I'm sitting here doing your books when these cops come and start asking questions about you and stuff."

Noelani dropped her tote bag on the sofa. "What kinds of questions?"

"Well, where you were and about the dead dude on the beach. Like I know anything about him, but they think you do."

Noelani passed through the living room and went down the hall to her bedroom, Wanda following in her wake. She opened her closet door, and then knelt and opened a safe, on the floor. She took her gun from her waistband, stowed it, and shut and locked the safe. "Sweetie, I spoke with the police. It's really just a misunderstanding."

Wanda said, "Cuz, I don't like being all caught up in the middle of your work stuff, especially since I'm already freaking out with your finances a total mess."

Noelani shut the closet, then, Wanda following behind, retraced her steps from the bedroom, through the living room, to the kitchen. She found Master Po, her flame-point Himalayan, sitting on the kitchen counter, eating granola from a knocked-over cereal box. "At least it's not bran flakes this time."

"Noe," Wanda said, "can we talk about your books?"

Noelani smiled at her younger, shorter, and much rounder cousin. "Wanda, I know things are a little messed up."

"You got more money going out than coming in and you take way too many pro boney cases, which makes it worse."

Wanda never had formal training in finance or accounting.

But she developed a knack for balancing the books and making sure the bills were paid on time while working as a receptionist for a group of doctors in Las Vegas. She quit the job shortly after divorcing her adulterous bartender husband, which, combined with intense homesickness, induced a move back to her native Big Island.

"Sweetie," Noelani said, "I appreciate you doing this for me, but it's always worse before it gets better." Noelani neglected to tell Wanda she still had a large reserve of cash in a secret savings account, money remaining from a hush-money tender she received in exchange for not spilling the beans about a sexual assault against her in Las Vegas several years earlier. The incident led her to relocate to Hilo and launch her career as a PI.

"Well," Wanda said, "you always come out ahead somehow, but I just wanted to let you know we ought to get these invoices out like now."

"A lot of those clients can't afford to pay me."

"Noe, be careful, or you'll wind up becoming a cliché."

Exhausted from a sleepless night and a long day, Noelani changed the subject. "Are you hungry?" She opened her fridge. "I have leftover Thai from last night." She removed two foam containers, one half-filled with khanom chin namya—rice noodles swimming in fish sauce—and the other about a third full of kai yang, a grilled chicken dish. Noelani heated each container in her microwave, and then the cousins sat at the kitchen table.

Wanda took a bite of chicken. "So the cops gave you the third degree?"

"It wasn't so bad. I know the lead detective."

"Is he cute?"

"He's married."

"You didn't answer the question."

"He's a handsome married man who has about fourteen years on me." Noelani wrapped noodles around a fork—owing to her clumsiness with chopsticks, despite her mixed Korean, Chinese, Japanese, and native Hawaiian heritage—and slurped them up.

Wanda said, "So you're gonna try and figure out how the

dude on the beach drowned, huh?"

"The cops told me to stay away from it. Besides the fact I really don't want to look into it."

"I dunno, Noe. Big time case like that? You figure out what happened to the bruddah, I bet you'd get some serious paying clients."

"The man drowned. End of story." Noelani ate more noodles. "I'll stick with philandering husbands and other cheats and scoundrels, thank you very much."

Wanda, her mouth full, said, "You're totally dodging the money thing on me."

"Yes, I am. But I appreciate your help. You know I can barely balance a checkbook."

The cousins finished their dinner, after which Wanda said she'd pray for a paying client to come Noelani's way. Noelani, an agnostic, nonetheless thanked Wanda for her spiritual concern and said she'd review her cousin's notes on her business finances. Then Wanda said she had laundry to finish at home.

After she left, Noelani checked her answering machine. There was one message, from a woman: "Hello, my name is Cinnamon—spelled C-Y-N-A-M-I-N—Allgood, and I need your help." Noelani called her back on her smart phone.

"Aloha, is this Cynamin Allgood?"

"It sure is, and who is this I'm talking to?"

"This is N. B. Lee returning your call."

"Oh hey, thanks for getting back to me so soon, hon," Cynamin Allgood said. "Look, I'd love to meet with you but tonight isn't good since the natural light's getting bad."

Noelani looked out her front, west-facing window. There were still a couple of hours left until the sun would set over Mauna Kea. "The light?"

"We'd prefer nice, early morning light from the east for a good shot."

We? Noelani stared at the receiver for a moment. "Oh. Okay."

"If you can—do you know the little jetty in the bay with the park benches on it, across from Lili'uokalani Gardens?"

"I'm sure I can find it."

"Great," Cynamin said. "Meet me there at eight tomorrow morning. If it's sunny again, and from what I hear it's supposed to be another gorgeous day, the producer said we'll have fantastic views of the bay in the background."

Views? "Producer?"

"Don't you worry none, though. He may have the title but everyone knows, I run the show."

Noelani closed her eyes. She felt a headache coming on. "Miss Allgood, I'm a little confused here. What is it you're asking me to do?"

"I need your help, especially since..."

Noelani waited a beat. "Miss Allgood, what's wrong? Are you in trouble?"

"You heard about the dead man they found on the beach this morning?"

"I wish I didn't know as much as I do, but, yes. Why?"

"Miss Lee," Cynamin said, "he was working for me."

Chapter Three:
The Rude Awakening

Tuesday morning, Noelani Lee snapped awake and looked at her alarm clock: six twenty-three in the morning.

Master Po, on a pillow next to her, purred and whipped his fluffy tail.

"I know. Food."

Noelani rolled from under the covers, sat on the edge of the bed, and ran a hand through her hair. She tried to remember what time she crashed, sometime after Wanda went home. Maybe eight thirty?

She rose and trudged to the kitchen. She opened a can of cat food and set it on the floor. Master Po dove in as if it were his last meal. Then she filled a coffee mug with tap water and nuked it, and then dropped in two bags of green tea, and returned to her bedroom.

There's something I'm supposed to do today.

Her phone rang. She answered.

"Good morning Miss Lee, it's Cynamin Allgood here. How are you today, hon?"

Oh crap. Her. "Good morning, Miss Allgood."

"Please, it's Cynamin to my friends, and you'll soon be my newest friend." Cynamin giggled. "Listen, I know it's kind of early, but it looks like lighting conditions will be perfect for our meeting on the waterfront at eight."

Noelani sipped her tea. "Uh huh."

"I'm wondering, could you wear something tropical? Like a loud, flowery print?"

Noelani shuffled to her closet. She opened it and perused the women's clothing hanging on the left side; she ignored the men's tee-shirts and jeans—her undercover wear—on the right. "I don't have florals."

"Then something bright, as long as it's not red," Cynamin said. "A blue or a green is fine. Purple, too. And shorts, preferably the shortest ones you own."

Even as she tried to comprehend what Cynamin was saying, Noelani looked down at her legs. She was proud of them and the compliments they generated, so if it was going to be hot—

"Also," Cynamin said, "how do you wear your hair?"

"Um." Noelani checked her reflection in the mirror hanging above her dresser. "It's kind of shaggy but not long or obnoxious. Why?"

"Outstanding. All right, see you then. And when you get there, just be yourself." Cynamin hung up.

Noelani stared at the phone.

Who is this woman?

***

When Noelani arrived at the jetty across Lihiwai Street from Lili'uokalani Gardens, she found an African American woman in a short red dress, basking in the morning sun.

The woman rose and smiled. "You must be Miss Lee."

Noelani offered a hand. The woman ignored it and instead gave her a crushing hug. Noelani caught her breath and said, "Yes, and you're Cynamin Allgood?"

Cynamin released her and motioned toward the jetty's rock wall. "Please sit down—to my right." She sat beside her and ran a finger on Noelani's blouse. "I love your top. Turquoise is an excellent choice."

"Oh, uh, thank you."

"I see you went with white capris instead of shorts, but it's okay since we're already solid in the twenty-five to thirty-four male demo."

Noelani squinted at her.

"Cute bag. Wherever did you find it?"

Noelani looked at the plain canvas tote in her lap. "This? Oh, it's just something I picked up at a—"

"Do you have one, flashier? For next time."

Flashier? "Miss Allgood, I'm not sure—"

"Now like I mentioned on the phone," Cynamin said, "just be natural and try to block out the cameras and crew."

Noelani scanned the park, but the only other people in sight were old folks doing tai chi and a pair of men with fishing poles. "Miss Allgood, forgive me, but I'm lost here."

"Please, call me Cynamin. It's how the world knows me." She adjusted her seat on the wall, allowing the short red dress to expose more of her long, lean thighs. A breeze tossed her black, waist-length extensions. "And don't worry about what we talk about today, because this won't air for another three or four months. So it's not like we're giving away any story lines."

Noelani rubbed her right temple and mentally scolded herself for spending almost twelve hours asleep instead of researching this Cynamin person. Noelani made it standard practice to find out all she could about prospective clients; in the past, she turned down jobs when she unearthed even a hint of sketchiness.

"Miss Lee, are you okay?"

"Yes, I will be." Noelani looked at Cynamin and guessed she was in her early forties, though her thick, almost theatrical make-up made it difficult to tell; it looked like Cynamin applied it with a masonry trowel.

"Anything you tell me is confidential," Noelani said. "I, um"—she again scanned her surroundings—"I never share client information with third parties, unless there's a subpoena or a court order involved."

Cynamin said, "Gotcha."

Noelani took a notepad and pen from her bag. "Last night, when we spoke, you mentioned Milt Nihoa was working for you."

"Yes, and it's a terrible shame what happened to him. He was so nice and professional. Did you know him?"

"Not well." Noelani flipped the notepad to a blank page. "I probably should tell you, I'm supposed to stay as far away from Milt's death as possible, so if you're asking me to look into it, I can't."

"Oh, I get it, there's some private eye professional ethics code, huh?"

"No, the Hawai'i Police Department told me not to."

Cynamin's mouth dropped. "Shut the front door. You're kidding me. You're kidding me." She smiled and closed her eyes and punched the air with her right fist. "Oh man, we're talking ratings gold."

"Ratings? What, ratings?"

Cynamin put both hands on her chest as she caught her breath. "Sorry, hon, but things like what you just said get me awful excited."

"No, it's all right," Noelani said.

"Miss Lee, I realize we haven't communicated well so far."

Noelani watched Cynamin raise her hem another couple of inches. *Any higher and she'll wind up flashing me.*

"I'm not asking you to investigate poor Milt's death," Cynamin said. "Although if you found the killer and we got it on camera, we'd most definitely kick those slutty 'real housewives'"—she bracketed the words with air quotes—"and all their collagen and Botox from here to the moon."

Noelani poised her pen above the notepad. "Miss Allgood, why exactly do you want to hire me?"

"I need you to find out what Milt was trying to figure out about the people who are trying to put me out of business."

"Okay. What kind of business?"

"I make beer."

Noelani stopped taking notes. "You make beer."

Cynamin patted Noelani's leg. "Let's take a walk. I'll tell you all about it."

Chapter Four:
The Queen of Beers

Noelani Lee followed Cynamin Allgood across the street and into the grassy expanse of Lili'uokalani Gardens.

Noelani said, "So, you said you make beer. It sounds like an interesting hobby."

"I know what you're thinking," Cynamin said. "It's unusual for a woman—and especially a beautiful woman of color, like me—to be brewing beer."

"No. Well, I mean, we all have our interests."

"And what are yours?"

The question sideswiped Noelani. Aside from her work, her cat, and her ukulele, she had precious few pleasures in her life. "Mmm, getting to know people."

"Let me get back to you on your whole 'I'm a people person' thing, hon." Cynamin winked. "I drink beer, too, although I limit my consumption to one a week, max." She ran her hands over her torso. "Too many empty calories and everything you see here? It goes to shit. And if that happens, so does my career."

Noelani opened her mouth to speak but changed her mind.

"Plus, it's not just a hobby. Hang on, hon." Cynamin stopped and took off her leopard-print stilettoes. She stood upright and said, "I make a little money from it, though not as much as I did at my last job."

"Which was?"

Cynamin put her hands on her hips. "You can't be serious."

Noelani blinked. "Sorry, I'm not sure—"

Cynamin took Noelani by the elbow and escorted her along the edge of Waihonu Pond, the park's watery centerpiece. "Like I was saying, someone—and I don't know who, which is why you're on set with me today—is trying to put me out of business."

"Your brewery."

"Yes, though technically it's a nanobrewery. Let me explain." Cynamin stopped and held her right palm several inches above her head. "Way up here are the big-ass corporate guys, like the ones in Milwaukee and St. Louis. They make cheap swill on huge assembly lines and they don't care if it's good or not because they're all about huge profits, and nothing else."

She lowered her hand level with her waist. "Here's where you have the microbrewers. They make smaller quantities and sell their product locally, in stores or at brewpubs." Cynamin blinked. "You do know what a brewpub is?"

"I've been to a couple. On cases."

Cynamin lowered her hand to her knees. "Down here are home brewers, who brew for the love of it—for themselves or their friends."

Noelani motioned with her pen, from Cynamin's knees to her head. "So where on the anatomical scale are you now?"

Cynamin lifted her hand halfway up her thigh. "I'm a nanobrewer. See, it's all based on how many gallons you make a year. I'll spare you the boring details, but here's a hint: my brewery's in my garage."

Noelani jotted notes as they resumed walking.

"Right now, I sell my product to several bars here in Hilo," Cynamin said. "It's all word of mouth. If the bartender likes it, maybe he'll recommend it to his customers. They fall in love with it, word spreads, and more and more people want more of it."

"How's this strategy working so far?"

"Awesome. The bars go through my kegs faster than anything else they have on tap." Cynamin's face erupted into a wide, bright smile. "Look, a Japanese footbridge. Imagine how it'll look on camera." She sprinted toward the stone span.

Noelani tried to keep up in her espadrilles, but the barefoot Cynamin arrived at the bridge's crest several seconds ahead of her. By the time Noelani joined her, Cynamin again stood tall in her stilettos.

"Don't worry about the running part," Cynamin said. "We'll edit it out later."

Noelani tried to catch her breath as she reopened her notebook. "All right, so you were about to tell me why you hired Milt Nihoa—something about stolen beer."

"Nobody's stolen my beer, Miss Lee. They're trying to steal

my ideas." Cynamin said, "This is the part where I give you backstory. The editors will cut it later, but you'll need to know it now. Get your pen ready."

Noelani took notes as Cynamin explained she began brewing beer after she and her husband moved to the Big Island a little more than year ago. She said it was a continuation of the hobby she developed when she lived in San Diego, but with a twist.

"I make pale ale with honey from Kona, and I use passion fruit for my lilikoi wheat ale," she said. "Sometimes I make a lager with pineapple. My macadamia porter is to die for, and you should hear what the beer snobs say about the stout I make with coffee from Pahala, down in Ka'u." She whispered, "Everyone else uses Kona coffee, but come on—who doesn't? Plus, I throw in some locally grown chocolate. Stuff'll make you glad you're alive."

Cynamin closed her eyes and turned her face to the sun. After a moment, she looked at Noelani and said, "I even made a batch with poi once, just for the heck of it. But it was god-awful nasty."

Noelani noted poi = nasty beer. "This is all fascinating, but how does it tie in with why you hired Milt Nihoa?"

Cynamin leaned against the bridge rail. Noelani noticed she wore neon orange nail polish decorated with tiny red stickers shaped like hibiscus flowers. "A month ago, a bar owner I know told me someone left a keg of honey ale by his back door. It had a note with an email address attached. It said, 'Try this—if you like it, I'll be back with more.' I thought he was joking, since I sold honey ale to this same bar once."

Noelani said, "You don't think it was a coincidence."

"I went down and we tasted the stuff. Now, it was close to mine, except it was way too sweet for most beer drinkers. But except for adding too much honey, it was almost like someone was trying to copy my recipe."

Cynamin said another client also found a keg outside of his bar, filled with the same honey beer. That's when she hired Milt Nihoa.

Noelani asked whether Milt had any theories.

Cynamin said he shared almost no information with her, although he claimed to have computer files and photos and documents stashed somewhere.

Milt's typical MO—keep the client in the dark just before you screw up or screw them over. "When was the last time you discussed the case with him?"

"A couple nights ago. He left me a voice message saying, 'I've got him, Cynamin. This time, the bastard's done.' He was excited, I could tell."

"But he didn't say who this 'he' is."

"Nope."

"Did he have any luck tracing the email address?"

"If he did," Cynamin said, "he didn't tell me."

Noelani asked who had access to her home brewery.

Cynamin said, "The only other people who get anywhere near it are my boys, Kawika Hailama and Jervy Salazar." She said they were local guys she hired to do odd jobs for her.

Noelani wrote the names in caps and circled them. "Can they get to your—is recipes the right word?"

"No, hon. I keep them locked away."

Noelani glanced at Cynamin's wedding ring. Other than a shiny gold watch on her right wrist and a key, of all things, hanging from a chain around her neck, it was the only piece of jewelry she wore. "What all does your husband do to help you with your brewing?"

Cynamin twirled the ring around her finger. "Edward's a writer and a historian. You've heard of him? Edward Vaughn. He's the reason we moved here." She explained her husband was doing research for his next book, a comprehensive history of African Americans in Hawaii and throughout Polynesia, which meant he was away from home weeks at a time.

Cynamin sniffled, and then wiped away nonexistent tears. "We hardly see each other, but we're still eyeball-deep in love. And I know one day, his book will be as big as my beer."

Noelani said, "It must be tough, being on your own while he's on the road."

Cynamin played with her hair, and then looked out over the park. "Come on, hon, this'll be a cool shot."

She grabbed Noelani's hand and led her down the bridge, past an Asian couple in matching aloha shirts, who smiled as another man prepared to take their picture. Noclani turned to look at him—Caucasian, in a white shirt with the sleeves rolled up, jeans, and a black baseball cap. As he readied to take the picture, he gave Noelani a slight smile.

Noelani returned the subtle greeting, then said, "Did Milt give you any indication if maybe Kawika or Jervy might be the ones trying to steal your information?"

Cynamin motioned Noelani to step closer, and then placed a finger over her lips. "You didn't get this from me, but Milt didn't trust them at all."

"Did he say why?"

Cynamin shook her head.

"Could it be someone else on the island who brews beer may be behind this?"

"Well, I know some of the other small brewers here in Hilo, but they're cool," Cynamin said. "Oh, there's a new microbrewery over by the community college, called Saddle Road Ale Company. Thing is, I heard they moved equipment in but they haven't started making anything yet."

Cynamin checked her watch. "Oh sweet Jesus, look at the time. Miss Lee, I need to run—we're setting up my next scene back at the house. Speaking of which, you'll come check it out, I hope."

"Of course, I'd like to take a look around," Noelani said. "Text me the address and call me if anything else comes to mind."

Cynamin smiled and hugged her. "Thank you, hon. Girls like us, we need to stick together."

Girls like us?

Cynamin held up both arms as she turned and walked away. "All right, everybody," she said, to no one in particular, "that's a wrap. Let's load up and move out."

Noelani watched Cynamin teeter away on her heels. Then she took out her cell.

"Wanda, you have today off, right?... Good. I need to talk to you."

***

Wanda Tess Fong gasped and slapped a chubby hand over her mouth. "No way, Noe, you're kidding me. You met Cynamin Allgood in person. No way."

Sitting in her cousin's apartment, Noelani said, "Yes, and it was a weird experience."

"Noe, I can't believe you don't know who one of the biggest reality TV stars of all time is. You're telling me you never saw American Election?"

"Sorry," Noelani said. "What can I say?"

"It was only the biggest thing to hit TV like five years ago," Wanda said. "See, what it was about was, this suburb near San Diego decided to become its own town. What do they call it?"

"Incorporation."

"The people who lived there couldn't agree if they should do it because they'd need an election for the city council and the mayor, but they couldn't afford it. So these producers—they're the same ones who came up with Celebrity Paintball Wars and I'm Sitting in WHAT?—they said they'd pay for the whole thing, but on the condition they could make a TV show out of it."

"And they did this? How on earth did they make it work?"

"Real simple," Wanda said. "They auditioned twelve people to run for mayor and followed them around while they did their campaign stuff and all sorts of things. Each week, they'd do a poll of the people in town to see who they wanted to eliminate from the race, which they combined with scores from the audience at home."

"Oh, now, hold on," Noelani said. "You're saying people sitting in front of their televisions in, like, Kansas, were voting for the mayor of this new town in California?"

"Viewer votes only accounted for about twenty percent of each candidate's overall score, but yeah. Cool, huh?"

"Wanda, please tell me you didn't do it, too."

"Sure I did," Wanda said. "I liked Cynamin from the start and I wanted her to win in the worst way, so I always voted for her on the network's website."

Wanda explained most of the contestants were old and white, except for Cynamin, a Hispanic man, a Chinese American woman, and a Guatemalan transsexual. Wanda said Cynamin became her favorite because she was the youngest and most outspoken and was expert at smacking people down when they said stupid things.

Noelani said, "I'm guessing Cynamin didn't win."

Wanda flashed a dimpled smile. "People in the town didn't like her since the place was like ninety percent old white people with sticks up their butts. But she had this really cool clothing store which got major props, and the rest of the country dug her because she got under everyone's skin. So she stayed on for weeks."

"I'm sure the producers loved keeping her around, too," Noelani said. "I believe the term I've heard recently is 'ratings gold.'"

"Then it all came down to the final elimination before the real election," Wanda said. "It was between Cynamin and this old preacher and a lady with six kids. They had a debate, but it went bad for Cynamin."

Wanda said the other two contestants/candidates, believing Cynamin's ridiculous national popularity might skew the election enough to help her win, teamed up to destroy her reputation.

"They said she made up having a husband since no one ever saw him as long as they lived there," Wanda said.

Noelani said, "Her husband wasn't on the show? How come? I mean, I bet the other two trotted out their spouses at every available opportunity."

"Cynamin said it was because he's this writer who travels a lot. She said he was away, something about a book about black people in the Wild West." Wanda said, "What happened was— and they got all this on camera—the old preacher and this lady followed Cynamin, took pictures of her having lunch with a guy, and then they slapped them all over the Internet like a day before the debate. They said it was proof Cynamin was having an affair."

"Wait," Noelani said, "the preacher and the lady claimed Cynamin wasn't really married, but when Cynamin told them she was, they believed her. Then they saw her having lunch with a man they'd never seen before, so they accused her of having an affair."

"You got it, cuz."

"And they put this on TV."

Wanda said, "Anyway, you should've seen the debate, Noe. It was an awful intense episode."

Noelani said, "Okay, well, how did Cynamin respond?"

"She said the dude was a friend who invested money in her shop, but no one could find him anywhere to see if she was telling the truth," Wanda said. "Like he just up and disappeared. Then Cynamin says the preacher and the other lady were spreading what she called 'disinformation' about her to keep her from winning. But when they calculated the scores after the debate, she finished third and didn't make the finals."

"Or what the rest of us call an 'election.'"

Wanda slumped back in her chair. "It didn't help when she said the preacher was hiding something himself but she couldn't prove it, and when she said the other lady should stay at home and make cookies for all her bratty kids."

"What happened to her after she lost?"

"She went on the morning talk shows and got interviewed in the celebrity magazines and said all the things the preacher and the lady said about her was all lies." Wanda said, "Turns out, the preacher went on and won the real election." Wanda grinned. "But dude got his in the end."

"I'm afraid to ask," Noelani said, "but I will anyway: What happened?"

"A year or so later, he got kicked out as mayor and lost his preachership when a reporter found out he knocked up a stripper and used city money to pay for her abortion."

Noelani laughed. "And of course, no one knows where the reporter got this information."

"Never gave it up, but since you're the detective, I bet you already figured it out."

"Sweetie, thanks for saving me from having to watch it all on Netflix." Noelani said, "Has Cynamin done any more reality shows since then?"

"Well, after American Election and all those interviews, she kinda went under the radar," Wanda said. "She moved away and nobody knew where she went."

Noelani parsed what her cousin told her as she mentally recapped her meeting with Cynamin.

Wanda said, "Now you're telling me one of the biggest all-time stars in the history of reality TV lives right here in Hilo, and she makes beer, too." She giggled. "Dang, how awesome is that?"

"You must have some time off coming soon," Noelani said. "I mean, you haven't taken any vacation since you moved back from Vegas, have you?"

"Not yet and it's been like seven months," Wanda said. "Mrs. Hanratty says I'm her hardest worker and I clean the most houses, but even she says I should take a break or else I'll get sloppy."

Noelani said, "Then maybe you can put in for a few days off and help me out with something."

"Anything for you, Noe. What's up?"

"Well, I need you to promise me one thing first, because it's really important."

"Yeah, sure."

"Promise me," Noelani said, "you won't get all bug-eyed when you meet Cynamin Allgood."

36

Chapter Five:
The Tahyo

Detective Ahuna looked at the business card in his hand, and then at the man sitting across the desk from him. The man wore jeans and a white shirt with the sleeves rolled up, and twirled a black baseball cap on his right index finger.

Detective Ahuna re-read the card:

DWIGHT BROUSSARD
Deputy U.S. Marshal
Criminal Investigator

"It's not every day we have a real US marshal come visit us in little old Hilo town," he said.

"I'm a deputy US marshal," Dwight Broussard said. He stopped twirling the cap and dropped it in his lap.

Detective Ahuna caught an accent, a slight Southern drawl—not Texan and not full-on Dixie, either. Somewhere in between. "You say you work in San Diego."

"The boys in Honolulu tell me you're a straight shooter. You don't get territorial nor do you get pissy when federal law enforcement agents come to you for assistance or, in my case, a courtesy call."

"I've never seen the point. We're all good guys in white hats."

Dwight held up the black cap. "Touché."

An embroidered gold design shaped like a half-peeled banana dominated the face of the cap's crown. Detective Ahuna said, "So how can the Hawai'i Police Department assist you today?"

Dwight unbuttoned his left breast pocket. He removed a small color photo, which he handed to Detective Ahuna. "Ever see this woman before?"

Detective Ahuna studied the DMV portrait of an attractive black woman. Long black hair framed her face—although, he thought she should have gone easy on the make-up. "No, I can't say I have."

"The population of Hilo, Hawaii, is about forty-four thousand," Dwight said, "of which, one-half of one percent is African American. That comes out to about two hundred black people. Not a hell of a lot. So if you could, Detective, please take another look, since I'm reasonably certain there are few women around here who look like her."

Detective Ahuna obliged and studied the picture a second time. "Like I said, she doesn't look familiar. Who is she?"

"She goes by the name Cynamin Allgood," Dwight said, "although she was born Clarisse Allenby in Baltimore, Maryland, forty-odd years ago."

"She must have done something bad if you're looking for her."

Dwight took another photo from his pocket and handed it to Detective Ahuna. "We believe she's either harboring this fugitive or knows his whereabouts."

The black man in the photo was bald, with a mustache. He reminded Detective Ahuna of a comedian he'd seen on TV—what's his name, Steve Harvey?

"This citizen's name is Landry Jenkins," Dwight said, "also known as Brian Junkins, also known as La'Voris Stanley, among about a dozen various AKAs."

"Lavoris? Like the mouthwash?"

"I think it's got a ring to it myself."

"What did he do?"

"For about ten years, Landry Jenkins convinced people to pour money into a company called CalPac Western Investments. This particular business bought wholesale liquor in Los Angeles and sold it for a sizeable profit to retailers in Las Vegas, Palm Springs, and Phoenix."

Dwight said, "We believe he fleeced his investors out of ten million dollars, of which, he blew who-knows-how-much on tail and foreign cars and a yacht and pro football parlays. But curiously, he dumped a chunk of it in Miss Allgood's failed campaign for mayor of Rancho de los Ancianos."

"Never heard of it."

"Just outside of San Diego."

"She's a politician?"

"No, but she played one on television."

"I see," Detective Ahuna said. "And when this Jenkins could no longer pay dividends to his investors, he disappeared."

"Like a gator in black water."

Detective Ahuna tossed the picture on his desk.

"The last time we had eyes on Jenkins was close to four years ago, in San Diego," Dwight said. "He started meeting Miss Allgood for lunch at a Mexican joint. Place has damn good shrimp burritos, by the way. But not long after, he's gone, and then she's gone."

"And now you think she's hiding him here in Hilo."

"We believe Jenkins is the husband she's claimed she's been married to for almost fifteen years, but who no one's ever seen in the flesh."

Detective Ahuna said, "Well, I can tell you, I've never seen him, either. At least anyone who resembles him."

Dwight removed another photo from his pocket. He studied it for a moment before he handed it to Detective Ahuna. "How about this one?"

Detective Ahuna accepted the picture and looked straight into a woman's deep brown eyes. "She looks, I don't know." He swallowed and licked his lips. "I may have seen her around town, though it's hard to say for sure."

"That so?"

"In her case, well, there's a hell of a lot more Hawaiians and people of mixed ancestry in Hilo than there are blacks, so it's—"

"Because I know you questioned her yesterday regarding the suspicious death of a gentleman named Milton Nihoa." Dwight made a motion with his right hand, imitating waves. "Shoot straight with me, Detective, or I'll have to tell the fellas in Honolulu all the nice things they said about you were pure bullshit."

Detective Ahuna stared into space for a moment, before he told Dwight the woman in the photo was a licensed private investigator named Noelani B. Lee.

"The B stand for something?"

"Yes. Bruce."

Dwight blurted a laugh. "Come on, now. You're telling me

a woman with hair like a Beatle but who otherwise ain't all half bad-looking has 'Bruce' for a middle name."

Detective Ahuna let himself smile. "I could explain but I imagine you'll get it from her."

"Save your breath," Dwight said. "Man, that's the richest thing I heard all week."

Detective Ahuna picked up a pen from his desk and began fidgeting with it. "May I ask what she has to do with this Allgood woman and Jenkins?"

Dwight said, "She met with Cynamin Allgood this morning at your park, the one with the Oriental statues and such next to the water. Say, can you fish in the pond over there?"

"It's connected to the bay, so when the tide's up, sure."

"I didn't hear everything they talked about, though I swear for some reason, I swear they mentioned beer," Dwight said. "But what I do know is, your friend 'Bruce' here had a funny look on her face almost the whole time. Like she couldn't get away from Miss Allgood fast enough."

Detective Ahuna grinned. Yep, that would be Noelani Lee.

Dwight asked him how well he knew Noelani Bruce Lee.

Detective Ahuna said they weren't close, but their paths had crossed several times over the years.

Dwight asked if Noelani Bruce Lee was a reputable PI or a typical scum-bucket like most of them he'd met in his career.

Detective Ahuna said as far as he knew, she had a solid reputation—even if, at times, her techniques were borderline.

Dwight said, "Define 'borderline.' As in, unethical?"

"She—and again, I hear things—in Hawaii we have what's called the 'coconut wireless,' our version of the rumor mill, so take this for what it's worth." Detective Ahuna said, "But, I'll put it this way: She's been known to bend the rules almost to the breaking point to get results for her clients."

"Ah, that's my kind of girl." Dwight twirled his cap once, twice, three times, before letting it fall in his lap. "Did she say anything to you about working for Miss Allgood?"

Detective Ahuna clicked his pen, twice. "No."

A moment passed. Then Dwight said, "You know, Detective, I have this nickname, *tahyo*." He plucked a stray dark thread from his shirt and dropped it to the floor. "I like it. Had it since I was a kid."

"What does it mean?"

"It's Cajun for 'big, hungry dog.' It fits me in my current vocation quite well, because when I'm after someone, I'm like a pit bull going after a teacup poodle." He twirled the cap.

Detective Ahuna said, "My wife sometimes calls me lapuwale, which means 'worthless.'"

"Yeah, well, don't let the old ball-and-chain get you down. My point is, based on what you told me, Noelani Bruce Lee and I have something in common. Besides our mutual acquaintance with Cynamin Allgood."

"What's that?"

Dwight fitted the black ball cap on his head. "By which I mean, plenty of rules are gonna get broken around here in the next few days." He rapped his knuckles on Detective Ahuna's wooden desk. "Just so you know."

Chapter Six:
The Fine Print

A thick, sticky film covered the floor at Wally's Dive Inn. Noelani Lee hoped it wouldn't leave a nasty residue on the soles of her new espadrilles as she entered the bar on Keawe Street in downtown Hilo.

She also hoped she wouldn't choke on the air in the joint, with its commingled aromas of spilled booze, puke, and numerous plug-in air fresheners, each emitting a different scent. Still, the place held a certain appeal to her. She attributed it to a design aesthetic she called "post-modern drunken frat boy meets Polynesian renaissance."

Noelani entered the bar under the watchful eyes of a large wooden tiki mask, which hung on a wall under string lights shaped like flamingos. Next to the mask, a framed poster of a busty, bikini-clad brunette straddling a cooler advertised a famous beer from the mainland. The decorations basked in the red neon glow of a hand-painted sign that declared, "It's Beer Thirty Somewhere!"

Noelani's shoes made smacking sounds as she crossed the gluey floor and sat on a black pleather stool. Behind the bar, a man in a blue tee-shirt with a silk-screened numeral "1" on the back said to her, "Brah, we ain't open yet. Come back bumbye."

She said, "What does a girl have to do to get a drink around here?"

Wally Yoshiro turned around and grinned. "Shoots. Noe, you forget how to say 'howzit' to a bruddah?"

"Howzit, Wally."

"Just trying to keep up with what the shit haters are saying on Yelp. And what about you? Too early for pau hana, yeah?"

Noelani noticed hairline cracks in the white Wally's Dive Inn script printed on his faded blue shirt. She'd never seen him wear anything else. "My work never ends."

"Speaking of which." Wally reached under the bar and produced a vodka bottle. "May I present your private reserve."

Noelani squinted at the twist-off cap's broken seal. "Please tell me it's something smooth for a change."

Wally placed a rocks glass on the bar in front of her, unscrewed the cap, and poured a couple of fingers. He garnished the rim with a lime wedge. "You tell me. Suck 'em up."

"Okole maluna." Noelani downed the drink in one gulp. She sat in silence for a moment, her eyes closed. She placed the glass on the bar and said, "Oh my, Wally. You're going to spoil me." Then she plucked the lime from the glass and sucked its juices.

"Business been good, so I splurged on the fancy French stuff," Wally said. "Next time you try convincing a moke you're drunk, you'll be drinking the best bottled water on the planet." He re-capped the bottle and returned it to its designated location under the bar.

"I'm glad to know you're spending my money wisely." Noelani dropped the lime rind in the glass. "Which reminds me, Tony down at the Flip-Side Too? Last time I went there, he swapped my water for real vodka."

"Ooo, ouch."

"Sometimes I think you bruddahs get together over many, many drinks, and try to figure out new ways to punk me."

"Not me, Noe," Wally said. "I like having you around here, even if you don't do nothing for my bottom line."

"Funny you mention it," Noelani said. "How much did Milt Nihoa do for your profit margin?"

"Milt. Yeah, bruddah had a problem. Played on my softball team, too. Bummer hearing he died. Good shortstop."

"When was the last time you saw him?"

Wally slipped Noelani's glass into a sink. "Had to been maybe Saturday night." He grabbed a towel and began wiping down the bar. "Dude came in all jacked. I asked what was up, and he started talking story about how he was close to solving this one case."

"What did he say? I mean, the man had a way of letting his mouth get ahead of him when he was blitzed."

"This time, not much. Just said he was gonna get paid big bucks. I figured he was being stupid so I started talking about softball." Wally draped the towel over his shoulder. "You hated Milt."

"Let's avoid the word 'hate'," she said, "until the cops figure out what happened to him."

"A couple of them dropped by earlier—they said Milt was in his softball shirt when they found him—they asked about you and him. They asked if you ever been in here."

"I hope you told them our version of the truth."

"Damn straight. I said I only seen you in here once, maybe twice, ever."

Noelani had visited the Dive Inn dozens of times—although on most of those occasions, she came as somebody else. "Did Milt happen to mention any names, like a Jervy, or a Kawika?"

Wally rubbed his chin. "Nah, he just said he was soon gonna be swimming in money. Then the bruddah damn near drank me dry till last call. I asked if he needed a ride home, but he said no, he was good. Got in his car and split."

Noelani asked about the car.

Wally said it was either a Toyota or a Honda, and either black or blue—hard to tell in the dark.

Noelani said, "Do you know—have you heard of a woman named Cynamin Allgood?"

"The disinformation lady."

"What did you call her?"

"She told me the name of her little brewery is the Disinformation Brewing Company," Wally said. "I got no idea what it means."

"Don't worry. I do."

"Whatevahs. I'll tell you this," Wally said. "For a black sistah, she makes awesome brews. And I mean a lot better than any of the haole brewers on the island, much less anyone else."

"How did you wind up drinking Cynamin Allgood's beer?"

"One day she calls and asks if I wanna try. I say sure, so she brings over her coffee stout—damn, Noe, it was ono." Wally said he also sampled Cynamin's honey ale and passion fruit wheat beer. "Cynamin says they'd be good on a hot day and women ought to dig them. Maybe even a teetotaler like you."

"I might consider it if she makes something non-alcoholic, with green tea," Noelani said. "So did you two come to an agreement to sell her beer?"

"I ordered a keg of her stout. Thing didn't last the weekend."

"It must be good."

"She sent over another one and one of her mac nut porter. Both tapped out damn quick," Wally said. "Then the weirdest thing happened."

"Oh? What?"

"She said she'd make me a batch of honey ale. Day or two later, I find this keg out back with a note—not signed, but it had this one email address on it—saying it's honey ale. Well, I tapped it and tried it and man, it was bad."

"How bad?"

"Too damn sweet. I called Cynamin and said, 'Hey, there's no way I can sell this.' She says, 'Can't be mine; mine's not finished yet.' She came right over and had a drink. Dude, she got so pissed, I thought she was gonna punch a hole in my bar."

Noelani asked Wally what he meant.

He said Cynamin told him whoever made the ale—except for adding too much honey—followed her secret recipe to the letter.

"She told me the same thing, but Wally, come on," Noelani said. "She figured out it was a knockoff, simply by drinking a small sample?"

"Sistah's got one awesome palate, what can I say," Wally said. "She knew how much hops and malt was in it, even over the taste of bee juice."

Noelani asked if Cynamin recognized the email address.

Wally said she didn't, but it didn't stop her from tearing the note to shreds. "Don't worry," he said, "I wrote it down first." He opened his cash register, took a wrinkled piece of paper from under the till, and handed it to Noelani.

She read: hibeerguy@bigisland.net. "Did you try emailing this address?"

"Nah. I figured, why bother. What, you think it's important?"

Noelani said, "What do you know about the Saddle Road Ale Company?"

"Couple months ago," Wally said, "this bruddah, friend of my aunty's cousin, got part-time work installing expensive brewing equipment got shipped in from the mainland. Down in this building over by the community college."

"Sounds serious." Noelani said, "What's happening there now?"

"Far as I can tell, nothing," Wally said. "I got curious one day a couple weeks ago, so I drove over. Just to see what was happening. But I never seen nothing go in and no one come out, only a couple cars in the parking lot."

Noelani said it seemed odd for a company to buy a building and make all those changes, and then do nothing with it.

Wally said yeah, especially after a package arrived at his bar one day in a plain brown wrapper. No return address, no note.

He reached under the bar and retrieved a tin sign and handed it to Noelani. "This is what it was."

Noelani studied the sign, which depicted the Saddle Road Ale Company logo: A banner with the company's name connected two stylized mountains, which she figured were symbolic of Mauna Kea and Mauna Loa. A curving black strip—the infamous Saddle Road, traversing a swath of wilderness between Hilo and Waimea—wound through the mountains, and terminated at a collection of buildings representing Hilo. Arching palm trees rose from the base of the town to form a circle.

She said, "How come you don't have it on the wall?"

"I probably could," Wally said, "but there's no point having a sign for a beer that don't exist yet."

"But it's a nice sign."

"Yeah, well, I doubt I'd save a tap for these guys anyway."

Noelani brushed her fingertips over the sign's raised letters. "You already have your mind made up about them."

Wally leaned over the bar. "Sometimes, big-ass corporate mega-brewers use fancy advertising and crafty-sounding names to fool people into thinking what they're drinking is a cool, new, local-made brew. They get away charging more for it, even though the stuff's like bottled horse snot."

"I'd imagine the micro-guys and people like Cynamin

Allgood can't be too happy about that sort of thing going on."

Wally pointed at a thin line of tiny white lettering, barely legible on the tin sign's black edge. "Check it."

Noelani bent over and studied the tiny letters. "Saddle Road Ale Company. St. Louis, Missouri?"

"Nice weather we're having here in the Midwest, yeah?"

***

At the Saddle Road Ale Company, in a refurbished warehouse on Kawili Street near the community college, Mitchell Ratliff peered at a metal plate welded to the side of a giant, stainless-steel brewing tank.

Beside him, a petite young woman holding an appointment book said, "Um, sir?"

He pointed at the metal plate and said, "Rowena, have you ever noticed the itty-bitty words on here?"

"No, sir," Rowena said.

"Says these things are made in Canada." He grunted. "Everything in here's from Canada. You'd think we could afford equipment made in America." He grinned. "No offense, in case you're some part Canadian."

"I'm half Samoan and half Filipino."

He watched a man drive past on a forklift laden with a pallet of hops in brown canvas bags. "Could be worse—we could've bought them cheaper from China. But imagine how often we'd be fixing or replacing them."

"Sir?"

"And considering the craftsmanship in Long Dong Province leaves a hell of a lot to be desired…" Mitchell stopped himself, and then whispered, "Uh, there's no Chinese in you, is there?"

Rowena pointed to an entry in the appointment book. "You're running late for your two o'clock meeting."

"What two o'clock meeting?"

"You said something about an off-site meeting."

"Yeah. Right. Almost forgot. Good thing I have you around, Rowena."

"Yes it is, sir."

He checked his watch. "Home office call today?"

"No, sir."

"The contract—did it come back yet? Signed?"

"No, it hasn't."

"Give me a break. I suppose she didn't call, either."

"No, sir, she hasn't."

Mitchell said, "Rowena, post a 'help wanted' ad. The home office is on my back and I need to make sure we have enough warm bodies in this place when we ramp up."

Rowena made a note in the appointment book. "Okay." She pointed toward the brewery's main entrance. "Two o'clock. Go."

Fifteen minutes later, Mitchell pulled his Jeep Cherokee into the parking lot at Rainbow Falls Park. Aside from a compact parked in a space at the far end, there were no other vehicles or people around.

He wandered to the overlook and watched the Wailuku River plunge eighty feet over a fern-lined lava-rock cliff into a deep, blue-black whirlpool.

Where's all this water coming from, and how can I turn it into beer?

A minute later, a pickup truck—its windows open, an indecipherable hip-hop song booming from its speakers—parked next to his Jeep. Two men in rubber flip-flops, tee-shirts, and baggy board shorts exited the cab. One was round and wore wire-frame glasses, and a black Kangol hat; he leaned against the truck, texting on his smartphone. The other one—lean, wiry, his long black hair tied in a ponytail—ambled toward Mitchell.

"Aloha, beer dude," he said, offering a fist bump.

"Jervy Salazar," Mitchell said, "tell me some good news."

"Come this way and we will." Jervy led Mitchell to the truck, where he said to the other man, "Kawika, show him what we got."

Kawika Hailama interrupted his texting frenzy long enough to withdraw a two-liter plastic soda bottle filled with a pale golden liquid from the passenger seat. He offered Mitchell the bottle with one hand as he typed furiously with the opposite thumb. "The sistah thinks she's outdone herself this time."

Mitchell twisted off the cap and sniffed the bottle's contents. "Floral. Fruity, and I'm getting a hint of grains." Then he took a healthy swallow. He closed his eyes, tilted his head back, and allowed the beverage to linger on his taste buds. Then he swallowed.

After a moment, his eyes still shut, Mitchell said, "I'm getting some kind of fruit up front, tangy, and, a lingering, sweet, yet pleasant aftertaste. Is that vanilla in there? Light-bodied, good mouthfeel. Just enough hops to make it interesting." He opened his eyes and looked at the bottle.

"Dude," Jervy said, "come on. It's just beer."

"Listen," Mitchell said, "even though my areas of expertise are marketing and promotions—"

"But you make it sound like some fancy-ass wine or shit."

"Yeah. Fine," Mitchell said. "But I do know a thing or two about what good beer is supposed to taste like." He held up the bottle. "And this, this is freaking awesome. Is she selling it yet?"

Kawika said, "Like she's gonna tell us. Says she makes it with lilikoi."

"With what?"

"How long you been here? Passion fruit, for you haoles." Kawika didn't look up, but instead kept his attention on his texting, as his thumbs—which, to Mitchell, more closely resembled overgrown big toes—danced across the phone's tiny keyboard. "You gonna try this one?"

Mitchell said, "I might have to," before he drank some more.

"Speaking of experiments," Jervy said, "how'd yours with the coconut thing turn out?"

"I put it on hold."

"For what it's worth," Jervy said. "Me, I'll stick with Corona."

Kawika said, "People putting coconuts and fruits and shit in their beer." He glanced up during a break in his typing. "Hey, I like the sistah; she's a nice person. Don't get me wrong. But it makes me wonder what the world's coming to."

"Guys," Mitchell said, "please. Haven't I taught you anything? It takes someone special to make product this good.

And we, and I mean me and the home office, need to brew something this good if we're going to crack the Hawaiian craft-beer market."

"If only you knew how to make beer," Kawika said.

"I know how to make beer," Mitchell said. "But I don't know how to make beer this good. You guys with your undeveloped taste buds don't get it, but she makes the best stuff I ever drank."

"Speaks volumes, you thinking hers is better than your own company's," Kawika said.

"Riddle me this, Mitch Man," Jervy said. "Why don't they send someone out bumbye to make the beer—what do you call it, da kine brewmaster?"

Mitchell said, "There is no brewmaster at the home office. Just a bunch of old geezers with the same last name who only know how to make two kinds of beer—dog piss and low-calorie dog piss."

"You got a sad way of expressing your company loyalty, man," Kawika said.

"They've made it the same way for a hundred and fifty years," Mitchell said. "Their mission is to make a gazillion gallons a day and sell it cheap. Quantity trumps quality."

"Explains the huge market share," Kawika said as his phone dinged, signaling an incoming message.

"Also explains why it tastes like wet donkey ass," Jervy said.

Mitchell rolled his eyes. "Those old bastards at the home office wouldn't know a good beer if you poured it over their pancakes. And two, they don't know shit about Hawaii."

Kawika said, "And you do? What, you lived here maybe eight months? Damn." His phone dinged again, which spurred him into another round of two-thumbed typing.

"You know all the instructions they gave me? They said, 'We're committed to this, so make it happen.'" Mitchell took another swig of beer. "Yeah. Right. Committed, my ass."

"Eh, well," Jervy said, "I believe in you, Mitch. Like the lady running for mayor says, we need more of the entrepreneurial spirit to improve the island's employment and the economy."

"I'm surprised you can hear what she says," Kawika said,

"when you got your eyeballs glued to her gigantic titties."

"Show some respect," Jervy said. "Lady's a born leader." He said to Mitch, "Dude, you're part of what's gonna be a tremendous economical turn-around, when she gets elected, and you hire more people and finally open the place, yeah."

"Maybe if she wins," Kawika said, "your girl can do the ribbon-busting ceremony with her bazookas."

"Guys," Mitchell said, "there's nothing entrepreneurial about what we're—what I'm doing. And I don't care about local politics. I only care about making quality product."

"Mitch, I know what you're thinking, and I'm telling you— there's no way we're getting anywhere close to her book," Kawika said. "And even if we could, she'd rip our dicks off."

Jervy smirked. "Probably make beer out of those, too."

"Jervy's Pecker Ale," Kawika said. "No flavor, no calories. Comes up short on everything."

"To recap," Mitchell said, "we need to establish the Saddle Road brand. To establish the brand, we need something to sell. To sell something, we need to produce it. And to produce it, we need to know how she makes hers, so we can get it on the mass-market—here, the West Coast from Seattle to Los Angeles, before she says we ripped her off."

Jervy said, "Can't she anyway?"

"Come on. She doesn't stand a chance against our legal budget." Mitchell unscrewed the bottle cap and gulped more passion fruit beer. "The home office gets sued every half-hour. And they never lose."

Kawika looked up from his phone. "Mitch, man, there's an easier way."

"Please, if you can, tell me where my years of experience are failing us."

Kawika slipped the phone in his pocket. "You said you tried to pay her off so she'd sell out and give up. You even talked to her, like, what, a bunch of times."

"Your point?"

"Well, how's it working out?" Kawika grinned. "Not to be critical or nothing."

Mitchell cleared his throat. "Go on."

"I'm telling you, ain't gonna happen," Kawika said. "No way, no how, and especially since those two or three bars in town are still working with her."

"True, but repeat after me: She still knows what goes in them, and—"

Kawika said, "You can't get the book, even though you tried. And we can't either. But dude, you got a man who can, and he's right under your nose." His phone dinged.

Mitchell squinted at him. "Come again?"

Kawika retrieved the phone, studied the screen, and commenced texting. "Brah, how is it I know more about your limited personnel resources than you?"

"But she's married."

"Rumor has it," Jervy said. "As far as I know, no one's ever met her man."

"I never did," Kawika said.

Mitchell leaned against the truck. "You're asking me to pimp the guy out."

"You make it sound like a bad thing," Kawika said.

Mitchell said, "And you believe he can get the key."

"Whole world's got a price'll make it do anything you want," Kawika said, "if you put enough zeroes on the end." His phone dinged; he looked at the screen, laughed, and muttered, "Yeah, no shit."

"Uh huh. Well, no amount of zeroes has changed Cynamin's mind so far." Not for lack of trying, too many times to count.

Kawika looked up from the phone. "Only because she's still got a ton of her old TV money."

"'Course," Jervy said, "if she went and made one batch of pakalolo beer, I'd be the first to forgive her for all the fruity shit."

Kawika laughed. "Bongwater brew. Plenty of crops down in Puna—never-ending supply chain, yeah? We could make a killing." His thick thumbs went into overdrive as he replied to another incoming message.

But Mitchell ignored them. Instead, he unscrewed the bottle cap and, between gulps of passion fruit beer, focused his energies on how to approach the man who he hoped could get his hands on Cynamin Allgood's recipes."

Chapter Seven:
The Original Gravity

Noelani Lee pulled up in front of Cynamin Allgood's home. Well, this isn't what I expected.

Modest for a woman who had attained international fame for starring on an infamous reality show, the cream-colored, single-story house with a separate garage sat at the edge of a cluster of houses on the far west end of Hilo, where two-lane Waianuenue Road became lane-and-a-half Piihonua Road.

Inside the open garage, Noelani found Cynamin Allgood sitting on a wooden stool, leafing through pages in a three-ring binder. She looked much different from when Noelani met her at the park; in the intervening hours, she had traded her dazzling red dress and leopard-print stilettos for jeans, a ratty tee-shirt, an apron, green rubber boots, and a straw hat. A bright purple towel lay on her lap.

Cynamin rose as Noelani approached her. "Miss Lee, I'm glad you could make it. Welcome to the Disinformation Brewing Company." She placed the binder and the towel on her stool. "I apologize for not being as glamorous as I was when you met me this morning."

"Well, you do look more, can I say, relaxed?"

"It's okay, though, because as you can see, the crews aren't here. They're off shooting B-roll at the volcano and won't be back today."

Noelani opened her mouth to say something, and then changed her mind.

Cynamin nodded at a collection of metal tanks and tubes and other equipment, which occupied most of the garage. "What do you think of my baby?"

"It's impressive, even though I have no idea what I'm looking at."

"Let me give you a tour." Cynamin provided Noelani with a brief explanation of the brewing process. "It all starts here, with the mill," she said. "The milled grains then go in here"—she patted a metal object—"called the mash tun. It's where they're combined with water. Then the mash goes here"—she tapped another shiny, cylindrical thing—"the brew kettle, and then on to the fermentation tank"—she pointed at yet another piece of equipment—"and then to the filter, before it goes to the conditioning tank. From there, I pasteurize it and keg it, and send it out to happy drunks all over Hilo."

Noelani said, "How long does it take to make beer?"

"It depends, but anywhere from ten days to two weeks per keg."

Noelani's cell buzzed; the call was from Detective Ahuna. She pressed Ignore. "I can tell you've put a lot of time and money into it."

Cynamin said, "I've been blessed with sufficient financial resources to make my dreams come true. As long as we can figure out who it is out there who's trying to screw things up for me."

Noelani asked her whether she kept the garage locked.

Cynamin said yes, unless she was working in it. She said no one else, except for her husband, had access to the brewery, adding that Kawika Hailama and Jervy Salazar could only get in if she was around to let them.

"You just missed them, too," Cynamin said. "They were here a few minutes ago. I gave them some of my lilikoi wheat ale to sample."

Noelani said, "Did they tell you where they were going?"

"Wherever it is guys with beer hang on a Tuesday afternoon."

"I assume you have a home office or someplace where you keep track of paperwork, bills, receipts, and all of that stuff?"

"I converted a spare bedroom," Cynamin said. "Come on in, I'll show you."

Despite its outward appearance, the home's interior felt expansive. It had an open layout that combined the living room, dining room, and kitchen. Furnishings consisted of teak chairs and a sofa, all with plain white upholstered cushions.

The place belied Cynamin's vibrant personality. There was no décor other than a generic seascape hanging on the wall above the sofa, and an empty crystal vase on the dining room table. No family photos, no tchotchkes or personal mementoes.

It looks like she's staging it for sale. "You have sort of a zen, minimalist style, I guess you could call it," Noelani said.

"I'm not much for clutter, hon," Cynamin said. "Here, my office is down the hall."

She led Noelani past a bathroom to an open door. Inside the room, a computer desk sat pushed against a wall; an open laptop—its screensaver running a slideshow with pictures of a younger Cynamin—competed with stacks of papers for space atop the desk. Next to it stood a four-drawer file cabinet, its top doubling as storage for three large, brown glass jugs.

Noelani said, "Does your husband share this office?"

Cynamin removed the key from around her neck and unlocked the second file drawer. "Edward works out of two laptops, a handful of flash drives, a couple tablets, a phone, and a whole bunch of cloud storage." She placed the notebook in the drawer, and then closed and locked it. "So he really doesn't need to."

Noelani's cell buzzed again: Detective Ahuna. She ignored the call. "Do Jervy or Kawika ever come in here?"

"Never." Cynamin held up the key for the file cabinet. "And they most definitely can't get their hands on this." She unraveled the chain and placed it around her neck and tucked the key under her tee-shirt. "Nobody does."

After a moment, Noelani said, "Do you have any chores planned for the boys?"

"No, not really," Cynamin said. "Why?"

Noelani smiled. "Here's what you need to do—make something up."

"All right," Cynamin said, "maybe I can call one of my suppliers, a guy over in Kona who I buy honey from, although I didn't plan on making honey ale anytime soon."

"That'll work," Noelani said. "And when you call the boys, let them know you've hired another helper to work with them."

"Oh, have I, now? And who are we talking about?"

As they spoke, neither woman heard an engine start up outside the house, nor did they see the vehicle leave Cynamin's neighborhood on a heading for downtown Hilo.

***

A half-hour later, when she finished detailing her plans to Cynamin Allgood, Noelani Lee said good-bye and climbed behind the wheel of her Nissan Sentra. As she did, her cell rang.

Her cousin, Wanda Fong: "Hey Noe, thought I'd call to see what's happening. Cops still all over your butt?"

"For the time being, no," Noelani said. She started the car and put Wanda on speaker. "What's up?"

Wanda said, "I did what you asked me to do."

"And what did you find?"

"Well," Wanda said, "Cynamin's got her own personal Facebook page and she's got another one for her beer-making. I friended her on both but she didn't accept me yet."

"Sorry, I think I distracted her from her social media duties," Noelani said.

"No worries. Anyway, she's got like thousands—and I mean tons of thousands—of friends on Facebook. Oh, she does Twitter, too. She has about thirty thousand followers, including some movie stars and NBA basketball players."

"Tell me about her Facebook, um, stuff."

Wanda said Cynamin's personal Facebook page offered little information—in fact, the last time she updated it was about three weeks ago. Most of her news centered on her husband's research for his book about the African American experience in Polynesia, interspersed with YouTube clips of her best moments from American Election.

However, Wanda said, Cynamin updated her Disinformation Brewing Company page at least twice a day. Most of the posts contained information on what types of beers she was brewing, when she expected they might be ready for distribution, and where people could find them in Hilo. Her last message, posted earlier in the day, mentioned something about her experimentation with passion fruit, and how she was eager to see whether her "test subjects" liked it.

"Noe," Wanda said, "I'm still totally surprised you don't get into the whole Facebook thing."

"Well, sweetie, I somehow find better ways to waste what

spare time I have. Listen," Noelani said, "I have to split, but I'll call you later. Oh, Cynamin gave me some beer for you, in a big jug she called a growler."

"Aw, sweet," Wanda said. "The lilikoi stuff?"

"I figured a gallon ought to last you through the weekend."

"If I'm lucky, right?"

Noelani ended the call and drove to her house on Iwalani Street. She arrived a few minutes later and pulled into her driveway. She removed her holstered Ruger from the glove box and slipped it into the back of her waistband, got out, and went to her mailbox. Inside was her electric bill, a brochure from the cable company beseeching her to upgrade her existing basic service, and a plain envelope with no return address. She felt a hard, thin object enclosed in the envelope. She studied the stamp and saw the post office had canceled it just yesterday, Monday.

As she pondered the anonymous piece of mail, she looked up and saw a man standing by her front door.

He was tall, close to six feet, with collar-length gray hair. He wore a white shirt with its long sleeves rolled up, jeans, black boots, and a black baseball cap with an embroidered fleur-de-lis on the front.

The same man she'd seen at Lili'uokalani Gardens, taking a picture of tourists.

She stopped and dropped her mail. He didn't move, just looked at her, his hands on his hips. Then she noticed his right hand was on the butt of a holstered sidearm.

"Sir," Noelani said, slinking her right hand to the Ruger in her back, "I think it's only fair to warn you I have a concealed-carry permit."

The man grinned. "Then we're just about even." He moved his left hand aside, revealing a star-shaped badge. "I have what you might call an open-carry permit."

Noelani let her right hand dangle at her side. "Is there something I can do to help you, Marshal?"

"First off, Bruce," the man said, "I'm a deputy United States marshal."

Bruce?

"Second, you might want to pick up your mail before it

blows away," he said. "And then, how about we go inside your dinky little house here and have us a conversation about Cynamin Allgood?"

Chapter Eight:
The Uninvited Guest

The thing about Dwight Broussard that caught Noelani Lee's attention—more so than his angular frame, or his shiny black alligator-skin boots—was his voice.

"I see you pack a Ruger," he said, pitched like Joe Pesci but with an easy Louisiana drawl instead of a New Jersey buzz saw.

She looked at the holstered gun in her hand. "Please sit. I'd offer you something to drink but I'm afraid all I have is water and fruit juice."

Dwight parked on Noelani's sofa. "See, I'm partial to the Glock 22 myself."

She sat in a chair opposite him. "Isn't that what the character on Justified carries?"

"He has a 17 as his standard sidearm with a 26 for a backup. Outside of that, it's a pretty good show."

She pointed at his boots. "Let me guess, you won a death match against the fellow who originally wore that skin."

"There are two million American alligators in the wilds of Louisiana," Dwight said. He drew it out as Loo-zee-anna. "Now, the longest gator ever recorded was north of nineteen feet, which makes him one huge son of a bitch because the average male is about thirteen feet long snout-to-tail and weighs upwards of six hundred pounds. Pure, prehistoric muscle. The damn things can run twenty miles an hour on land, so trust me, I don't let a gator get anywhere near me unless I'm wearing him or putting him in my belly."

"Is it true they taste like chicken?"

"Ever use yours?"

Noelani set the gun on an end table. "It's strictly for personal protection."

"In case some pissed-off cheater of a husband decides to ruin your day."

"Or if a big lizard from Loo-zee-anna walks through my front door."

"They are amazing swimmers." Dwight studied the living room. "You know, Miss Lee, you've got a nice place and all as far as it goes. But I've seen bigger shotgun shacks back in Plaquemines Parish."

"I have eight- hundred square feet," she said. "Three beds—well, two and an office—a bathroom, decent kitchen, and you can't tell me this living room isn't comfortable."

Dwight ran his hand over the sofa's blue-and-white striped slipcover. "Still and all, I figured a private eye of your considerable renown would be living in something, I don't know, bigger. More impressive."

Noelani took a moment to inventory the room—a television; her ukulele case leaning against the TV stand; framed photos of her mom; finger-painted pictures of houses and birds, from Wanda Fong's nieces on the mainland.

She said, "I didn't know I had 'considerable renown.'"

"You bought it from your mother when she moved to Kauai?"

She hesitated before she said, "We—yes, I did."

"How's she like it over there?"

"It's a slower pace, which she finds appealing."

"Huh. I don't know how much slower you can get from this town," Dwight said. "Then again, it's got to be a hell of a lot more laid-back than your father's current place of residence. Lompoc, as I recall."

"He didn't have much of a choice."

"What was it, racketeering? He got himself mixed-up with the Korean Mafia in Los Angeles. Something about the sex-slave trade and a bunch of other incorrigible offenses."

Noelani didn't respond. Instead, she watched the way his mouth moved when he spoke, how he enunciated each word, clear as a bell. She decided he had a nice mouth.

"Life with no parole," Dwight said. "Must put quite the damper on holiday get-togethers."

"These days it's just me and Mom, but I'm over it," she said, not bothering to mention her two elder, distant sisters living on the mainland. "I've been over it, considering I was just a kid when he went away."

"Nine years old, by my calculations," Dwight said. "He's the one who gave you 'Bruce' for a middle name?"

"Bruce Lee was his favorite actor," she said. "Since he already had two daughters when I was born, he was hoping I'd be a boy." But I came close. She decided to keep her mild hyperadrenalism—a hormonal imbalance which left her with some minor masculine traits—a secret from the Cajun lawman.

"Back in the day, my Pop had the hots for Mamie Van Doren," Dwight said. "You know, one of those blonde bombshell actresses, like Marilyn Monroe and, uh, the other one, she damn near lost her head in a car crash."

"Jayne Mansfield."

"Same big bosoms, but not nearly as talented. So if my old man had followed your old man's child-naming conventions, I could've been Dwight Mamie Broussard."

Noelani tried not to smile. "It's sort of regal, you have to admit."

"Yeah, but Pop never forgave Ike for making Dirty Dick Nixon his running mate," Dwight said. "Besides, it's not nearly as catchy a name as Cynamin Allgood."

Noelani now regretted ignoring Detective Ahuna's calls, no matter how much crude appeal the marshal exuded. "You realize there's no point in asking what she and I talked about in the park this morning."

"Or at her house this afternoon," Dwight said.

"I guess you've already figured out how to get around town," she said. "It seems you won't need a tour guide."

He said, "I only wish I had time to explore the island's many wonders. But if I did, would you be offering?"

"Well, I—" She froze and soon caught herself staring into the man's deep-set, bluish-green eyes. When he blinked, she said, "Not my specialty. Besides, I'm more into marital infidelity, slip-and-falls, and insurance fraud."

"Skiptracing?"

"On occasion." Then she said, without thinking, "Why, do you have something in mind?"

"Sort of." Dwight removed a color photo from his pocket and handed it to Noelani.

She studied the picture of a man, African American, bald, with a mustache. Dwight explained the subject was a fugitive named Landry Jenkins, who had several known aliases and probably more nobody knew about. He said the feds wanted Jenkins for running a Ponzi scheme, which bilked too many people out of too much money. He went on to tell Noelani about the man's past connections with Cynamin Allgood, including donations to her reality show mayoral campaign.

Noelani said, "Wouldn't he have changed his appearance by now?"

"Look closer, on his neck, under his right ear," Dwight said. "He's got a dime-sized birthmark shaped like an upside-down Ping-Pong paddle."

"Well, Deputy, I'm pretty sure Cynamin isn't hiding him at her place," Noelani said. "Since you apparently know it's smaller than mine, then you know she doesn't have room for a permanent houseguest."

Dwight said, "I didn't say she's hiding him, but more to the point, I have no interest in Cynamin Allgood."

"Oh?"

"She's irrelevant to my investigation of Jenkins outside of the fact I believe she may have information on his whereabouts. And besides," he said, "your business with her is your business, I understand, although it could eventually overlap with mine."

"Unless you're into home-brewed beer," Noelani said, "I doubt it."

"I'm more of a tequila man, but I keep an open mind."

"And you think I can get it out of her."

"What I'm thinking is you can do it without interfering with whatever it is she hired you to do."

"Technically," Noelani said, "she hasn't hired me to do anything and I haven't even explained my fees to her."

"Which are?"

"Seventy dollars per hour, plus mileage and expenses."

Dwight laughed. "You make a living from that?"

"Look around. Like I said, I'm comfortable." As comfortable as a woman who lives alone with a cat can be. Noelani said, "Why don't you interview her yourself, since you're here anyway and you know where to find her?"

"On more than one occasion in San Diego," Dwight said,

"Miss Allgood made it abundantly clear to me she, and I quote, 'had no idea where the motherfucker went because he up and split without telling me shit.'"

"Sounds convincing."

"She also demanded I promise never to talk to her again about Jenkins, and so far, I've kept my word."

"I get it," Noelani said. "You lack a velvet touch when it comes to women."

"All thumbs is more like it. If you need proof, ask my ex-wives."

Ex-wives, plural. "And you believed her."

"When she said she didn't know squat about Jenkins?" Dwight said, "But if I'd been totally persuaded, I wouldn't be discussing it with you now, would I?"

"So you believe Jenkins is in Hawaii."

"I have no idea where he is, Miss Lee, which is why I'm hoping you can lend a hand with Cynamin Allgood. Prime the pump, as it were."

"Maybe you'd have better luck working with the police," Noelani said. "Have you talked with any of them yet? There's a detective who's—"

Dwight silenced her by holding up a hand. Then he took his wallet from his left hip pocket, and from it, extracted a folded piece of paper, and handed it to her.

She unfolded it to reveal a Marshals Service wanted poster, complete with Landry Jenkins's photo, a list of his known aliases, his birthdate, a detailed physical description—down to the birthmark under his ear—and a summary of his crimes. What caught her attention, though, was a line reading "REWARD: A reward of up to $25,000 is offered for information leading directly to JENKINS's arrest."

"What this tells me," she said, "is that you think he is on the island."

"Or one of them, maybe," Dwight said. "You see, Landry and Cynamin, well, she told you about her supposed husband, I'm sure."

"The writer, the one nobody is sure exists. Are you one of those people? You don't think she's really married."

"No, I do believe she's married. To Landry Jenkins."

Noelani stared at Dwight for a moment before she turned her attention back to the wanted poster. Then she closed her eyes and rubbed her temples, a fresh headache. This fed's holding something back. He must be, if he's good at his job.

Dwight said, "You all right, Miss Lee?"

"Fine and dandy."

"I'm not asking you to do anything that'll compromise whatever it is you agreed to do for her. Nothing illegal either."

"Except?"

"Paint the edges, mention Jenkins and see how she reacts," Dwight said. "Be her friend to the point she'll tell you anything. Hell, I saw how you two got along in the park."

"Deputy," she said, "I don't screw over my clients. It's unprofessional, not to mention impolite and disrespectful."

"Unless of course your client is an accomplice to a wanted felon or at the very least is hiding a fugitive."

"But you don't believe it yourself."

"You're a pro." Dwight rose from the sofa. "You'll figure it out. And when you do and you get something that can lead me to Jenkins, the good people of the United States of America will make sure you're generously rewarded for your efforts." He asked her for Jenkins's DMV photo, which she handed to him. He slipped it in his shirt pocket. "Sorry to cut the visit short, but I need to make some calls."

Noelani stood and escorted him to the door. Standing beside him, she smelled his cologne—a crisp, warm aroma, both woody and citrusy. Quite masculine. "I'm sure you're aware what kind of awkward position you're putting me in."

"Yeah, but you must be accustomed to this sort of business." He stood in the open doorway, one hand on the doorknob. "I'm only interested in finding Landry Jenkins. As far as I'm concerned, Cynamin Allgood is, well, all good." Dwight stepped outside, turned to face her, and said, "Listen, I was thinking of maybe getting a drink later. Care to join me?"

She wondered how he drank, whether he did it with the same self-assuredness he displayed when talking with her. Or, did he go for the gusto and pound shots? "Considering I don't drink and I have work to do," Noelani said, "I'll have to decline your invitation."

"So I suppose you can't tell me where I can get an adult beverage with an old friend who's also in town."

Noelani said, "There's a place downtown called Wally's Dive Inn. The bartender's a friend of mine. Tell him the first round's on me."

He put on the ball cap and handed her a card. "I'll be in touch."

Noelani closed the door behind him. She looked out her window and watched him climb into a SUV and drive off. Then she picked up her cell and called Detective Ahuna.

He said, "I tried to warn you but you didn't answer."

"I'm beginning to think you care about me."

"Did you know he calls himself 'Mad Dog' or something weird like that?"

"I'm not terribly surprised."

She heard the detective slurp something over the phone. "It was the least I could do, considering you're officially still a murder suspect."

"I guess this means I'm going to miss the elk hunting trip I had planned in Montana."

"Eh, they're not in season anyway," Detective Ahuna said. "Now, what did you and him talk about?"

Noelani relayed her conversation with Dwight Broussard.

Detective Ahuna said he had the same discussion earlier in the day. "Why do I get the feeling, based on your tone of voice—"

"And inflections," Noelani said. "Don't forget my inflections."

"Why is it you think he's not telling the whole story?"

"Because he's not, and because you don't think he is, either."

"Of course I don't. But what is it you think he's hiding?"

"I wish I knew," Noelani said. "There are ways of finding out, though."

"Yes, well, I'm betting you're already on it," Detective Ahuna said. "On another note, we found Milt Nihoa's car, in the parking lot out at Rainbow Falls."

Noelani pictured the lot and the falls. She also envisioned the Wailuku River's path from the falls to Hilo Bay. As a kid, she had spent many a day exploring the river with her sisters. She remembered, when flows were low—as they were now, due to the drought—much of the river's rocky bed stood exposed. Meaning, if someone had dumped Milt in the river below the falls, his body might have hung up on rocks downstream instead of floating to the bay.

She said, "And what about the autopsy results?"

"We should know more tomorrow." Noelani heard the sound of shuffling papers. "So I suppose this means you're going to have another sleepless night."

"Bad things happen when I sleep, and they only get worse when I wake up."

"You are an unusual person, Miss Lee," Detective Ahuna said. "But with this one, well, just be careful."

"I plan on it," she said. "In fact, I think I'll take a break and go out for a drink."

Chapter Nine:
The Loyal Son

In his fourth-floor hotel room on Banyan Drive, with a view of the street and tree tops—the ocean-facing rooms being out of reach of his meager travel budget—Dwight Broussard almost called the office in San Diego. But he stopped himself.

It was a force of habit he would have to remember to forget.

A moment later, his cell buzzed and a picture of his father, the tough bastard Owen Broussard, appeared on the phone's display.

"Hello, Pop."

"Where yat, Tahyo?"

"Awright, Pop."

"You killed the nigger yet?"

Dwight stepped outside of the room, onto the lanai. "For starters, no one with any sense or morals uses the n word anymore, and I'm ashamed for you for saying it."

"Give me a break, son. You know I get along good with the blacks. Some of my best friends back in Port Sulphur was black."

"Pop, you had no choice but to get along with them. Almost half the town was black."

"Good, nice, God-fearing Christians, too," Owen said. "And you know, I've met some real nice black folks here. Lady lives across the street's one of them. She came by the house and brought me sweet potato pie yesterday."

"Pop, the doctor said you're not supposed to—"

"Nice lady. Husband's dead, going on eight years. He was retired Navy."

"Sweet potato pie—you know the doctor told you to cut down on that stuff."

"But the fella you're looking for is not black," Owen said, "afos he gives all blacks a bad name. Hell, he gives all humans a bad name. Therefore, the man's a nigger."

Dwight knew from decades of experience it was futile to argue Owen's primordial socio-political views. "I told you a hundred times, Pop, if I told you once, we wouldn't be in this mess in the first place if you weren't so damn gullible."

"He said I'd triple my money after three months and every couple months thereafter, for true," Owen said. "C'mon, boy, how was I supposed to know he'd take off with all of it?"

A hundred thousand, give or take—every penny Owen Broussard had to his name. "You should've asked me first, when something sounds too good to be true."

"Son, I'm thinking it's a California thing."

"You—what?"

"'Pop, come live with us in San Diego; weather's great out here and there's no hurricanes,'" Owen said, in a dead-on imitation of his son. "Wildfires and earthquakes, you left them out of the sales pitch."

"Pop."

"I pack up what shit Katrina didn't blow to Baton Rouge and moved in with you and Gina, and next thing I know, you two are fixin' to get divorced. Gets me thinking maybe I'm in the way, maybe I should move out and make it on my own with what precious time I got left on God's green earth."

Dwight said, "Pop."

"Some slick dude in a shiny suit finds me, knocks on my door and he sees me for the coon-ass I am," Owen said. "He promises to make me rich, at least real comfortable until the Lord calls me home. What would you do?"

"I wouldn't answer the door."

"Your son's divorcing his second wife and he's got a job takes all his time and even then, I never know when he's gonna come home dead. I figure I'm either gonna need to boost my retirement or pay for your funeral, whichever comes first."

Dwight watched banyan leaves rustle in a breeze. "You think me killing him is going to solve all your problems?"

"Yeah, you right, Tahyo," Owen said. "Any man who calls himself after a mouthwash is a blame fool to begin with."

"If he's even on this island. And if I do find him and kill him, then it's guaranteed you'll never see your money again."

"Hell, it's way gone anyway," Owen said. "Why not put a bullet in his head like you said you would and square things up, huh?"

"You're not the only person he ripped off," Dwight said. "A lot of people want him brought to justice and locked away for what he did. I can do that. It's my job."

"Don't tell me you have second thoughts now you're waist-deep in the shit."

Dwight closed his eyes and said nothing for several long moments.

Owen Broussard broke the silence. "You find the girl? The feisty one from the TV show, what with the dress shop?"

"Yes, she's here."

"Dapremond she knows where he is, from what you told me. You got to know she wants his ass dead, too."

"I haven't talked to her, yet, because there won't be much point, owing to our past history," Dwight said, "but I've got some local help and no, I am not going into detail with you."

Owen laughed. "None needed, son. But that's welcome news."

Dwight went back inside and sat on his unmade queen bed. "So what did the doctor say? You saw him today, right?"

Owen said, "They never tell you nothing, doctors."

"You have to listen to what they say, Pop. Now I know you don't understand medical terminology and all but at least you could ask him questions."

"Well, what he did say was the heartbeat's still irregular. He called it—what is it he called it?"

Dwight said, "An arrhythmia."

"It's why I'm always short of breath and get dizzy sometimes, he says."

"I should be there taking care of you, instead of over here on a wild goose chase."

"Seen any hula girls?"

"I've been busy since I got here."

"Take yourself to one of them luaus, son. Celebrate once you kill the son of a bitch. Have some of them boat drinks, too."

Dwight checked his watch. His next appointment was in an hour. "Are you sure you're feeling okay?"

"Listen to me," Owen said. "The ticker's messed up all to

hell, but I know I'm gonna live long enough for you to square this shit."

Dwight bent over, his elbows on his knees. "I can be on the next plane home if you need me for anything. Just say the word."

"This ain't home. Home's Port Sulphur."

"Home blew away in aught-five, Pop."

"You can do this one thing, Tahyo," Owen said. "You're tough as me. Hell, you still got some of Saddam's shrapnel in you, after all."

Dwight never paid much attention to nor made a big deal of the tiny piece of mortar shell, smaller than a penny, embedded in his right calf since January 1991. It only irritated him when the weather changed, or when he had to explain to TSA agents why he set off metal detectors.

"As for me," Owen said, "there's a big slice of sweet potato pie in the icebox with my name on it. Talk to you tomorrow, son." He hung up.

Dwight sat in silence for a couple of minutes. Then he got up, went to the bathroom, and peeled off his shirt. He took a quick field shower, wiping a wet, soapy washcloth over his face, neck, arms, and chest. He toweled off and slipped into a dark blue polo shirt. He retrieved a sealed envelope from the nightstand, which he folded into quarters and slipped inside his wallet. Then he left the hotel.

Dwight had considered driving to the downtown bar the Lee woman recommended. But because one of his goals for the evening was to get stupid drunk, he thought better and chose instead to hoof it. Maybe take a cab back when he was done.

He arrived at Wally's Dive Inn about a half-hour later. As his eyes adjusted to the bar's darkness and his nose accommodated its stink, he observed several men and women gathered around a pool table in one corner, drinking, laughing, and playing 8-ball; next to them, a pair of guys talked smack as they shot darts. He looked in another corner, to a small stage, where a quartet played reggae on guitar, bass, keyboards, and drums. Almost everyone, including the band, stared at him as he walked in.

Scouting for a place to sit, Dwight noted groups of loud, laughing, inebriated patrons filled the tables in the middle of the tavern's sticky floor. So he turned his attention to the bar, where a butt occupied almost every stool, except for three at the far end. He clomped across the floor and perched himself on one, which afforded a clear view of the entrance.

The bartender, a medium-height, round man in a blue tee-shirt, dropped a paper coaster in front of him. "Howzit," he said. "What can I get you?"

Dwight looked past him to rows of booze bottles lined up on shelves against a mirror behind the bar. "What's your name?"

"I'm Wally, like the sign says."

"Okay, Wally, what kinds of tequila do you have?"

"All of them. You got a favorite?"

"Yes, but forty bucks says you don't have it."

Wally laughed. "Shoots, you're on, brah."

"It's called Tres Idiotas, but I'm warning you, it's hard to find."

Wally turned and grabbed a bottle from the shelf and showed it to Dwight. He recognized the label, with its cartoon drawing of three Anglo men in serapes and sombreros, each hoisting a shot glass, and with exaggerated, vapid expressions on their faces. Having visited the distillery outside of Puerto Vallarta, Dwight knew the characters represented drunken college gringos on spring break.

"Añejo, no less," Dwight said. "I suppose this means I owe you a couple of Jacksons."

"Brah," Wally said, setting a shot glass on the coaster, "you give me a twenty, I give you the bottle, and we're even."

"You're damn kind."

Wally placed a second glass on the bar. "As long as I get some, too, since I never tried this one before."

Dwight cracked the bottle and poured shots. Wally lifted his glass, said, "Okole maluna," which Dwight assumed meant "cheers," and then they both gulped the tequila.

Wally slammed his glass on the bar. "Damn, that's some serious-ass firewater, chief."

Dwight savored the tequila on his taste buds before he

swallowed. "Are you sure you should be drinking on the job?"

"This ain't work; to me, this is play. Besides, my name's on the place."

"I just don't want you in any sort of trouble with the local authorities."

"Do that good enough on my own already," Wally said. "Now I know you're not from around here, so what brings you to Hilo? You a tourist? We get some here but most of them go over to Kona side."

"No, I'm here on official business." Dwight poured himself another shot. He offered one to Wally, who waved a hand over his empty glass.

Wally said, "What business you here on, or are you gonna say 'none of your'?"

"You got it." Dwight drained the shot.

"Listen, it's cool with me. As long as you don't do nothing illegal in my establishment, we're cool."

Someone puked at the other end of the bar. The ensuing mix of profanities, laughter, and groans from other patrons prompted Wally to excuse himself.

As Dwight watched him walk away, a man in dark sunglasses, jeans, a long-sleeved tee-shirt, and a green-and-gold Oakland Athletics baseball cap, its bill pulled down his forehead, sat next to Dwight. When Wally returned a minute or so later, he lifted a bottle of vodka onto the bar and placed it and a glass in front of the man, who focused his attention on the television above the bar.

Dwight stared at the man for several moments before he said, "Excuse me."

The man ignored him.

"I said, excuse me."

The man turned to face him, but his cap and sunglasses kept Dwight from reading his eyes. "Yeah, what do you want?" he said, in a voice that sounded like Sean Penn.

"I'm saving this seat."

"For who?"

"For my personal space," Dwight said. "Now, the definition of what constitutes personal space varies from person to person, which stands to reason, although most experts agree the typical range is two feet. Mine happens to be about eighteen to twenty inches, and as you can see, these stools are much closer. So, could you please save me some anxiety and move down one?"

The man took a slug from the vodka bottle. "Dude, what's all this you're talking about, man?"

"Listen, it's only fair of me to tell you—"

The man jumped up from the stool, maintaining a grip on the vodka bottle with his left hand. "Wanna scrap? Huh? You want beef, haole?"

Dwight sat stone still and sized him up. Maybe about five eight and a buck-twenty or -thirty, max. If it came down to it, Dwight knew he could toss the twerp out of the bar and across the street with one hand. The man couldn't even stand up straight; Dwight figured he'd probably been drinking for most of the afternoon.

But Dwight didn't want it to come to that, especially because most of the other patrons were watching in eager anticipation of what might happen next. Except for the band, which Dwight heard singing something about every little thing gonna be all right.

"Listen," Dwight said, "all I am asking you to do is move down one stool. Nothing more. You can still watch Vanna turn her letters up there on the TV—"

"She don't turn them no more. She taps the screen things and they change."

"At the same time, you'll give me room to breathe and not leave me feeling boxed in. Now, isn't that fair?"

Even in the subdued light, Dwight could see the guy's nostrils flare and his temples throb. But just as the drunk tightened his grip on the vodka bottle, Wally snuck up behind him and grabbed his shoulders.

"Dude, come on," Wally said, "show my new friend here some respect and just move down a seat. Come on, yeah?"

"Haole comes to my bar and tries messing with me," the guy said, "it ain't right."

"Brah, it's my bar, not yours, no matter how much you come here." Wally lowered the drunk onto the next empty stool.

"Just chill, all right?"

The man looked at Wally, and then at Dwight. Without another word, he swiveled on the stool and resumed watching TV.

Wally apologized to Dwight. "I'd eighty-six him but he's the only regular I got who pays his tab."

Dwight poured a shot of Tres Idiotas. "It's over now, so don't worry about it."

As Dwight slammed the shot, he saw another, older man enter the bar. The newcomer, in a blue floral aloha-print shirt and loose-fitting white chinos, ambled along the bar until he reached the empty seat next to Dwight.

"Wouldn't do that, I was you," the drunk with the vodka said, without looking at either Dwight or the new arrival. "Haole there's got what you call a short fuse."

The gray-haired man looked at the drunk, and then at Dwight. "There's nowhere else to sit."

"Never mind him," Dwight said. "Please, have a seat."

The older man did, and then asked Wally for a club soda with a lemon slice.

As Wally served the drink, Dwight gave the new customer the once-over. Using what little illumination the bar offered, Dwight noted the man had pale skin, at least two chins, and an overabundance of crow's feet around his eyes. Dwight had him at five nine and a couple hundred pounds. The man's thick glasses reflected a backlit whiskey display behind the bar.

Dwight poured another shot and swigged his tequila and watched television as the man sitting next to him sipped his soda. Dwight noticed the drunk, two stools down, appeared to have passed out, with his head on the bar and both hands wrapped around his half-empty vodka bottle.

Dwight said to the older man, "So, you visiting friends here or are you on vacation?"

"Neither," the man said.

Dwight nodded. "Business?"

"In a manner of speaking." The man fished the lemon from his drink and dropped it on a cocktail napkin. Then he removed the straw from his glass and gulped the remainder of his soda.

He flagged down Wally and ordered another round.

Dwight said, "I heard a good joke the other day. Want to hear it?"

"Sure," the old man said, "why not."

"Okay, a politician and a preacher walk into a bar—" Dwight smacked his forehead. "Wait, I think I may be telling it wrong."

The old man glared at him.

"Yeah, see, it's because the preacher and the politician are the same person. Well, damn. I guess I just screwed up the whole thing. Sorry to ruin it for you."

The old man blinked at him. He paid no mind to the fresh drink Wally delivered.

Dwight said, "So what do I call you? I mean, you're not Mayor Paul Templeton anymore, and you certainly aren't Reverend Paul Templeton. Hell, you haven't been either one for quite a while."

Paul Templeton nodded at the tequila bottle. "How much of that poison have you been drinking?"

"All this time and you still carry a grudge." Dwight refilled his shot glass. "Aren't you familiar with the old saying about water under the bridge? Better yet, you could maybe get around to turning the other cheek."

Paul Templeton swiveled on his stool to face Dwight. "I did not come all the way to Hawaii to hear you of all people lecture me about letting bygones be bygones. I asked you to find her. I didn't ask you for your typical condescending, pedantic garbage."

"I'm just trying to figure out how your mind works, Paul. Why you can't let go of something you haven't been able to prove after all this time."

"Let it happen to you or someone you care about, then get back to me." Paul blinked. "Oh, wait. Something like this did happen to someone you care about. Silly me."

Dwight sniffed. Then he removed the envelope from his wallet, placed it on the bar, and pushed it toward Paul. When Paul tried to grab it, Dwight maintained a firm grip.

"All I ask," Dwight said, "is you let me make one more run

at her. Then you can do whatever stupid bullshit it is you're thinking of doing."

"So you can get off the island first."

"There's something to be said for plausible deniability. And, whatever it is you're plotting, it better not involve death, dismemberment, or any other form of bodily harm."

"I hired you to find her," Paul said. "What happens next is none of your concern."

"You don't have it in you."

Paul said nothing, just blinked.

"Since I've been here," Dwight said, "there's something I learned about our friend Cynamin. Something which might behoove you to know, and which, sad as this may sound, I am honor-bound to share with you."

Paul withdrew his hand from the envelope.

Dwight nodded toward Paul's club soda. "I see you still abstain from alcohol."

"In all its vile, evil forms, unlike some idiotas I know."

"Then I can only imagine what you must think of a woman who makes beer, at her home, out here, in the middle of the Pacific Ocean," Dwight said. "What I hear is, she's pretty good at it, too. And she sells a bunch of it, kegs galore, even to this very bar." Dwight pulled the envelope back. "It's in here. If you prefer I refund you your deposit, well, then, fine. I still have my real job to do—"

"Real job?"

"—and what you'll get is wasted time, unless all along what you've been aiming for was a nice Hawaiian vacation. But the fact remains, you keep your hands off her."

Paul said, "Even considering what she did to me."

"She didn't do shit to you, Paul. All she did was call you out on some insanely stupid stunts you pulled." Dwight said, "Personally, I think she did the taxpayers a favor. By the way, how old was that girl? She have daddy issues?"

"Don't cast stones."

"See, Reverend, I don't give a flying rat's ass about you or your sorry vendetta, unless you go completely off the rails. Then you will answer to me."

They sat in silence for several moments, before Paul said, "The soul of every living thing is in the hands of God."

Dwight said, "And don't you forget it."

He pushed the envelope toward Paul.

Paul snatched it and stuffed it in his breast pocket, swapping it for another, much thicker envelope, which he handed to Dwight. "Go ahead and count it if you want."

Dwight nodded toward the drunk in the baseball cap as he leaned back on his stool and shoved the envelope in his jeans pocket. He sat up and held his shot glass at eye level. "Do you know the proper way to taste tequila, the way they teach you in Mexico?"

"Why would I care?"

"You're right. Look who I'm asking." He raised the drink to his lips, but instead of slamming it, he sipped it. "This is really good stuff. Sure you don't want some?"

"I got what I came for."

"Almost."

"Done yet?"

"Uh, well, now that I'm flush with cash, the least you can let me do is get the next round."

"You're getting all my rounds," Paul said. He stood and pushed the stool aside. "Call me when you're done with her."

"Don't be stupid, Paul. Subtlety goes a long way. Take my word for it."

Paul turned on his heel and left Wally's Dive Inn.

Dwight watched him walk out as the band slowed the pace with a song about no woman not crying. He sipped his tequila and caught a glimpse of Vanna tapping the screen things to reveal vowels. He listened to the pool players laughing and giving each other shit. He caught snippets of conversation from the partiers at the tables, and barely paid attention when the drunk in the baseball cap got up and threw him a dirty look. The drunk tossed a folded twenty on the bar and said something unintelligible to Wally, before he staggered out of the bar and into the encroaching night.

As Wally swiped up the twenty, Dwight noticed something inside the bill. It looked like a piece of paper.

Wally capped the drunk's vodka bottle and hid it in a space under the bar. Dwight finished his shot and asked Wally if he'd do the same with his unfinished Tres Idiotas. He said he'd be back tomorrow night for more.

Wally said it was no problem; whenever Dwight was ready, he'd lock it up.

Dwight thanked him. Then he thought about his ailing father, Owen, as he stuffed the thick envelope in his pocket.

This one's for you, Pop. You ornery old coon-ass.

***

Wanda Tess Fong, in her Honda Accord across the street from Wally's Dive Inn, tried to walk like an Egyptian in her seat as the Bangles' song blared on her post-market stereo.

Then her cell buzzed with an incoming text:

Start the car.

Wanda turned the ignition at the same time the passenger door opened. "So what's up, Noe?"

Noelani Lee, in sunglasses, a long-sleeved tee-shirt, jeans, and an Oakland Athletics baseball cap, climbed in and shut the door. "Wanda, did you see an older gentleman leave the bar a couple of minutes ago?"

"Yeah, gray-haired dude. He had on a blue aloha shirt and white pants."

Noelani removed the cap and tossed it in the back seat. She opened the glove box and took out a packet of make-up remover wipes. "Which way did he go?"

"He went that way"—Wanda pointed over her shoulder—"then I lost him."

"He didn't get in a car? Nobody picked him up?"

"No, he was walking. Why, what's going on? Who is he?"

Noelani wiped dark theatrical make-up from her cheeks. "Sweetie, let's go. We need to find him."

Wanda started the car and the cousins negotiated downtown Hilo's one-way streets—turning right on Waianuenue Avenue, and then making another right on Kamehameha Avenue. They veered into the parking spaces fronting the colorful, historic buildings facing Hilo Bay; Wanda slowed the Accord to a crawl.

As they stopped at Haili Street, Noelani pointed at the old man, who turned right and continued strolling past storefronts—a snorkel rental shop, a restaurant supply store, a gift shop. He stopped to check out merchandise displayed in a fireplace store's window.

"Oh wow, Noe," Wanda said, "I know who he is. He's the old preacher went and dissed Cynamin on the show."

"Pull up there," Noelani said, pointing at an empty space to their left. Wanda parked the Accord and killed the engine.

Noelani turned to face her and said, "I need you to follow him, but don't get too close. You're out window-shopping, okay?"

"Yeah, sure, no worries."

"I'd do it but he's seen me. You have your cell, right?"

"Yeah, of course."

"Good," Noelani said. "Just be careful."

Wanda hopped out of the car and walked toward the shops. She pretended to window-shop as Paul Templeton—he was shorter than she remembered him from American Election—stuffed his hands in his pants pockets and meandered down the street. When he stopped, she stopped; when he walked, she walked.

A couple minutes later, Wanda saw her Accord leapfrog her and turn into a side street, between a gas station and a dive shop. Wanda turned her attention back to Paul Templeton, who turned onto Punahoa Street. When Wanda reached the corner, she looked to her right and saw him stroll past a furniture store. Then she looked across the street and saw her Accord on the curb, next to a grassy park dotted with palm trees. Behind the wheel, Noelani motioned for her to get in the car.

Wanda slid into the passenger seat. She looked outside as Paul Templeton crossed Punahoa Street and turned right, and then entered an unremarkable wood-frame building.

"What's that place he went into, Noe?"

"It's a hotel," Noelani said. "More like a B&B."

Wanda nodded. "So now what, cuz?"

Noelani started the car. "Now," she said, "you get to meet Cynamin Allgood."

Chapter Ten:
The Huddle

Noelani Lee and Wanda Fong pulled into Cynamin Allgood's driveway early Tuesday evening, just as the reality star-turned-brewer closed her garage door.

"Miss Lee," she said, as the cousins climbed out of the Accord, "what's with the clothes? You look so much less fabulous than last time I saw you."

"We need to talk, Miss Allgood," Noelani said.

"Mmm, the crews are gone for the day but I guess it's okay." She smiled at Wanda. "Let me guess, is this your cousin, the beer lover?"

"Cynamin, this is Wanda Fong," Noelani said, "and she's easily star-struck."

"Hi Miss Allgood," Wanda said. A giddy grin overwhelmed her face. "I'm your biggest fan."

"Aren't you terribly cute," Cynamin said. "So did you try my passion fruit beer yet?"

"I didn't have a chance," Wanda said. "You see, I was about to but—"

Noelani said, "Can we talk for a few minutes? This is kind of important."

The cousins followed Cynamin into the house. Noelani hesitated when she heard voices down the hall. "Are we interrupting anything?"

"Ah, no, I left the TV on in my bedroom. I guess I forgot about it." Cynamin motioned toward the dining room table. "Won't you please sit down?"

Cynamin sat next to Noelani. "I hope you have good news for me, Miss Lee, about whoever it is who's stealing my beer ideas."

Noelani retrieved a folded piece of paper from her pocket. "No, but some other issues have cropped up and I—what I need for you is to be honest with me."

Cynamin sat back. "I, um. What are you talking about? I've been totally up-front with you about my problem."

"This has nothing to do with your beer recipes or Milt

Nihoa," Noelani said. "But why was a federal marshal waiting for me at my house this afternoon with this?" She unfolded the paper and handed it to Cynamin.

Cynamin's eyes widened as she studied Landry Jenkins's picture on the wanted poster. She said, "Oh sweet Jesus. This marshal, he has like a Louisiana accent?"

"He thinks you're hiding Landry Jenkins," Noelani said, "or he thinks you know where he is."

Cynamin dropped the poster on the table. "No way. I am being completely honest with you, Miss Lee. I haven't seen that scoundrel in years."

"So why is the marshal coming after you if you haven't?"

Wanda said, "On the show—and I wanted you to win so bad and I was bummed when you didn't—"

Cynamin glowed. "Aw, thank you."

"I remember the old preacher and the lady with all the kids said bad things about you and this Jenkins bruddah."

Cynamin looked at Wanda, and then at Noelani. "I was not having an affair with Landry Jenkins. I mean, please. Compared to him, my Edward could be Denzel Washington's long-lost twin."

Noelani said, "Okay, but what kind of relationship did you two have? It must have been something; otherwise, this fed wouldn't have come all the way to Hilo to question you again."

Cynamin flattened the poster with both hands. Noelani watched as the corners of her client's mouth formed an almost imperceptible smile. "Landry invested money in my boutique. Not a lot but enough to keep me afloat when I hit a rough spot."

"In addition to helping fund your campaign for mayor," Noelani said.

"Come to find out later from this redneck marshal, Landry was using me to launder his dirty money."

"So you had no idea, when Landry gave you this money, it was stolen?"

"He said he heard about my boutique and came one day to meet me for lunch," Cynamin said. "Something about how he wanted to help me. Because the boutique, he told me, could make a killing."

Noelani said, "How much did he give you?"

"Close to seventy thousand. Helped me with marketing, advertising, getting the word out." Cynamin smiled. "Smooth talker, that one was."

"And right now you have no clue where he is."

Cynamin said no.

Noelani studied her for a moment. "The marshal thinks Landry is your husband."

"Oh, yes, hon, I heard it from him firsthand I don't know how many times."

Cynamin's wispy smile was still in place. Noelani said, "Well, I just wanted you to know this marshal is going to drop by soon."

Cynamin raised an eyebrow. "He knew you'd come to me first, before he did."

"You still need to tell him the truth. Which leads me to my second piece of information."

"Does it have something to do with your wardrobe? If I didn't know any better, I'd figure you for some nerdy dude."

Wanda said, "She didn't tell you about her disguises? Noe's got tons of them."

Noelani said, "There's another man on the island who apparently paid the marshal to find you." She explained what she overheard and saw at Wally's Dive Inn, about the envelope swap and the conversation between Paul Templeton and Dwight Broussard.

"I saw him walk up close," Wanda said. "So, yeah, it's him."

Cynamin said nothing.

Wanda leaned over and said, "You're the one told the reporter about the Templeton dude and the pregnant stripper and the abortion, yeah?"

Noelani watched the expression in Cynamin's eyes harden. She said, "What do you think Paul Templeton's capable of doing? I mean, since he blames you—correctly, so it seems—for being booted from office and bounced from his pulpit."

"I'm not the one who knocked up the stripper, Miss Lee, and I definitely did not tell her to kill her unborn child as a consequence." Cynamin stuck out her chin. "But when I found out, well, you know, there's no way I'm keeping it a secret after what he and his prissy housewife friend did to my reputation. I won't apologize for nothing."

"He's probably not expecting you to fall on your knees and beg for mercy." Noelani said, "When does your husband get home?"

"Maybe a day or two; could be as late as Friday. He never knows."

"Call him and tell him to get back as soon as he can," Noelani said.

Wanda said, "There's no way you should be home alone, with those mean dudes hanging around the island."

"I think I can handle myself with Paul Templeton."

"Don't take any chances," Noelani said. "He may be older, but he's carrying a big chip on his shoulder. And besides, the marshal's a whole other story."

"Yeah, well," Cynamin said, "I know how to deal with him, too."

Noelani said, "Just so we're clear, I'm still going to do what you hired me for. We're all set for tomorrow morning, right?"

"Yes. The boys said they'll be here about nine o'clock."

"Which is closer to ten in Hawaiian time." Noelani noticed, for the first time, Cynamin wasn't wearing the key chain around her neck. "Now, there isn't much we can do about the deputy, except you have to tell him the truth whenever he shows up."

Cynamin nodded.

"In the meantime," Noelani said, "Wanda and I will do what we can to make sure Paul Templeton keeps his distance."

"What exactly am I supposed to do?" Cynamin said. "You've seen how hectic my life is. I mean what with the producer and the crews hanging around all the time, and me with my beer."

"Do what you do, normally," Noelani said. "But the first thing you should do is call your husband—"

"If I can get him. He doesn't always have his cell turned on."

"Text him. Leave a message. Something so he knows it's urgent." Noelani looked at Landry Jenkins's picture on the

Marshals Service wanted poster and recalled Dwight Broussard's theory. "Convince him to come home. Make up something if you have to."

Cynamin waved a hand. "Fine, fine."

"Then the next thing I need to know is," Noelani said, "what does Landry Jenkins's voice sound like?"

***

Twenty minutes later, after Noelani Lee and Wanda Fong drove away, Cynamin Allgood went down the hall to her office. She sat at her cluttered desk and opened a drawer. She took a letter from the drawer, on Schneckenkorn Brewing Company letterhead, and read it for probably the hundredth time.

Damn, that's a lot of zeroes.

Cynamin had disregarded Mitchell Ratcliff's other offers but this one, wow, he was serious. Sounded desperate, too:

As a legally authorized agent acting on behalf of the Schneckenkorn Brewing Company dba Saddle Road Ale Company, I am prepared to tender a lump-sum payment in the full amount as described above in the form of a cashier's check. In return, as outlined in the enclosed contract, the Schneckenkorn Brewing Company dba Saddle Road Ale Company would assume total and immediate control of your brewing operation, including but not limited to all durable equipment, formularies, and any and all intellectual property and applicable software you may currently possess.

Miss Allgood, please understand, this offer is not open-ended; time is of the essence. I appreciate your prompt attention and response. Please call me as soon as possible.

If she signed the contract, she'd make more money with the stroke of a pen than she ever earned from American Election and her boutique in San Diego combined. If she didn't sign it, she could continue making her beer the way she wanted, not selling out.

Then she heard gunshots.

Cynamin folded the letter and slipped it back in the drawer and went to her bedroom. She pointed a finger at a man she saw sitting up in her bed, watching a cop show on TV. Cigarette butts filled an ashtray on his lap.

"Get your sorry ass out of here," she said, "and I mean pronto."

It's a good thing the crews got back in time for this.

Chapter Eleven:
The Key

Tuesday evening, the empty Saddle Road Ale Company's brand-spanking-new but non-functioning brewery on Kawili Street was damn near spooky, as far as Mitchell Ratliff was concerned.

Even with all the life-draining fluorescent lights turned on, Mitchell couldn't help but look over his shoulder every few seconds, just in case.

Mitchell's sense of vulnerability swelled when he realized, all he had to defend himself with as he walked toward his office was a two-liter plastic bottle, half-full of passion fruit-flavored beer.

What a difference from St. Louis, where the cacophonous bottling lines at the Schneckenkorn Brewing Company, in continuous operation since 1866, produced the signature Schneckenkorn Lager—"the beer of worldly men worldwide." It long ago dominated the market and cemented its reputation as the go-to cheap brew for backyard barbecues, ball games, and fraternity hazings from coast to coast.

Mitchell settled in behind his desk, opened the bottle, and poured beer in a coffee mug emblazoned with the Saddle Road logo. The logo he designed. He took a gulp.

He had to admit, Cynamin's brews were phenomenal. Every single one he tasted blew his mind. This one was no exception. She knew what she was doing, unlike Mitchell, who was a whiz at marketing and operations, but couldn't make beer to save his life. So when Mitchell first tasted her homemade product at one of Hilo's dive bars, he reported it to the home office. They immediately ordered him to put her out of business, but only after he figured out how she made it.

When Schneckenkorn dispatched Mitchell to Hawaii, they gave him orders to conquer the state's microbrewers—as he had done previously with their stealth craft-brew operations in the northern Rocky Mountain region and New England. After quick visits to Maui and Oahu, his initial scouting trip ended at the Big Island. Within a day or two, he deemed the island ideal for the company's purposes: it had a dearth of competition and a wealth of natural resources, and enough retail outlets to generate good sales and buzz. With the company's blessing and a pile of its cash, he bought an empty warehouse on Kawili Street in Hilo to house the newly named Saddle Road Ale Company.

The name he made up.

Through a mutual friend, Mitchell later met Jervy Salazar and Kawika Hailama, Cynamin's helpers. He suggested they accept Cynamin's product in lieu of cash. The idea went over like a fart in church since they preferred mass-market crap like Schneckenkorn. So he sweetened the deal with authorization from the home office to pay off their car loans and cover their rents for a year.

In a private small-batch room he installed inside the brewery, Mitchell tried to replicate Cynamin's beers using samples the guys brought him. But he failed with a thud, as his honey ale experiment drew zero requests for refills. He got the same results with the coconut ale.

Mitchell hid those flops from St. Louis, which had shipped sparkling new brewing equipment to Kawili Street. When they suggested he buy Cynamin out, Mitchell called her with an informal proposal. He did his best to convince her selling out to Schneckenkorn would be the ultimate win-win: her unique local brews produced in ginormous quantities by the world's largest brewer, for sale throughout Hawaii and the West Coast. The entire West Coast! In exchange, she'd get a shitload of cash up front and a generous check year after year for the rest of her life.

But she disregarded his messages, as she did a proposal he snail-mailed to her. So he tried again, with more zeroes. Same result.

She called one day and told him she wished to remain friendly rivals. "My beer's too good for you people," she said. "Beat me if you can, hon."

Arrogant and stubborn. Quite the combo.

But Mitchell admired Cynamin. He conceded she was a bit like him.

He kicked his feet up on his desk and drank more passion fruit ale. Damn but it was good.

Her recipes. I need to get my hands on her recipes. If she'd only accepted my offers, we'd both be better off.

Kawika's idea about using one of his employees to get the formulas? It had merit. But the notion made Mitchell nervous, just as another former employee's mere mention of Cynamin's name made this other guy damn near jump out of his skin.

I can't do that to him. Dammit, Jervy and Kawika can figure it out themselves. No more free rides.

As he drank the last of the beer, he held the mug to the light and smiled.

What a damn fine logo.

***

Noelani Lee picked up her favorite mug—with the logo of the United States Association of Professional Investigators printed on each side—and poured hot water over a green tea bag. "Did you notice how weird Cynamin was the whole time we were talking with her?"

Wanda Fong, sitting at the kitchen table with a glass of guava juice, said, "Yeah, you brought up Paul Templeton and she got this look like she wanted to rip his guts out. Don't blame her."

Noelani sat down. "True, but she got revenge on him in the end."

"You're talking karma there, cuz. The old man had it coming, what he did to her."

"But when I mentioned Landry Jenkins, she got mushy." Noelani sipped her tea. "And she barely spoke about her husband, only to say he's ultra-busy and she has a hard time getting in touch with him." Noelani stared at the tea bag floating in her mug. "Wanda, you're divorced—"

"I'm thinking of going back to my maiden name. The farther I put that cheating weasel behind me, the better."

Noelani always liked the name Wanda Mahalua. "And there's the exact response I expected from Cynamin, about Landry Jenkins."

"Yeah, but she wasn't married to him."

As far as we know.

"Anyway," Wanda said, "what's all this got to do with Cynamin and her beer problem?"

"Nothing, maybe. Who knows. But now this other thing with the marshal creeps up and I'm not sure what I can do to help her or protect her."

"Oh, Noe," Wanda said, "don't sell the sistah short. She's tougher than you think."

The cousins spent the evening finalizing their plans for the next day. About eleven o'clock, Wanda said good night and retired to Noelani's guest bedroom.

In her own office, Noelani booted up her PC and launched a background check on Kawika Hailama and Jervy Salazar. She didn't find much—minor youthful indiscretions, shoplifting, underage drinking. A couple of years ago, Jervy earned probation after he got popped breaking into a tourist's rental car.

Day jobs—Kawika worked part-time in maintenance for the county's parks and recreation department. Jervy had two part-timers, one with an auto repair shop and the other at a feed and farm supply store.

Finished with her research, Noelani went to the living room. She picked up her ukulele and played random blues riffs. Her hands created background music as her mind sorted through Cynamin Allgood's beer situation and what the late Milt Nihoa may have uncovered in the course of his investigation. She also pondered this guy named Landry Jenkins and the unpleasant Paul Templeton and what Cynamin wasn't telling her about them.

Much less Deputy US Marshal Dwight Broussard, with his black alligator-skin boots and his high-pitched but otherwise pleasant drawl, and his Glock and his love of tequila.

She decided he wasn't quite handsome but also realized his was a face you couldn't ignore. Well, his face and his presence, commanding and conveying piles of confidence even though he wasn't much taller than her. What was the word? Swagger. Dwight Broussard had swagger to spare. Like he knew what he was doing no matter what he was doing, a fine trait for any human being but one that fit the lawman like a perfect pair of jeans.

Which he wore well.

Against her brain's wishes, Noelani's hands began playing "Born on the Bayou."

Her cell buzzed. She looked at the incoming caller ID. "Detective Ahuna, fancy hearing from you at this late hour."

"Hello, Miss Lee. I trust I didn't wake you up."

"My cousin and I are having a slumber party. Come over and play Truth or Dare?"

"I appreciate the invitation, though I'm not sure what kind of truth I'd get out of you, Miss Lee."

Not this again. "Detective, like I said, I was working when Milt—"

"Speaking of which," Detective Ahuna said, "the preliminary results of Mr. Nihoa's autopsy would seem to indicate you couldn't have killed him."

Noelani sucked in a breath. "You're saying he didn't drown."

"No, he did drown. His lungs were soaked like a sponge. It's just, he didn't drown in the traditional sense."

Noelani said, "There's an untraditional way?" She rubbed her right temple with her free hand. "You're losing me here."

"Based on what the ME was able to determine, it appears as if Milt's last swim was in beer."

"Wait. What did you just say?"

"He didn't drown in the bay, or the river or a pond." Detective Ahuna said, "Unless you were around a pool of the stuff, which I get the feeling is unlikely owing to your non-alcoholic reputation, then I believe you."

Milt drowned in beer?

"Now for the bad news," Detective Ahuna said. "My next step will be to question your client, Cynamin Allgood."

"But, uh, she'd have no reason to kill him. He was working for her."

"Maybe he figured something out she didn't want him to figure out. It would give her some incentive. Wouldn't you agree?"

Noelani again rubbed her temple.

"Looking at it objectively, I mean," he said.

"I suppose I need to keep my mouth shut next time I talk to her."

"Perhaps you'll sleep well tonight."

When he hung up, Noelani wandered to her kitchen. She saw the day's mail on her table. She'd left it there when Dwight Broussard paid his unexpected visit.

Setting the uke aside, she opened the plain envelope, the one minus the return address and with a hard object enclosed. Inside was a sheet of paper, which she unfolded. As she did, a key fell to the floor. She picked it up and studied it: small, shiny, brass, with the letter G engraved on one side above the numbers 4562. It was unremarkable and could have fit any of thousands of locks on the island.

She turned her attention to the paper, a black-and-white photocopy of the Marshal Service's Landry Jenkins wanted poster. Whoever sent it to her had circled the photo in bright orange highlighter ink and drew three large exclamation points above it.

Noelani blinked at Landry Jenkins's image. Then she picked up her phone.

***

Hubert Kang, locksmith, wearing a green flannel bathrobe over his red-and-blue striped pajamas, yawned and scratched the back of his head. "You do know what time it is. Don't you?"

Noelani Lee, on the other side of the counter of Hubert's shop in downtown Hilo, said, "I'm really sorry, but you know I wouldn't have called if it wasn't important."

"Uh huh."

"And you are the best in town. Thirty-plus glorious years in the biz, right?"

Hubert extended his left palm and wiggled his fingers. Noelani dropped the key in his hand. Hubert held it up to the light, examined both sides, and then laid it on the counter.

"Well?" Noelani said, "What's it for?"

"Technically, my workday doesn't start for another six or

seven hours."

"You live above the shop. I'm the only person I know who has a shorter commute."

He stuffed his hands in the bathrobe's pockets and nodded toward the key. "It's for a file cabinet."

Noelani said, "You can tell just by looking at it?"

"I know my keys. It's how I make a living. During normal working hours." Hubert yawned. "It's from a company called Gruber, in Iowa. Probably one of a pair since keys for file cabinets usually come in twos."

"So it's not a copy."

"Nope. See? It has the manufacturer's markings—the letter and the numbers."

"Good to know." Noelani picked up the key. "Hubert, I owe you."

"Good night, Miss Lee."

Chapter Twelve:
The Convergence on Piihonua Street

Wednesday morning, driving down Waianuenue Road, Kawika Hailama said, "You believe she's got us doing this?"

In the passenger seat of Kawika's pickup, Jervy Salazar said, "Too damn early for me. I don't know what she was thinking."

"Makes me wonder where the sistah's head is."

Jervy rubbed his eyes. "Then she says she got a new guy going with. What's the bruddah's name?"

"She didn't say," Kawika said. "Just said the dude's geeked to learn about beer-making."

Jervy opened the glove box and grinned. "Damn, brah." He reached in and removed a baggie full of weed. "When'd you get this? You been holding out, yeah?"

"It's for laters. When we get rid of the new guy." Kawika's phone signaled an incoming text. He read it and said, "Told you, we meet you bumbye."

"Is that who I think it is?"

"He's all impatient." Kawika dropped the phone in an empty cup holder. "Since I called him last night, dude's wound tighter'n my old lady during her monthly."

"Give him some of this, mellow him out. For reals." Jervy replaced the baggie in the glove box, and then peered at a cooler in the back seat of the truck's twin cab. It contained a six-pack of lite beer, several Spam musubi, four ham sandwiches with extra Swiss and mayo, and a dozen Reese's Peanut Butter Cups—Kawika's traditional road trip provisions. "I just hope the new bruddah don't have a weight problem, otherwise, he ain't fitting in here with us."

Kawika adjusted his Kangol hat. "Last one in's the first one off."

*****

Deputy US Marshal Dwight Broussard parked his rented SUV in the shade a few yards down from Cynamin Allgood's house on Piihonua Road. He killed the engine and drank oily convenience store coffee.

Cynamin's car sat in the driveway, in front of the closed garage door. Over the past couple days, Dwight had driven by when she'd been working in the garage, checking gauges and doing whatever else it is people do when they're involved in the tedious process of making beer. He figured she'd spotted him once, direct eye contact. Since then, the garage door remained closed.

As did the curtains in her living room. From his vantage point, Dwight couldn't see in. There was no sign of life inside or outside. He sipped the bitter coffee and grimaced.

A minute or so later, a blue Honda Accord pulled into the driveway. Dwight watched as a man in ultra-dark sunglasses and an Oakland Athletics baseball cap crawled out from the passenger seat.

Dwight stopped drinking coffee mid-swallow. He checked his watch: nine thirteen a.m.

The Accord backed out. Dwight could see the driver was a woman, but he was too far away to get a good look at her. He made a mental note of the license number as the car departed.

The man in the ball cap approached Cynamin's front door. Dwight watched the door open and the lady of the house invite him in.

Well, it is a small world after all. Then he opened the window and poured out his remaining coffee.

Cynamin said, "You know the redneck marshal's sitting outside in an SUV."

The disguised Noelani Lee said, "I knew he'd be here, since he's planning on paying you a visit soon."

"But he saw you, hon."

"No, he saw the same dude he encountered at the bar last night. Besides," Noelani said, "he's not our immediate concern, as long as you're polite with him."

"Easier said than done, since he's in cahoots with Templeton."

"Remember what I told you. We'll do what we can to keep Templeton at a distance. Did you call your husband?"

"Yes, but the best I could do was leave him messages." Cynamin checked her watch. "The boys are running late, as usual."

"Island time, you know."

"I just wish the producer and the camera crew were here," Cynamin said. "We'll have to do another take and I'm betting the marshal won't go for it."

Oh, this again. "Before they do," Noelani said, "do you mind if I conduct a quick security sweep? You know, just to make sure no one can get in without you knowing."

About nine thirty, Cynamin led the guy in the Oakland Athletics ball cap from the house to the garage and opened the door. Her shiny brewing gear reflected the morning sun. Dwight watched the guy in the cap take a step back and say something that made Cynamin laugh. Then the pair stepped inside, out of Dwight's field of vision.

Figuring the guy might be there for a while, Dwight sat back and got comfortable, seeing as he had nowhere else to go until he could corner Cynamin alone.

***

In the tiny dining room of an intimate B&B in downtown Hilo, Paul Templeton picked at macadamia nut pancakes and Portuguese sausage links, distracted by the expensive piece of paper with Cynamin Allgood's address.

Paul considered skipping breakfast, maybe get to Cynamin before Dwight Broussard did. This despite the marshal's warning to wait until he'd questioned her first about her boyfriend/husband/whatever, the fugitive Ponzi schemer.

He read the address again, on something called Piihonua Road. Dwight had provided no directions.

The B&B's proprietor, a woman Paul figured was in her early sixties, approached him and said, "Mr. Templeton, how's your breakfast this morning?"

"It's good, thank you." He glanced at his barely eaten food.

"It's just, well, I'm not as hungry as I thought I was."

"Are you enjoying your stay with us?"

"Sure, yes I am."

"What are your plans for today? If you're going to the volcano, I know people who can take you there by boat. Right up to the lava flow, where it goes into the ocean. As close as they can legally get."

"Sounds amazing."

The woman said, "They give all my guests a nice discount. The best time is just before dark. You can get some dramatic photographs around that time."

"To be honest," Paul said, "there's an old friend of mine from way back I want to visit, here in town, but I don't know how to get to her house."

The woman blinked at the paper next to Paul's plate. "Did you try calling her?"

"No, uh, I want it to be a surprise, since it's been a long time." He handed her the paper. "Any idea where this is and how I get there?"

The woman read the address. "Kind of in the middle of nowhere if I remember right. Would you like me to pull up directions on the Internet?"

"I would appreciate it." Paul showed her his 1990s-era flip phone. "See, technology and me? I'm a dinosaur."

The woman smiled and said she'd be right back. Paul nibbled on the sausage and had a couple more bites of pancake. He hoped the woman wasn't looking up who lived at the address on Piihonua Road; Hilo being a small town, it wouldn't have shocked him if Cynamin and the woman knew each other. His anxiousness subsided when she returned a couple of minutes later with a computer printout of turn-by-turn directions.

"Here you go," she said, handing him the directions and the address. "It's easy to get there, even if it's far away. Just don't let all the Hawaiian street names confuse you."

"Where I live in California," Paul said, "the streets are in Spanish. My house is at the corner of Via de Viejas Cabras and Avenida de las Vacas Viejas."

"Goodness."

"So this," he held up the printout, "is nothing. You just have more vowels and Ps and Hs here, is all."

Minutes later, Paul stepped out to the parking lot behind the B&B. He climbed in his rental car and studied the directions, turned the ignition, and then hung a right on Ponahawai Street. He continued on, turning right on Komohana Street. A few blocks later, he stopped at a chain pharmacy, where he paid cash for a 100-ounce bottle of detergent, a roll of heavy-duty duct tape, and a large-tipped, red permanent marker.

The cashier smiled and offered a polite aloha. "Did you find everything you were looking for today, sir?"

"Almost."

"Oh, I'm sorry, what else can we help you with?"

"No, see, I'm sorry, I have all I need," Paul said, as he picked up his purchases, "for the mind of man plans his way, but the Lord directs his steps."

"Yes, he most certainly does." The cashier handed him his receipt. "And God bless you too, sir."

***

Kawika Hailama parked in Cynamin Allgood's driveway and said, "He the bruddah?"

Jervy Salazar studied the dude, in jeans, shades, a long-sleeved tee, and a ball cap. He was talking with Cynamin inside her garage. "Must be. She tell you his name?"

"Something started with an A."

He and Jervy got out of the pickup. Cynamin greeted them with a beaming smile. "Hey guys, sorry about messing up your morning."

"No worries," Kawika said. His phone bonged; he checked the incoming message, which he ignored.

"Well, it means a lot to me since this is a last-minute thing, so thank you."

Jervy said, "This the new guy?"

Cynamin introduced the new guy, Augie. She said he heard about her beer-making skills and said he wanted to learn how to do what she did. "Naturally, I won't be sharing all my secrets, but since he's eager to learn from the best, who am I to argue?"

Kawika looked sideways at Jervy, who bit his lower lip. Then he looked at the new guy, who rubbed his nose to hide a smirk. "Howzit, Augie?"

They exchanged a combination bro handshake and hug. Augie said, "All right, brah."

He sounded like some white actor, though Kawika couldn't place the name. And he was soft, with no muscle to speak of.

Cynamin said, "I think you guys'll get along, especially since you have a big road trip ahead of you today."

"Yeah, right," Jervy said. "So what's up?"

"I need you boys to pick up honey from my guy. His name's Stewart."

Kawika sniffed. "Honey? Again?"

"He'll meet you in Honoka'a," Cynamin said. "No need for you to schlep all the way to Kona this time."

Jervy said, "Aren't you making da kine lilikoi beer? Didn't you tell us you had orders for it?"

Augie said, "Miss Allgood says this one bar asked for the honey brew."

"And my new friend Augie here says he'll help me adjust the recipe." Cynamin put an arm around his shoulder. "See how eager he is to learn?"

Jervy said, "Uh, you're changing it? Because I like it as is, yeah."

Kawika coughed to disguise a laugh.

"Just a minor tweak," Cynamin said. "A little experiment."

Kawika's phone bonged. He looked at the incoming message, and then typed a quick reply: back in ten.

A moment later, a response: ???

***

Wanda Fong parked on Noelani Lee's front yard. She hopped out and dashed to her cousin's Nissan Sentra, which she then drove downtown. She parked outside of the B&B on Punahoa Street, positioning the car with a clear view of the inn's entrance. Her job, Noelani said, was to keep an eye out for Paul

Templeton.

And if need be, she would have to execute Plan B.

Wanda hoped it wouldn't come to that. Since she'd moved back to Hawaii from Las Vegas a few months ago, she helped Noelani doing computer stuff, mostly research on social media, since Noelani avoided Facebook and Twitter as if they carried a disease. But to this point, she hadn't asked Wanda to stake anyone out, much less follow them around town.

Wanda rolled down the window, the sun beating on the car's roof and turning its interior into a sauna. A soft breeze blew in from the bay, but the relief it offered was slight and temporary. She refreshed herself with a long sip from a sugary, forty-four-ounce cola.

A minute later, a small car emerged from the inn's parking lot. The driver looked to his left, and then pulled out onto the street.

"Oh geez," Wanda said. "Oh geez."

***

A few seconds after the three Hawaiian dudes—the one in the ball cap, the one in a black hat, and the one with the ponytail—got in the twin-cab pickup and left, a red coupe flew up the narrow street. It slowed in front of Cynamin Allgood's house before it rolled past Dwight Broussard.

Dwight looked down and recognized the driver. "You have got to be shitting me."

Piihonua Street being too narrow for him to flip a U-turn, Dwight started the SUV and slammed it in reverse. In his rearview mirror, the red car slipped into a driveway a few houses down. When the car's back-up lights illuminated, Dwight accelerated and slid to a stop behind it. He jumped out and in two strides blocked the driver's door, gripping the car's roof with both hands. "What the living hell are you doing here?"

Paul Templeton glared at him. "What do you think I'm doing? I'm going to make the black bitch pay for what she did to me."

Dwight spotted a huge jug of generic detergent, duct tape,

and a big red marker on the passenger seat. "I told you to back off until I had a chance to question her."

"If it goes as good now as it did all those other times in San Diego, then you may as well quite now," Paul said. "And when exactly are you going to have your pointless little chat?"

"I have no idea what you're planning to do with that stuff—"

"I have laundry and a hole in my suitcase."

"Whatever it is, it better not involve bodily harm to a material witness in an ongoing federal investigation." Dwight smacked the roof.

Paul smirked. "Oh, come on. You don't care about her one iota. And besides, do you really think she'll give him up now?"

"If anything bad happens to Cynamin, and I find out you're responsible, I'll make double-damn sure you're doing a long-ass stretch in Club Fed," Dwight said. "Speaking of asses, here's some advice: If you drop the soap, don't bend over to pick it up."

"Suddenly you're all about law and order."

About then a screen door screeched open and a shirtless man emerged from the house. His arms, legs, and torso were polluted with tribal tattoos, geometric patterns mixed with Hawaiian petroglyph symbols. "What the hell you haoles doing in my fucking driveway?" he said. "I need to get my gun and shoot your asses?"

Dwight turned so the man could see his star and his Glock. "I'm a deputy US marshal. If you're dumb enough to threaten me with a firearm or any other weapon, I will be within my rights to blow a hole in your giant, tatted gut."

The man stopped and studied his giant, tatted gut. "You fulla shit, haole."

"On another note," Dwight said, "if you continue to interrupt me in the pursuit of my duties, I will book you for obstruction of justice, punishable by a fine and five years in a federal penitentiary. If I'm given any say, it'll be the shittiest shithole in the system. And I'll throw in a charge of felony stupidity, just because I can. Any questions?"

The man took a step back and covered his considerable

midsection with both hands. "You serious, haole?"

"What I'm serious about is you getting back inside your house, locking the doors, and closing the windows. And don't go aiming any cameras or phones out here or blab this to any of your cousins, aunties, or uncles. Are we cool, brah?"

"Shoots," the man said. "Two no-account white dudes hanging in my driveway, and I'm the one treated like the criminal." He turned his ink-covered back on Dwight, said, "Whatevahs," and retreated into his house.

Paul said, "Still making friends and influencing people, I see."

"Here's the deal," Dwight said. "Cynamin knows I'm on this rock, and there's a good chance she knows you are, too."

Paul sneered. "If you said anything to her, so help me—"

Dwight said, "What you're going to do is give me two days."

"I fly home tomorrow night."

"Extend your stay. I'll get her to talk, then I'm done with her. Two days, Reverend." Dwight slapped the car's roof with his left palm. "Give me a second and I'll move my rental, so you can get to your laundry and luggage repairs."

Dwight backed up the SUV and waited for Paul to leave. Then he watched him crawl past Cynamin's house before gunning it down the road.

Back at his original spot in the shade, Dwight noticed for the moment, Cynamin's house was devoid of visitors. The twin-cab was long gone and the garage door was closed. He waited a moment, and then he opened the driver's door—

—just as a white Nissan Sentra flew into the driveway.

Oh, for Christ's sake.

He watched the driver, a short, chunky Hawaiian woman in a brown tee-shirt and denim shorts, bounce from the car. She stood next to her open door and looked up and down the street. Then she stepped away from the car and repeated her survey.

Dwight slumped behind the wheel and waited, until he heard a car door slam shut. He sat up and observed as the woman, now with a black satchel over her left shoulder, waddled from the car toward Cynamin's front door. She knocked and

Cynamin greeted her with her patented glowing smile and a long hug and led her inside.

It was almost ten o'clock. The sun was heating up and he had nothing cool to drink. He rolled down the window. He heard birds singing and he smelled flowers, probably the ones in Cynamin's neighbor's front yard. He took off his cap and wiped sweat from his forehead, and then closed his eyes.

Paul Templeton was a classic jerk, but Dwight knew he was right about one thing: his previous attempts to question Cynamin were unproductive. She bitched about Landry Jenkins taking her for a fool, about how she accepted his money because he wanted to see a woman of color succeed in a snow-white San Diego suburb. And she took his money again when she ran for mayor on that stupid show, thinking he sincerely wanted her to win the made-for-TV election for the same reasons he propped up her boutique.

But Dwight remembered, it wasn't always what she said about Jenkins, but how she said it, often with this glazed-over expression. Which, in Dwight's playbook, meant she was hiding something.

The last time Dwight questioned Cynamin, she claimed she didn't know where Landry Jenkins was hiding or where he ran to. She swore up and down, if she found him first, she'd cut off his balls and flush them down a toilet.

Now she was maybe a hundred feet away, in her house. All Dwight could do was wait for her endless parade of visitors to be gone so he could sit down and talk with her and maybe convince her to tell the truth for a change. Then he'd assure her the prosecutors would go easy on her if she confessed to the whereabouts of Landry Jenkins/Edward Vaughn.

He'd also get one more opportunity, perhaps his last, to admire her high cheekbones, her long legs, and her enigmatic personality, up close. The excessive make-up—well, he'd forgiven her for it years ago.

But any of which Paul Templeton harmed in any fashion, Dwight would have no problem giving the bastard a proper beat-down.

He heard an approaching car and opened his eyes. A silver

sedan pulled up in front of Cynamin's house. Then he got a look at the driver: a familiar face.

Now what the hell?

Chapter Thirteen:
The Questions

Kawika Hailama peered in the rearview—the mirror vibrating in time to Damian Marley, cranked high. Augie, the new guy, sat in the back seat, nodding off beside the big cooler. "Yo, wake up, brah."

From the passenger side, Jervy Salazar said, "You all hung over or what?"

"Nah," Augie said. "It's just the black sistah, she wen' get me up all kinds of early this morning."

"You ain't the only one," Kawika said.

"Most definitely not cool." Jervy typed a text on his phone.

Before they hit the road, Cynamin Allgood instructed Kawika, Jervy, and the new bruddah to meet some haole named Stewart at the Malama Market in Honoka'a Town, to pick up a case of honey in jars.

Kawika said, "How'd you meet her?"

"Who?" Augie said, "The black sistah?"

"There another one?"

"Asked about her at this one bar I hang out at. Wally's."

Jervy said, "Oh yeah, I know the place. Go there after work, pau hana, couple times a week. Maybe I seen you there?"

"Coulda been. I drank this one beer there," Augie said. "It was good, so I asked the bartender; he says some black sistah makes it. I ask who it was, since there ain't a lot of black chicks in Hilo. He tells me."

"It wasn't the nasty shit she makes with coffee," Kawika said, "was it?"

"No, man. This one had like pineapple in it."

"And you drank it anyway."

"Dude, I was thirsty."

Jervy said, "What do you think of her?"

"Woman's all kinds of funny kine."

"Heard that," Jervy said. "Not to talk stink, yeah."

Jervy's phone buzzed. He read the incoming text, and then said to Kawika, "Ho brah. This ain't good." He held up the phone.

Kawika read the message. "Damn."

Augie said, "What ain't good?"

"Bruddah we know is having a bad day," Kawika said. "And it ain't getting any better."

***

Cynamin Allgood said, "Won't you please sit down, Officer—"

"Detective Ahuna."

They each took a seat in Cynamin's living room. Detective Ahuna said, "Is your husband here, by chance? I mean, I don't want to interrupt your day in case you have anything planned."

"He's away on business." Cynamin looked over her shoulder, down the hallway past her kitchen.

Detective Ahuna clicked a pen and opened a notebook. "Then I won't take much of your time, Miss Allgood. I know you probably have better things to do than talk with me, so we'll make this quick."

Cynamin offered him something to drink; he declined. He said, "I've heard you make beer, correct?"

"I do. Have you had it, maybe someplace in town?"

"Not yet, but I've heard good things."

"You've heard true things." She giggled.

He looked at her for a moment, and then said, "The reason I'm here is to ask you some questions about a gentleman named Milton Nihoa."

"Aw, I heard what happened to him, poor man," Cynamin said. "What do you suppose he was doing out in the ocean like that?"

"I've come to learn he was working for you. Based on files we found in his office, I mean."

Cynamin told Detective Ahuna she'd hired Milt a few months ago to look into the possibility someone was trying to undermine her brewing operation. She also mentioned the voice message Milt left on her cell.

Detective Ahuna took notes. "And was this the last time you saw him?"

"No, hon, I didn't see Milt then," she said. "He called. I figured he was close to, what is it you cops say, 'cracking the case'?"

"But he didn't tell you what he knew."

"No, sorry."

"Did you return his call?"

"I tried but it went straight to voicemail." She put a hand over her mouth, hoping as she did the hidden camera crew had a good angle to catch her reaction. "Oh. He may have already died by the time I called him, do you think?"

Detective Ahuna flipped to a fresh, blank note page. "Miss Allgood, what sorts of information did he share with you about his investigation, up to then?"

"Not much, but I didn't care, just so long as he nailed whoever's trying to screw me."

"And you had faith he'd do that."

"He said he would, and since I was paying him, who am I to call the man a liar?"

"When was the last time you saw Mr. Nihoa in person?"

Cynamin tilted her head back and closed her eyes. "It had to have been, I think, Friday night. He dropped by for expense money. He said he needed it because he had overdue bills."

Detective Ahuna asked her to describe Milt's state of mind.

Cynamin said he seemed normal, maybe a little drunk but not scary sloppy.

The detective said, "Have you by chance met a local private investigator named Noelani Lee?"

She nodded. "Yes, she's working for me now, too."

"And are you aware she and Mr. Nihoa did not get along?"

"Well—"

"The fact is, they detested each other, I'd call it passionately," Detective Ahuna said. "Professional rivalry, which got personal."

Cynamin again covered her mouth with her hand, and again hoped the crew was taping all this. "My God, you don't think she killed him, do you?" She gasped. "Lord, I'd hate to think she could kill a man. She doesn't seem the type, to me."

Detective Ahuna wrote something in his notebook. "What

did you think of Mr. Nihoa? You must have known him long enough to form an opinion."

She waited a beat. "He seemed nice enough. When I first called him to ask if he'd help me, he was here in under ten minutes."

"Would you describe him as professional, sloppy? Maybe, I don't know—what about his personality?"

"Like I said, he was nice to me," Cynamin said. "Even though I have a feeling he had no idea who I am."

"I ask because acquaintances have told me all sorts of things. It seems like everyone had an opinion," Detective Ahuna said. "I'd just like to hear yours."

Cynamin said, "It seemed to me he drank a lot. You know, he always smelled like booze. And he wasn't all too worried about his appearance, what he wore or if he was clean. Unlike you, hon. Did your wife pick out your shirt?"

"Did he ever tell you about other cases he was working? About friends, enemies, other people he encountered?"

Cynamin shook her head. "We never got into those sorts of details."

"What about people he encountered while working for you? What did he tell you about his investigation of your, uh, situation?"

"Like I told you, all he said was he was close to nailing the bastard. He didn't give details."

Detective Ahuna blinked at her. "How secure is your equipment?"

"Secure as it can be. I don't have children, so it's my baby, and I protect it like a mama bear looks after her little cubs."

Detective Ahuna clicked his pen and closed the notebook. "I wonder if I could impose upon you to show it to me?"

Cynamin led him to her garage. She opened the door and Detective Ahuna approached the intimidating stainless-steel equipment. Cynamin described each apparatus's role in the making of her fabulous beer. As she did, Detective Ahuna studied the tanks and their interconnected hoses, pipes, and gauges. The top of each tank—the mash tun, brew kettle, and fermentation tank, she called them—was level with the detective's chin.

He said, "The lids for these things, do they come off?"

"Yes, they have to, so I can sanitize them."

"Have you cleaned them lately?"

"I'm getting ready to start a new batch so, yes, I needed to sterilize them. Why do you ask?"

"A set-up like this must have set you back a pretty penny."

"It's all new. I couldn't live with myself if I made my beer with equipment someone else used first, see what I'm saying?"

"And you do all this by yourself."

"As far as the brewing goes. I mean I have some boys who help me with pick-ups and deliveries, but no one but me works in here."

He asked their names; she gave them, and wondered aloud as Detective Ahuna wrote them in his notebook if he thought Kawika or Jervy had something to do with Milt's passing. "It would be weird because I don't think they ever met him but once."

Detective Ahuna said, "You're telling me, nobody else can unlock the garage door? They can't access it, right?"

"No, no one can."

"You leave it closed and locked when you're not working? The one over here on the side, too?"

"This is a big investment," Cynamin said. "If someone got in and messed up my stuff and I found them and got my hands on them, I'm afraid you'd probably have to put me in jail."

Detective Ahuna examined Cynamin's brew kettle. "I sure hope it never comes to that, Miss Allgood."

***

Wanda Fong emerged from Cynamin's bathroom with a copy of People and walked down the hall toward the living room. But neither Cynamin nor the cop who'd arrived a few minutes earlier were in sight.

She peered out a window and saw them standing in front of the garage, Cynamin facing her, the cop with his back to her. Wanda smiled at Cynamin, who returned the greeting. Then

Wanda turned to look at an empty SUV across the street.

Something in the corner of her eye distracted her. She turned to look, thinking she saw movement in the front yard, but there was nothing around. So she backed away from the window and let the curtain fall into place.

Wanda went to the kitchen and took a bottle of water from the fridge. Then she retraced her steps back down the hallway, past Cynamin's office and her master bedroom, to a spare bedroom in the back of the house. A sliding glass door afforded a view of the backyard and a small, covered concrete lanai, sitting right outside the bedroom. She opened the sliders.

A picnic table sat smack in the middle of the concrete slab. Wanda noticed how everything was neat and tidy out there, except for a big clamshell on the table, full of cigarette butts.

Weird. I could've sworn she don't smoke.

Wanda closed the sliders and left the bedroom and tiptoed down the hallway. Still not hearing Cynamin or the police detective in the house, she went into the office. She scanned the room, and then sat at the cluttered desk.

Oh, Cynamin, trust me, this ain't my idea.

Then she opened the file cabinet's bottom drawer.

***

Deputy US Marshal Dwight Broussard waited a minute or so after Cynamin invited Detective Ahuna into her house before he got out of the SUV and jogged across the street.

He climbed over the lava-rock wall fronting the property and snuck along the chain-link fence separating Cynamin's yard from her neighbor, until he reached some shrubs and a puny palm tree at the corner of the house. He waited for several moments, eyeballing the house next door and straining to hear human voices above the birds and a steady breeze that blew around the house. From the garage, he caught snippets of muffled speech—Cynamin and Detective Ahuna. Then he slid around the corner until he came to a window. He stopped when he heard noises from inside a room.

Dwight removed his black cap and peeked in.

It was a small office, a desk with a laptop beside a file cabinet, its bottom drawer open. Sitting at the desk, the same chubby woman he'd seen earlier pored over what looked to Dwight like a ledger book. She typed numbers into a calculator, and then transcribed something onto a notepad.

Dwight heard her say, "Huh?" He watched her perform more calculations, scratch her head, and write something else on the pad. She said, "Dang, this can't be right."

He crept past the office to another window. A bedroom: wooden African tribal animal carvings—elephants, lions, zebras—collected dust on a dresser; a huge portrait of Cynamin, in a sheer gown, dominated the wall above the headboard; and a paperback sat atop one of two nightstands.

The bed was unmade. Both pillows had indentations.

He eased around to the backyard. There wasn't much yard to speak of, though, mostly trees and a concrete slab with a propane grill and a redwood picnic table, outside sliding glass doors. A large clamshell rested on the table.

Dwight crossed to the table and peered into the shell. Inside it were about a half-dozen cigarette butts, each imprinted with a thin band of red ink at the base of the filter. But no ashes.

Then he looked through the glass door into another bedroom. This one was pristine: the bed made, carpet vacuumed—as if no one ever used it.

He heard voices again: Cynamin and Detective Ahuna. They sounded polite enough, although Cynamin's was different. He remembered, all those interviews in San Diego, when she got nervous, her pitch dropped.

Something's not right.

✳✳✳

Detective Ahuna said good-bye and got in his car and drove away. Cynamin offered a half-hearted wave. Then she exhaled and shivered.

This cop's interview, she decided, was worse than any the cracker marshal had given her back in San Diego.

She tried to get a grip on what just happened: But Milt

drowned. And I sure as hell didn't toss him in no ocean.

And did they get this on tape? She surveyed her front yard and assumed the cameras, as usual, were hidden. Forget "ratings gold." We're talking platinum here.

She turned toward the front door and went inside. Wanda Fong, Noelani Lee's cousin, sat at the kitchen table, her hands clasped around a water bottle.

Wanda said, "Things go okay with the cop?"

"Yes, just fine, hon," Cynamin said. "No sign of the old man, huh?"

"Nope. Maybe he decided to stay away."

The doorbell rang, followed by a knock. Cynamin said, "Yes, I'm coming," as she went to the front door. She opened it and froze.

"Hello, Cynamin," said Dwight Broussard. He removed his black cap. "Long time no see. May I come in?"

Cynamin looked at Wanda. Wanda put a hand on her chest. Cynamin looked at Dwight. "It's okay, hon."

"I'm sorry." Dwight said, "Do you have company?"

"Yes, a friend."

"Ah. You were expecting someone else?"

Cynamin stepped outside and closed the door behind her. "Look, you know full well his cheating, dishonest, unborn baby-killing white ass is on this island."

"Who are you talking about?"

"You know who. The old man, Paul Templeton."

Dwight blinked. "No, I don't, and how would I?"

"Don't lie to me," Cynamin said. "I...you—just forget all that crap. I'll take care of him if he comes around."

"I might remind you, anything you say that may be construed as a threat to any person—"

"Knock it off, please, Dwight." Cynamin felt her face getting hot. She lowered her voice. "I told you once, I told you a million times—I don't know where Landry Jenkins is and I moved here to get away from him anyway so he couldn't find me, either."

Dwight said nothing.

"What he did to me he did to your daddy, if what you told

me is true. Which makes at least two of us wondering why you haven't caught him and tossed him in jail instead of asking me the same old questions over and over again."

"Just doing my job."

"Like you did before. Do you see what it is I am saying?"

"Perhaps I can have a moment or two with your husband."

"He's not home," Cynamin said. "Maybe he'll get back tomorrow."

"Too bad," Dwight said. "I still haven't met the lucky man. Always wanted to."

"You got to the count of three," Cynamin said, "to get off my property and never show yourself in my presence again."

Dwight said, "I read about a report awhile back. It was by one organization or another that found cigarette smoking reduces life expectancy of women smokers by, on average, eleven years. Twelve years for men."

Cynamin squinted. "What are you talking about?"

Dwight held up a cigarette butt. Cynamin felt the air in her lungs escape in a rush.

Dwight said, "I know you don't smoke. Never have, or at least as I remember, you claimed you didn't. You always said it messed up your smile, made your hair smell bad, all the things that could ruin how you presented yourself on camera and how the morning talk-show hosts would perceive you."

Standing in the warm sunshine, Cynamin felt a chill.

"So, I have to ask," Dwight said, "who's the woman, or man, who's going around shaving a decade-plus off their life by inhaling this nasty shit?"

Chapter Fourteen:
The Honey Pot

Almost to Honoka'a, Kawika Hailama said to the new guy, "You don't talk much. You all right?"

The whole way from Hilo, along the Big Island's Hamakua Coast, as they rolled past cane fields and through pinpoint-sized towns, Augie checked his phone nonstop. He kept lowering his green-and-gold cap over his eyes until Kawika couldn't see them anymore, and then would stare out the window.

"Nah," Augie said, "I'm cool."

"All right," Jervy Salazar said. "Just a lot quieter than the last bruddah we hung out with."

Kawika noticed, in the mirror, the new guy sat up. Looked like he came to life.

Augie said, "What bruddah was that?"

"Just some moke," Kawika said, "named"—he looked at Jervy—"what was his name? Fred, right?"

"Yeah, Fred," Jervy said. He turned to face Augie. "Not like you at all. Bruddah talked his head off, even when he was sober."

Kawika grinned. "Which wasn't often."

Augie said, "What's this guy look like? Sounds like someone I know."

"Huh, maybe your height, not real fat," Jervy said. "Big drinker. We'd go to bars and shit and the bruddah was always getting cockeyed."

"Completely shitfaced is more like it," Kawika said. "But yeah, dude asks lots of questions, especially when he's drunk. I'm telling him, 'Brah, shut up already.'"

"Yeah," Augie said, "has to be the same guy."

"Surprised he never mentioned you," Jervy said.

"Haven't seen him in a long time."

"Us either," Kawika said. "What, last week one day?"

Jervy nodded. "No sign of him since, like, last Friday, huh."

Kawika said, "Came over my house with a case of the Schneckenkorn beer he just bought. We talked story all night, him going on about the black sistah, asking about what beers she's making, how she makes it, where she keeps things. All this stuff is inappropriate."

Augie said, "Why's it inappropriate?"

"'Cuz it was none of his damn business," Jervy said.

"My wife kicked him out of the house," Kawika said, "when he started talking stink about some other sistah. See, she don't go for mokes who disrespect women."

"Drunker he got," Jervy said, "he was saying stuff like she, this sistah he was talking about, she was a total raving bitch and a know-it-all, yeah. Always going on how much smarter she is than him."

"Uh huh," Kawika said. "Before he left, he said he had something he was gonna snail mail to her, said it would make her all jealous and show her he's better'n her after all."

"Whatever that means," Jervy said. "All I know is, his ass was sloppy by then, but he still got in his car and drove away."

Augie said, "Yeah, same dude."

For the first time, Kawika noted, the new guy smiled. Augie said, "The black sistah?"

Kawika said, "What about her?"

"I don't get the whole TV thing. Pretending there's like cameras and stuff around."

"Ho brah," Jervy said. "She ain't right in the head, far as I can tell."

"You know she was on one reality show," Kawika said.

"Right, but she ain't now," Jervy said.

"In her mind she is," Augie said.

Kawika steered the pickup off Highway 19 onto Plumeria Street, on a heading toward downtown Honoka'a.

"First time I meet her is today," Augie said, "and she stands there and tells me she'll pay me with her beer. No money, beer. But I don't need no beer. I need money."

"Shoots," Jervy said, "she don't pay us money either, no way. Same deal, says 'thanks' and end of story."

"Then why do you keep doing stuff for her?"

Kawika looked at Jervy. "Eh, something to do. Whatevahs." He adjusted the Kangol cap. "Anyway, she's not all bad once you get to know her. She might be a little crazy, but all together, she's okay, yeah."

"Reminds me," Jervy said, "are we gonna get back in time for the debate?"

"I hope so," Kawika said, "so you can get an eyeful of your new hot girlfriend."

"Shut up."

Augie said, "Girlfriend?"

"Big debate on TV tonight," Jervy said. "Last one before the election. She does good, I think she'll win."

"Jervy here's all tied up in the mayor's campaign," Kawika said. "My boy here's got a serious crush on the lady running in it."

"Sistah's got a solid platform, job creation and all," Jervy said. "She also wants to crack down on crime, which is cool."

Kawika said, "And she's got some huge-ass tits."

"It don't hurt she's good-looking, but don't go making it like I'm all shallow."

Kawika looked at Augie in the rearview. The new guy squinted at a message on his phone, and then rubbed his head. "Guess you ain't into politics, yeah."

"Nah," Augie said. "Just trying to get along."

Kawika turned left into a parking lot in front of a market and pulled into a stall.

Jervy said, "What's the dude driving?"

"She said a panel van. See it?"

"Not yet."

"I'll be back." Augie opened his door. "Gotta take a leak." He hopped from the truck and walked toward the market.

Kawika waited a beat. "Something's off with the bruddah."

"Heh." Jervy nodded. "I thought it was just me."

***

Wanda Fong's cell buzzed. "Noe, what took you so long?"

"Sorry I couldn't get back to you right away," Noelani Lee said.

"Where are you now?"

"Staring at a shelf full of baked beans. What's going on?"

"Well," Wanda said, "the old dude, he was here at Cynamin's house but then he disappeared. I mean, he never came near the place. It was weird because he drove out here from downtown."

"I guess that's a good thing."

"The police detective was here awhile ago, and now the marshal's here, too."

After a beat, Noelani said, "What's he doing?"

Wanda peered out Cynamin Allgood's kitchen window. She saw Cynamin and Deputy US Marshal Dwight Broussard in the front yard, engaged in an animated conversation. "I don't know, but him and her are outside talking up a big old storm. He keeps showing her something looks like a cigarette butt."

Noelani said, "Can you hear anything?"

"No, nuh-uh. I didn't hear much the cop said when he was here, either, except they were talking a lot about the Milt Nihoa bruddah."

"Like I knew he would."

"Then they went outside to check out Cynamin's brewery and I didn't hear anything else before he split."

After a moment, Noelani said, "What else did you find?"

Wanda said, "Noe, maybe we can talk about it when you get back."

"Bad?"

"More like, unexplainable."

"Okay," Noelani said. "Be careful in case Paul Templeton shows up, okay?"

"Yeah, no worries, cuz," Wanda said. "Hey, did you spring your surprise on those buggahs yet?"

"Nope, but soon."

"Think it'll work?"

"Sweetie, they won't be able to resist."

***

The panel van pulled into the parking lot the same time Augie emerged from the market. The van parked two stalls down from Kawika's truck. He and Jervy motioned the new guy to join them.

The driver, the white man named Stewart, got out of the van and approached them. "You must be Cynamin's guys," he said.

"Just us," Kawika said, "and this is Augie. He's new."

Augie sauntered over next to them. "Howzit."

Stewart opened the van's back doors. Kawika looked inside at a case of glass jars filled with honey. "She didn't say how much she needs," Stewart said. "Any left over, maybe you guys can use what she doesn't."

"Get the wife to slap it on some ribs," Kawika said. "Thanks, brah."

"No worries. All Cynamin said was she needed it quick."

Jervy lifted the box from the van. "You sell this stuff for a living?"

"Stores carry it," Stewart said. "Bakers, restaurants—they all buy it."

"Yeah, but there's not many people making beer with it, right?" Kawika said.

Stewart closed the door. "She's the only one I know of."

"Figures," Jervy said. "Who ever heard of honey beer?"

"Hey, I'd try it," Stewart said. "Tell her to save me some, yeah?"

"Not a problem," Kawika said. "Speaking of beer, we got some in the truck. You thirsty at all? Hot day, long ride home."

"Wish I could." Stewart checked his watch. "I need to get going. Tell her I'll email her an invoice." He got in the van and drove away.

Jervy shoved the box in Augie's chest. "Here ya go, new guy."

Kawika sent a text, and then said, "All right. Time for a snack break."

They drove out on Honokaa-Waipio Road to the Waipio Valley overlook. Kawika parked the truck and helped Augie hoist the cooler from the back seat. "Heavy for you?"

"Nope."

"Good. You carry it."

The three men walked down to the overlook area below the

parking lot. There, Kawika surveyed the wide, green, sun-splashed valley below. White surf crashed on the black sand beach. A silvery ribbon of water cascaded down the face of a gray lava cliff on the valley's far west end.

In the shade of a pavilion, Augie lifted the cooler onto a picnic table. Kawika said, "You ever come out here much?"

"Nah. Not some place I wanna drive to."

Jervy opened the cooler, reached in, and distributed musubis and sandwiches. "What, too touristy for you?"

"Beer me," Kawika said. "New guy, you want one?"

"No, brah, not allowed."

"I didn't know anyone needed permission to have one beer, yeah."

"Not my idea. I'd be violating my probation."

"Dude." Jervy looked at him. "You too? What'd you do?"

"Nothing big," Augie said. He took a bite of sandwich. "Damn, brah, how much mayo you went put on this thing?"

Jervy popped open a beer. "Truth is, I'm not 'allowed,' either." He took a swig. "But no one has to know, am I right?"

Kawika opened a beer with one hand and unwrapped a sandwich with the other. He turned to face Augie. "Seriously, what did you do to get probation? See, I'm asking because you don't look like the criminal element to me, yeah."

"Got an aunty lives Kona side," Augie said. "One day I was visiting, I went to this store. I see a couple shirts I like. Long-sleeve, like this one."

"I can't believe you wear that," Jervy said, "on a day like today."

"What? I like them."

Kawika said, "You're making me sweat just looking at you."

"What happens is, I take the shirts up to the cash register," Augie said. "Chick working there, she's talking story with this bruddah. So I wait and wait. I'm getting bored and I know my aunty's got dinner ready, like, soon." He said, "I figure, well, if this chick's gonna blow me off, maybe I can give myself da kine ten-finger discount."

"Oh shit," Kawika said. "You didn't."

Augie said, "I pick them up, walk out. Big as you please."

Jervy washed down the sandwich with beer. "Then what?"

"Halfway down the street, I'm home free. Then the dude from the store, the one talking with the cashier chick? He runs up and tackles me."

"Man," Kawika said. "Anyone get it on video?"

Augie wiped mustard from his chin. "Turns out, buggah's an off-duty cop."

"Oh hell no," Jervy said. "That's all kinds of fucked up."

"Especially since you aren't all that big," Kawika said, "or got muscles."

"Turned out not so bad," Augie said. "Judge takes pity on me, being a first-time offender. Gives me probation, and I've been a good boy ever since."

Kawika pointed his sandwich at Jervy. "Unlike some losers I know."

"Fuck you." Jervy pounded what was left of his beer.

They ate in silence for several minutes, Jervy downing a second beer, Kawika chasing his sandwich with a Spam musubi. Augie barely finished his sandwich.

Kawika noticed Augie playing with a chain around his neck. "Brah, what's that?"

Augie looked at him, and then at the object in his hand. "Just a key."

Kawika looked at Jervy. Jervy looked at Kawika, and then at Augie. He said, "Oh, so your house key or something, yeah?"

"Nah. Found it at the Cynamin sistah's house."

"Where at?"

"Sitting in her garage. Where she's got all the beer-brewing stuff."

Jervy said, "So you just took it? You being a good boy, huh?"

Augie grinned. "Didn't say I was always good."

Kawika adjusted his cap. "What's it for?"

"I don't know. Probably nothing."

Jervy looked at Kawika. "Hey, we need to get back to Hilo town."

"Yeah," Kawika said. "Miss Allgood's waiting for her honey."

They climbed the hill from the overview to the parking lot. As Jervy jumped in the shotgun seat, Augie loaded the cooler in the truck's bed. Kawika heard Augie say something and saw him bend over to pick something up.

Kawika said, "You okay, dude?"

"Yeah, dropped my wallet," Augie said. He held it up and opened the empty billfold. "Nothing in it anyway, as usual."

"Eh, well, no worries. Maybe we can fix that for you bumbye."

Kawika got behind the wheel and they began the hour-long return trip to Hilo.

As they hit the main highway, Jervy exchanged texts with someone on his phone, and then grinned at Kawika.

Kawika said, "What'd he say?"

"Says he's happy now," Jervy said, "and I quote, 'as hell.'"

Arriving in Hilo, they parked beside a white Sentra in Cynamin's driveway. Cynamin Allgood was in her open garage, tending to her brewery and reading something in a notebook. She held it to her chest as Kawika, Jervy, and Augie got out of the truck, Augie tasked with hauling the case of honey.

"Hey boys," Cynamin said. "I'm glad you're back."

"Miss Allgood," Kawika said, "you okay? You look all shook up."

"Oh, no, hon, I'm fine. Everything went well with Stewart?"

Jervy nodded toward Augie's load. "It's all right there. We didn't take any."

Cynamin directed Augie to set the box on a bench. "I'd give you some beer," she said, "but I don't have any left. Now that I'm going to start the new one, it'll be a couple of weeks until it's ready."

"No worries," Kawika said. "You got a visitor?"

Kawika watched Cynamin's gaze wander from the Sentra in her driveway to the street. "Yes, I forgot to tell you, a friend of a friend came by. She's inside. If you want, I can introduce her."

"No, I gotta get to my real job," Kawika said. "Half-day today, yeah."

Jervy nodded. "Yeah, me too. Boss'll get mad if I'm late."

Cynamin looked at Augie. "What about you, hon? If you want, you can stick around and I'll teach you everything you'd ever want to know about brewing great beer."

Augie bit his lower lip and looked at Kawika. "Uh, no thanks. Got things to do at home."

Cynamin reached into her pocket. She took out cash and handed each of them a twenty. "Listen, guys, I know I impose on you a lot, so since I don't have beer for you today, maybe you can each get lunch or something."

The three men accepted the money. Kawika said, "Geez, Miss Allgood, this is real nice of you."

"Yeah," Jervy said, "I'm always good with your beer."

Leaving Cynamin's house, Augie said to Kawika, "Apartment's on Mililani Street. Can't miss them. Buildings're yellow."

They entered the complex, three buildings in a U-shape. Kawika pulled into a covered space. "Hey, brah, nice meeting you, man."

They exchanged fist bumps. "Yeah, you too."

Augie jumped out of the truck. As he did, Jervy asked to use his bathroom.

Augie said, sure, just don't stink it up, and led him upstairs. Kawika stayed in the truck, listening to Black Uhuru full blast.

Augie unlocked the apartment and led Jervy inside. He turned and said, "It's right down there."

The first blow struck Augie in the midsection. It emptied his lungs and doubled him over. Jervy's next punch was an uppercut to the chest, which knocked Augie on his butt in the middle of the living room.

Clutching his sternum and his gut, Augie fell to his side. He struggled to breathe. He looked up as Jervy straddled him and bent over and grabbed the chain around his neck. Jervy pulled, snapping the chain. Then he stood up and showed Augie the key.

"Hey, check it, I don't need to go pee anymore," Jervy said. He shoved the key in a pocket and turned toward the door.

Jervy descended the stairs and got in the passenger seat. Kawika raised his voice over the music. "Everything come out okay?"

Jervy said, "How fast can you get me downtown?"

"Fast enough. Why, what's up?"

"Probation officer. Hates it when I'm late."

Chapter Fifteen:
The Do-si-do

Noelani Lee winced when Wanda Fong applied an ice pack to her chest.

"Dang, Noe," Wanda said, "the buggah nailed you but good."

Lying on her cousin's bed, Noelani struggled to remove the Oakland A's ball cap and her sunglasses. Wanda gave her a hand, setting the props on a nightstand. She said, "He took the key? Right off your neck?"

"Things didn't happen the way I'd hoped." Noelani pressed the ice pack against her aching sternum. "The good thing is, he doesn't have much of a punch. Do you remember, a couple months ago, the woman I caught trying to sneak out of the fitting room wearing four dresses?"

Wanda said, "It looked to me like your eye was gonna stay swollen forever."

Noelani said nothing for a few moments. Then she picked up her smart phone and pressed an app. An aerial image of Hilo appeared on the phone's screen, with a cartoon depiction of a car moving toward a collection of warehouses and businesses near the airport.

Wanda asked her what she was looking at.

"GPS device I attached to Kawika's truck," Noelani said. "I wanted to see if they're going where I assumed they'd go."

"Did they?"

The truck was on Railroad Avenue, less than a mile from Kawili Street, where she expected it might be. He's at the Parks and Rec maintenance yard, at work. "No, not this time. Um, can I have something to drink?"

Wanda went to the kitchen and returned a few seconds later with a beer for herself, a water for Noelani. "You got that look on your face, cuz. I mean, not counting the pain."

An intense throb knifed through Noelani's chest as she sat up. She took the water from Wanda. "What did you find out today?"

"Something can't be explained." Wanda pulled a folded

sheet of paper from her hip pocket and handed it to Noelani. "I made a copy on her scanner when her and the detective were talking."

Noelani sipped water while she read the document. "Those are a lot of zeroes."

"I know, right?"

She read it again. Then she wondered why someone named Mitchell Ratliff, with the Saddle Road Ale Company, would make such a generous offer to buy out Cynamin.

Wanda said, "Maybe the Ratliff dude got those bruddahs to take the key from you. You said they were sending lots of texts today. No coincidence, huh?"

"But why would he go to the trouble of having them do it when he wants to buy her out anyway?" Noelani rubbed her aching chest. Jervy's punch had landed right between her tiny breasts, catching nothing but bone.

After a moment, she said, "Did you hear anything between Cynamin and Detective Ahuna?"

Wanda said she only heard parts of the conversation before the detective and Cynamin went to the garage. She said she saw the detective get in his car and leave, and not a minute or two later, the US marshal showed up. Then she asked Noelani whether she figured out who mailed her the wanted poster and the key.

Noelani said no, it just came out of the blue, unmarked.

"You know, cuz," Wanda said, "there was something else I saw there at Cynamin's house that was big time weird."

"What do you mean?"

"Well, see, the whole time she was on the American Election show," Wanda said, "Cynamin would go on about smoking and how bad it can kill you."

Noelani clutched the ice pack tighter to her chest. "She's not far off the mark."

"Plus she said one time she thinks smokers are pigs, and how she and her husband don't want smoke around them at all. She said she kicked a friend out of their house for lighting up in the bathroom."

Noelani said, "Are you telling me you caught her smoking

today?"

"Oh, no way, Noe. But when she and the detective were outside," Wanda said, "I was looking around the house and went out to her backyard. Well, there sitting on a picnic table was this big shell, and it was full of cigarette butts. Smelled nasty."

"Were there a lot of them?"

"Hard to tell. I mean, I didn't get close enough to check them out, since I didn't know how long she'd be talking with the detective. And besides, you wanted me to snoop around in her office."

"Wanda, I believe my exact words were 'take a look and see what you can find.'" Her head starting to ache, Noelani rubbed her temples. "Hang on, sweetie." Then she picked up her phone and dialed a number. It rang twice, three times.

Then someone answered. "Hello, Miss Lee."

"I sure hope I didn't get you at a bad time, Detective Ahuna."

"None better or worse than any other. What do you need?"

Noelani said, "I assume you've searched Milt's office and his home."

"If you're interested in anything related to what he was doing for Cynamin Allgood," Detective Ahuna said, "I'm afraid I can't share it with you. Much less tell you about it. All I can say is, hypothetically, there may have been nothing."

"No hard copy files? Anything on his computer?"

"Again, Miss Lee, I can't tell you we didn't find anything on his computer."

"Uh huh."

Detective Ahuna said, "Any more quick questions?"

"Just one," Noelani said. "Did you, hypothetically, find anything related to Landry Jenkins?"

Four seconds of silence. Then, "How did you know—Miss Lee, I can't tell you we found a file Milt had compiled on Landry Jenkins."

"You—wait." Noelani said, "Hypothetically, then, if such a file existed, have you shared it with a certain Cajun lawman?"

"Right now, I'd say no."

"What's in it?"

Detective Ahuna said, "If there was such a file, and a considerable one at that, it would indicate your buddy Milt had been looking for Jenkins for the better part of a year and only recently found him."

"Here? In Hilo?"

"It probably would contain notes, photos, times, dates and places—the usual."

Noelani said, "I guess you also aren't allowed to tell me if there's anything in it directly linking Milt with the marshal."

"No, I'm not. Besides, it took us a long time to get into his file drawers."

"Why?"

"We didn't have a key. It seems to be missing. Now if you'll please excuse me, Miss Lee, I have work to do." He disconnected the call.

Noelani stared at the phone for a moment.

Wanda asked her what the detective said.

Noelani relayed the important parts.

Wanda said, "Noe, I don't get it. Why would the dead dude you hated—"

"The feelings were mutual."

"Why would he send you the poster, and his key, even?"

"One thing about Milt Nihoa," Noelani said, "was he liked to rub my face in it. Remember when those people got busted for the fake slip-and-falls at markets all over town?"

"I think I do. Why?"

"Milt figured it out. Of course, a goldfish with ADHD could have, too. But afterward, I got these anonymous newspaper clippings in the mail. I ran into him one day and he said, 'Hey, Lee, read the papers lately?'" Noelani said, "So, no, Milt wouldn't be above gloating about a twenty-five-thousand-dollar reward from the feds, especially if he was close to finding Jenkins."

The theory worked for her. What she didn't understand was why, if Milt in fact had sent her the poster, he had included the file cabinet key. Which now was in Jervy Salazar's hands.

Her head throbbed. She closed her eyes and rested her head against a pillow.

Wanda drank more beer. "Did you try the email address Wally gave you yet?"

"Not yet." Noelani opened her eyes. She took out her smart phone and set up a fake email account, and then wrote a message to hibeerguy@bigisland.net.

"Sweetie," she said, "let's see what happens next."

***

Inside the Saddle Road Ale Company on Kawili Street, Mitchell Ratliff felt his phone buzz. It was an incoming email:

FROM: sales.chick@hilo-hi.net
TO: hibeerguy@bigisland.net
SUBJ: Marketing job

My bud Wally Yoshiro says you can help me
get a job working in marketing and sales in
the beer industry. I'm good at it. Please text
or call me, (808) 555-5059.

Mitchell re-read the message. He knew of a bar in downtown Hilo called Wally's Dive Inn, where he'd left a keg of honey ale. But he couldn't remember discussing job prospects with a Wally Yoshiro or anyone else in town, for that matter.

He called the number.

A woman answered. "Aloha."

"Who is this?"

"Um, I could probably totally ask you the same thing."

Sounded like Kate Hudson in one of her rom-coms. "You just sent me an email with your number."

"Oh yeah," she said. "You got a name?"

"It's Mitchell Ratliff."

"Eh, howzit, Mitchell Ratliff?"

"Well, it'll go a lot quicker if you tell me who you are."

"Oh, yeah, my name's Amber and like I said, I'm buds with Wally Yoshiro. You know Wally, right?"

"Guy owns the Dive Inn."

"Uh huh. Well, he like suggested I touch you—he says he thinks you can help me get a job marketing your beer, when you get it going, I mean."

"He did, did he?"

Amber said, "Well, I'm totally into marketing and all that and I think I'm good at it and he actually thinks I can do an awesome job for you." The woman waited a beat, and then said, "You know, you sound kind of hot."

"Well, thanks."

"And," Amber said, "he says if you get me this job, he'll literally put all your beers on tap, no exceptions. I'm not like a bar person, so, is this a good thing?"

Mitchell smiled. They do the same thing here, huh? "It will be."

"Awesome. So like can we meet and talk about this in person?"

"I'm kind of pressed for time but if we can meet tonight?"

"Sure, awesome. At Wally's place? Have you been?"

"Bring your resume and references, just to make it look official. I'll text a time later."

"Oh, I'm literally tingling. Mahalo, Mr. Mitchell."

Mitchell disconnected the call. He picked up his keys and went to the brewery's reception desk where his assistant, Rowena, was playing solitaire on her PC. "Do you know if I've ever met a guy named Wally Yoshiro?"

Rowena stopped playing the game and pulled up an electronic calendar. She did a quick search, and said, "Uh huh, a couple months ago. Why?"

"Nothing special, just the name rang a bell." Mitchell said, "I have a meeting. I'll be back in a few."

Rowena turned back to the calendar. "You do?"

"Where's Donald?"

"He's out back, having a smoke."

"I should have known."

After Mitchell left, Rowena went through the brewery to a

back door, which led to the building's loading dock. Out in the sunshine, she found her husband, Donald, puffing a cigarette.

"Hey boo," she said, "what're you up to?"

"Not much of nothing," Donald looked at her with no expression, "since I got nothing else to do."

"Well, I can think of a way we can pass the time." She grinned and stepped closer and looked up at him, being five inches shorter. "Mitchell just left."

"Oh, he did."

"Something about another meeting he doesn't have on his schedule."

"Seems he has lots of those."

"Now we have the whole place to ourselves."

Donald dropped the cigarette. He didn't crush it, just let it burn down, as he took Rowena in his arms. "So you're saying daddy left the kids home all alone?"

"Uh huh. Geez, do you know how bad I want to do it in his secret room?"

Donald laughed. "Makes two of us, but he put the lock on it. Not that we could get in it before anyway." He bent over and kissed her.

Rowena giggled. "Your scratchy beard. I love it." She looked him over. Not terribly handsome but he treated her well and she knew he loved her madly.

She studied the lines on his face, his beard, and the diamond studs in his ears. Then she stopped and squinted, something caught her attention.

Donald said, "Ro, what?"

"Boo, have you been spending more time in the sun?"

"No more than usual. Why?"

"You need to be careful about skin cancer," she said. "The spot thing on your neck looks a lot darker."

Chapter Sixteen:
The Tête-à-tête

Early Wednesday evening, walking across the lobby of his hotel on Banyan Street in Hilo, Dwight Broussard felt his phone buzz.

"Hello, Pop."

"Where yat, Tahyo?"

"Awright."

"Did you take care of my business?"

"Not yet, Pop."

But it wasn't for lack of trying.

After his interview with Cynamin Allgood, Dwight spent most of the day roaming Hilo, showing people Landry Jenkins's picture. He got blank stares and shaken heads in return. Visits to businesses in the seedier parts of town, metal buildings filled with people working in boat repair and welding and auto shops, resulted in the same reactions.

Civilians in the town's few black-owned and -frequented businesses were no more helpful. A barber asked Dwight why he was so dumb to think a bald man would set foot in his shop. A lady serving up greens in a soul food restaurant accused him of racial profiling.

A handful told Dwight he wasn't the first person to ask them about the man in the picture. Dwight asked whether the other person was a police detective.

No, they said, a Hawaiian woman who looked like she was part Asian. And awhile back, a local man who smelled like a liquor cabinet.

Dwight sat on a rattan sofa. The seat afforded a view of the bay outside. "Don't worry, Pop. I'm getting closer. I can feel it."

"Same way all those years the Saints kept getting closer to winning the Super Bowl."

"They eventually did."

Owen said, "What was you doing last night?"

"I might have had a few too many."

"You and the Mexican hooch don't mix." Owen laughed. "Son, you can't do the job when you all chockay."

"Pop, I was nowhere close to falling-over drunk," Dwight said. "I just had enough to get myself to a pleasant cruising altitude. You know what it's like."

"Ain't what I want to hear, Tahyo," Owen said. "Besides, remember what happened to your departed mother."

"I always do, Pop."

"What I want to hear is you tell me you're gonna send the thieving macaque to meet his maker."

Dwight said, "Pop, these days no one refers to anyone, and especially anyone who's African American, as a 'monkey.'"

"Yeah, yeah, yeah, but you know what I'm getting at," Owen said. "Anyways, how much longer is this gonna take you?"

"Give me a couple more days, Pop. I know he's here." Somewhere.

"You met up with the Allgood woman, I'm betting."

"For what it was worth," Dwight said. "This morning."

"I recall, she's quite the charmer." Owen pronounced the word as chawmer. "Too bad for you she's married."

"Rumor has it."

"But Tahyo, you know you can't fool me none. You've had the hots for her since day one you met her."

Dwight brushed imaginary lint from his jeans. "So, Pop, how're you feeling today?"

"Great. Took me a long walk this morning and didn't even get winded. First time all week."

"Good to hear."

"I tell you we got new neighbors down the block? I think they're Jaypan or something. Come across as nice people; he's an architect, I think, and she's—"

Dwight looked to his left at Noelani Lee, in a bright yellow top and white linen pants, a plain canvas bag over her shoulder. "Pop?"

"Yeah, Tahyo?"

"I'll call you back later."

"Well okay, get it done and get back here so we can go fishing," Owen said.

Dwight noted his father's continued refusal to call San

Diego "home."

Owen said, "Ocean's full of rockfish and yellowtail just begging to be caught."

"I will, Pop. Take care."

Dwight disconnected the call as Noelani approached him. He stood and offered her the seat next to his. "Hello, Miss Lee."

She sat, resting the bag in her lap. "I'm sorry. I interrupted an important phone call, didn't I?"

"Just my Pop. I always check in on him to make sure he's doing okay. Heart problems."

"Oh, I'm sorry. How is he?"

"He's still old and stubborn and breathing, so, yes. He's doing great." Dwight said, "I see you found my home away from home."

"It's nice, though there's a cute bed-and-breakfast downtown I hear is pretty popular."

"I've never been one for those myself," Dwight said. "My first wife noted that particular romantic failing when we finalized."

"Years ago, I had a boyfriend who took me to one. On Maui," Noelani said. "Really quaint, secluded. Then a few months later, he dumped me and had the nerve to spend a weekend at the very same inn with a ballroom dancer from Australia. In the exact same room, even."

"And you know this, because?"

"Give me a little credit. I did eventually get over him."

"I suppose that's a good thing," Dwight said, "even though he should have his head examined."

She blinked at him. "Meaning?"

"You really need an explanation? It's a compliment. Take it." Dwight said, "You been busy today, with all your PI business?"

"The clock never stops." Noelani sat forward. "And how was your visit with Cynamin? Productive?"

Dwight bit his upper lip. "Miss Allgood and I had, well, let's call it a pleasurable reunion."

"You crazy kids got caught up on old times."

"As if they never ended."

"Perhaps I shouldn't ask, but did she shed any new light on what she knows about Landry Jenkins?"

"As I said, Miss Lee, it's as if it never ended."

"Too bad," Noelani said, "especially since Milt Nihoa probably would have provided you with more help than she ever could."

Dwight sat back and watched her take a paper from her tote. She leaned over and handed it to him. He unfolded it to reveal a copy of Landry Jenkins's wanted poster. This one had orange exclamation points jumping off a circle around Jenkins's picture.

He saw her grin, which radiated gotcha. "You expect me to believe," Dwight said, "Milton Nihoa sent this to you."

"He was a cheeky fellow when he wanted to be," Noelani said. "The cops have all his files now, especially since they think his death was suspicious."

Dwight handed the poster back to her. She tucked in her bag. Then he crossed his left leg over his right knee. He wiped dust from his black alligator-skin boot. "Official word I heard is he drowned."

"You'd have to ask Detective Ahuna to be sure, since I can't speak for the police. But what will they find in those files, if I may ask?"

Dwight stopped wiping his boot and waited a beat, and then said, "Where you're going with this, it could get slippery."

"Marshal, I—"

"Deputy US marshal."

"Forgive me." She smiled. "Look, my job is to find out who Cynamin thinks is trying to torpedo her beer brewery. Now I'll admit, I assumed she was exaggerating, considering her flair for the dramatic."

"She comes loaded with it."

"But after today, now I'm convinced she's been right all long."

"Something happen to alter your outlook?"

"An uppercut to my chest."

Dwight winced.

"Long story."

"Are you all right?"

"I'm tougher than I look," Noelani said. "Ask my cousin, if you get a chance."

"Fair enough." Dwight said, "Well, Milt Nihoa never discussed Cynamin Allgood or her beer-making with me. And if he had, I would have asked him what the hell it had to do with anything."

"Could be he asked her about Jenkins, while he was working for you?"

Dwight looked away. "I doubt it."

"Cynamin tells me she doesn't know where he is," Noelani said, "and I believe her. Maybe you should, too."

A clamshell full of cigarette butts, with red-ink bands, the same brand Landry Jenkins smoked before he vanished. The indentations on two pillows in Cynamin's unmade bed, and no husband in sight. "Miss Lee, perhaps you're familiar with the word 'bullshit'?"

"It rings a bell."

"I won't bore you with the complete etymology," Dwight said, "but linguists believe the author T. S. Eliot was the first person to use the term in writing. He titled a poem 'The Triumph of Bullshit' sometime around 1910. Funny thing is, he never used the word in the poem. Read it if you get a chance; it's funny as hell."

"It's a shame you think Cynamin's feeding you a line of crap."

"He ends every stanza—they're called stanzas in poetry— he ends each stanza with 'For Christ's sake, stick it up your ass.' Cutting-edge stuff for his time."

"No one is criticizing you, as far as I can tell," Noelani said. "Except for Cynamin, who thinks you're trying to set her up for a fall."

"All she has to do is be truthful with me. You did pass my promise along to her, I hope."

Noelani said, "I did."

"And?"

"She said it was bullshit."

Dwight felt the corners of his mouth turn upward. "You

have style, Miss Lee. How about you let me buy you a drink?"

Noelani Lee couldn't remember the last time any man offered to buy her a drink, much less any man who she was pretty sure wasn't interested in getting her in bed. "Did you forget? I abstain. From alcohol."

"A Shirley Temple won't kill you. Maybe a virgin piña colada or something equally poofy. Besides, I have some time to kill." He smiled. "Come on."

They went to the hotel's lounge and sat at a small table overlooking Coconut Island and the bay. A waitress took their orders—soda water for her, bourbon neat for him.

"You're a tequila man."

"This is just a warm-up," he said. "And an ode to some friends in Kentucky."

"Am I to assume," she said, as the waitress walked away, "this means we're done talking shop?"

Dwight sat back, relaxed. "What would make you come to such a conclusion?"

"The fact you offered to buy me a drink," Noelani said. "Here, in a nice lounge, with a sweet view of the water. It's not exactly the kind of place you end up talking about fugitives and white-collar crime."

"I can talk about that anywhere," he said. "Even here, if I decide I want to. But I figured it might be nice for us to discuss ourselves for a while."

"Why?"

"Because I like to know who it is I'm dealing with."

"But you already know all about Mom living on Kauai and my dad living in a federal penitentiary. And I have two older sisters on the mainland, in case I forgot to tell you about them."

For so many reasons, she wanted to avoid conversation about Anela, a nun at a convent in Missouri, and Okalani, owner of a successful lesbian tattoo parlor outside of Boston. She hoped he wouldn't ask.

He didn't.

Dwight said, "Jambalaya has lots of stuff in it—I mean, beyond the basic meat and vegetables—all kinds of tasty things provide its distinctive flavor. Consequently, because no two versions are exactly alike, you sometimes have to ask the cook for the recipe."

"Do they always share it?"

"Sometimes."

"You know my basic ingredients, my job and my cat. What else is there?"

"Why you do what you do. What you get out of it. What motivates you. Where do you go on vacation?"

"There was only one question in there," Noelani said, "so I will answer it by saying, 'hardly anywhere.'"

"Because you live in paradise."

"No. Well, maybe."

The waitress delivered their drinks. Dwight raised his glass and offered a toast. They drank.

Dwight said, "It can't be about the payday. I mean, I know people in your line of work, in California, who charge three, four times as much as you."

"I have a lot of low-income clients," Noelani said. "They pay what they can afford, if they can pay at all."

"As I can well imagine," Dwight said, "what with Hawaii having one of the highest poverty rates in the country. Seventeen percent, adjusted for cost of living, last time I checked."

"You looked it up?"

"I have a curious mind."

"Which is why you do what you do."

"You haven't answered me on that one first."

Noelani sipped her soda water, and then said, "I've been screwed over and taken advantage of, by men, in the past. Two of them were lawyers."

"Lawyers? I hate to Monday-morning quarterback, but you should've seen it coming."

Like I haven't heard it before. "The first one ran off with his partner's nubile young niece; the second one—the one I mentioned, about the bed-and-breakfast—he ditched me for the Aussie dancer," she said. "This was after I graduated. I earned my criminal justice degree and was working as a court reporter. Mom always hoped me marrying a lawyer would be my ticket to a long, happy life. But then, my dad wound up being one of the slimiest scoundrels this state ever produced, so."

"So you get some sort of moral reward from going after cheating husbands and such," Dwight said, "something to make up for how those idiots treated you."

"Them, and some others who I care not to discuss." In Vegas.

"Your restraint is admirable. But what about men who're on the receiving end?" Dwight sipped his bourbon. "Are you an equal-opportunity avenger?"

Noelani wiped condensation from her glass. "I don't discriminate. But how did you handle it?"

"Well, the first one," Dwight said, "met her back home, went to high school together. She was all lovey-dovey when my mother passed." He pointed at his drink. "Too much of this stuff."

"Your father?"

"Moved to live with me after Katrina. Well, me and my second ex."

"Nice of you to take him in."

"Yeah, well, he and I have had some stumbles," Dwight said, "mostly centered on money. Pop is gullible, easily taken for a ride. The last one left him flat-ass broke."

Noelani nodded and wondered whether Dwight's search for Landry Jenkins was as much personal as professional.

"My first wife, about three years into our state of holy matrimony," Dwight said, "started accusing me of heinous things I absolutely did not do—the thing women hire you to figure out. Well, after my transfer to San Diego, she started slumming in redneck bars, sleeping with any trash who'd have her, which was most of them." He picked up his drink. "I did what I needed to do, then come to find out, she was later diagnosed as a schizophrenic."

Noelani watched him gulp down half of his drink. "What about number two?"

"A stark raving bitch." Dwight placed the glass on the napkin. "Plus she never warmed up to Pop. Nor him to her. I know this doesn't explain why I do what I do, unlike your situation, but I always wanted to be a cop because it's bad-ass. And being a US marshal? The bad-assest of them all."

Noelani weighed her next words, what she wanted to say versus what she ought to say. She came down the middle. "Must work with the ladies, too."

"Mmm, not as much as you'd think. Sometimes the star turns them on; other times, they think I'm full of myself. Which is true to a certain extent, but I cover for it with considerable charm." He pronounced it chawm. "Wouldn't you agree?"

Why, yes. Yes, I would. "Should I ask Cynamin for her opinion?"

Dwight grinned and pointed at her. "Good one. And you? Do men dig on you being a PI, or does the concept of dating someone who can access every deep, dark nook and cranny of their miserable existence make them run and hide?"

She said, "My profession can sometimes be hazardous to my private life."

"Too bad," Dwight said.

Noelani saw something warm in his eyes. "Why do you say that?"

"No real reason, other than I get the feeling you'd be a challenge."

She sat forward. "You think I am already."

"I also think you'd be fun to work with, what I know of you so far."

"Aren't we working together now?"

"If you say so, although you are a step ahead of me, if what those folks at the barber shop and the soul food restaurant were being truthful," Dwight said. "I've just been waiting for verbal confirmation."

"What they confirmed to me was a man named Milt also was going around, asking about Landry Jenkins."

"Uh huh."

Noelani sipped her soda. "So tell me, you're completely convinced Jenkins is here because you believe he's Cynamin's husband, even though you have nothing to hang that theory on."

"My gut never fails me."

She said, "What happens if you don't find him in Hilo? I

mean, I know I wouldn't get to claim a twenty-five-thousand-dollar reward, which most definitely sucks. But what about you?"

"Then I guess I get to take home the satisfaction of having visited Hawaii, catching up on old times with Cynamin Allgood, and meeting you."

Noelani adjusted her butt in her seat.

"Who knows," Dwight said, "I might even stick around a few extra days, have myself a little vacation. I haven't seen much of this island and I know people've been here who say you have some fantastic sights."

"Lots of them," she said. "The volcano, beaches, even some with black sand. Oh, you could kick bullshit at the ranches up in Waimea, with those gator-skin boots."

"Now you're talking." Dwight finished his drink and lowered the empty glass to its napkin resting spot. He checked his watch. "As much as I hate to end this pleasant tête-à-tête, I really should be heading out." He took out his wallet and called the waitress over. He gave her a twenty and told her to keep it.

Dwight said to Noelani, "I can walk you to your car if you'd like."

She smiled as they both stood. "I'm pretty sure I can find it. But thank you." Noelani offered a hand. He shook it. His grip was that of a man who knew how to shake hands with a woman, firm and warm. "By the way, I just remembered something."

"Yes?"

"Do you know a Paul Templeton? I've been told he used to be a preacher in California. Somewhere around San Diego, I believe."

Dwight scratched his chin. "The name's familiar. Wasn't he on the same silly reality show as Cynamin?"

"Rumor has it, he's been seen on the island," Noelani said. "She told me all about him and their history. Something about a stripper and an abortion. Sounds messy."

She waited for a reaction, but he didn't give one away. "Tawdry, is more like it," Dwight said. "From what I know about the show."

"Anyway," she said, "it's probably all just a coincidence, if he's here."

He nodded. "You're probably right."

She could tell his eyes were focused on something in the distance. Something not in the lounge.

*****

In his room at the B&B, Paul Templeton thanked the Lord in Heaven for providing him with the strength of character and the wisdom necessary to understand what he was about to do to the black bitch was perfectly acceptable in the eyes of God.

"Amen."

Then he opened his eyes and surveyed the materials distributed on his bed: The big jug of liquid detergent. The roll of duct tape. The red marker.

After the marshal ordered him to keep his hands off Cynamin Allgood—what gives him the right, since I paid him to find her in the first place?—Paul retreated to the inn and prayed and meditated, until divine guidance led him down a path of holy retribution.

However, this updated version of God's infinite justice did not involve duct-taping her to a chair, washing her mouth out with detergent, and scripting a big red J as in Jezebel on her face.

He tossed the duct tape and marker aside and hefted the detergent from the bed. The jug contained a hundred ounces of super-concentrated cleaning power—enough for up to sixty-four loads—with an easy-pour spout and a pleasing, mountain-fresh scent.

Oh, this isn't nearly enough. I better get more.

Chapter Seventeen:
The Rejection

Around sunset on Wednesday, Mitchell Ratliff said to Cynamin Allgood, "I wish you would change your mind."

Cynamin looked at him and said, "Oh, hon, I know you do. It's just it'll never happen."

Inside her garage, Mitchell watched her inventory bags of hops and malt. The relaxed lady brewer in jeans and rubber boots and an apron. "Cynamin," he said, "I'm serious. This is your last chance."

"What, so you can get your hands on all I've worked for?" She said, "You take it and buy me off and then you forget about me. And then my show gets canceled."

What show? "Fine. Listen," he said, "it's one hell of a payday. You'd be set for a long, long time. You'd get stock options and all the other perks, just like those guys in Montana and Vermont did."

"Well, it doesn't make it any more right."

"St. Louis is dropping the hammer on me to get this thing off the ground."

"Mitch, you make it sound like I should care. Besides, I know about you. You can't make beer."

"I'm getting better at it."

"You can sell it, but making it is a skill set you lack." She said, "Tell your bosses, if they hire me as your brewmaster, I'll sign."

Independent of the home office, Mitchell had pondered this option before. No doubt, Cynamin knew her stuff. But her expertise scared him; whether it was the brewpub he ran with his friends in Seattle, or at Schneckenkorn's stealth breweries in Montana and Vermont, someone else always made the beer. People who knew their shit. For once, he wanted to do it, to be known as a brewmaster, not just a marketing guy.

He said, "All right. The least I can do is ask."

"Think about it," she said. "We'd get a TV deal, a show about a beautiful African American woman making the best beer Hawaii's ever seen. Think about the publicity and how you could market it."

Mitchell decided not to respond.

"Plus, I'd get a salary twice what other brewmasters make," Cynamin said, "all those hipster white boys in Colorado and Oregon."

Mitchell held up a hand. "Now, hold on. The company's last offer was exceedingly generous." Even though brewmasters don't make squat.

"Well, I'd say it's more 'okay' than it is generous."

"Cynamin, I'm just not sure if the home office will pay you anything beyond what's called for in the contract."

"Oh, well, I suppose I shouldn't be surprised to hear that, hon." She scratched behind her right ear. "Then I guess if I don't sign, all you're left with is flat-out stealing my ideas."

"Wait. Hold on. I have never stolen anything from you."

"Sorry, I gotta call you out on that one."

"I don't know what you mean," Mitchell said. "You're the envy of every beer-making nerd on this rock. Please. Come on."

"All of which explains why you're trying to steal my recipes instead of making me your brewmaster and paying me accordingly."

He decided against defending an offense he hadn't committed. "So you at least read the offer."

Cynamin approached him and wrapped her arms around his neck and pressed her body against his. Mitchell felt her heat, her modest breasts pressing against his chest through her apron. He inhaled her—she smelled like spice—and felt relieved she wasn't wearing excessive make-up for a change.

"Yeah, you're right. It's generous as far as it goes." She said, "But just imagine how much my stuff will be worth when it's on national television. When we're on national TV."

Mitchell tried to suppress his erection. He put his hands on her hips. "You're making the honey ale next, aren't you?"

"What, did a little bird—or two of them—tell you?"

"There's an unopened case of honey sitting right over there."

"It doesn't mean a thing. You'll just have to wait and see."

She leaned closer. "Edward's flying back soon. He'll be

home for a couple weeks."

Mitchell stayed quiet, just felt her breath on his skin.

Cynamin drew herself closer, her mouth next to his ear."When he leaves next time—Samoa this time, I think, or is it New Zealand?—anyway, maybe then we can continue this little negotiation of ours."

All Mitchell could say, with his heart pounding and his dick getting hard, was, "Right, okay."

Then Cynamin released him and took a step or two back. "When we do," she said, "do me a favor, and leave your nasty cigarettes at home."

He peeked at the peach-scented electronic smoke in his shirt pocket. Nasty?

***

Kawika Hailama wrapped up his half-day shift and was getting into his truck when his cell buzzed. "Yo, Mitch, what up?"

Mitchell Ratliff said, "Kawika, you busy?"

"All pau, brah, heading home. Wife's got stew on the stove. Why, you need something?"

"Yes. I do," Mitchell said. "If you have a minute, let me fill you in."

"Does this have to do with the black sistah?"

"Uh huh. And when we're done, call Jervy. See if he can help you."

Chapter Eighteen:
The Night on the Town

Before leaving home, Noelani Lee prepared for a night on the town by donning an auburn wig, a red-and-white striped peasant top, navy blue shorts, bright yellow espadrilles, and sunglasses with lenses the size of Frisbees.

"When I lived in Vegas," Wanda said, "I knew a girl named Amber. Now that I think about it, she kinda dressed like you are now."

"Well, Vegas."

"Did you use up all my lipstick?"

Noelani checked her look in the rearview. "Almost. And your rouge, too. Sorry, I'll replace it."

"No worries," Wanda said. "So you think this'll work?"

Noelani smiled. "Let's hope so."

They parked across the street from Wally's Dive Inn. The bar was almost empty, except for some mokes sitting around a table, drinking beer and laughing at a stand-up comic on TV. They paused their revelry when Noelani led Wanda into the bar. They maintained their focus on Noelani's legs until the cousins sat at a table in the corner. Then they turned their attention back to the television and resumed drinking.

Noelani nodded at Wally, tending bar, who responded with a wink.

Wanda said, "Okay, Noe, now what?"

"We wait," she said, taking a twenty from her wallet. "First round's on me. You fly, I'll buy."

A minute or so later, Wanda returned with the drinks—a draft beer for herself, a club soda for Noelani. "So how will you know this guy?"

"Wally's familiar with him. He gives me a signal, then I go to work."

"And what do I do?"

"Hope I get the job. Positive vibes, sweetie."

They drank for a few moments, until a man wearing black boots and a ball cap entered the bar.

"Oh great." Noelani covered her face and dropped her

chin. "What's he doing here?"

Wanda looked over her shoulder. "Uh oh. The marshal." She turned to face her cousin. "I have some extra eye shadow if you need it."

Noelani watched Dwight Broussard take a stool at the end of the bar, the same one as the other night. Then she watched Wally pull a bottle of tequila from under the bar. "He didn't see you at Cynamin's place, did he?"

Wanda said, "I'm kinda sure he didn't."

Noelani took a pen from her tote and scribbled on a napkin. She handed Wanda the note and asked her to deliver it to Wally, who was pouring a shot for Dwight.

When Wanda returned, she said, "Does this screw things up?"

"I hope not."

A few minutes passed. A couple came in and sat at the bar. Two of the mokes at the table got up and started playing darts. A third went to the men's room. An older couple came in and sat at a table. The bar's lone waitress took their drink orders.

"Noe," Wanda said, "what if he doesn't come?"

Noelani kept her face hidden even as she snuck glances at Dwight. "He will, Wanda, he will."

Another minute went by. Then a man entered the tavern. He was average height, maybe five ten, clean-shaven, with brown hair. He wore a short-sleeved button-up shirt, jeans, and well-worn hiking boots. He approached the bar and said something to Wally. They shook hands and the man sat down. Wally picked up a towel and laid it over his right shoulder.

"It's him," Noelani said. "Okay, sweetie, go sit at the bar, between him and the marshal, okay?"

"Sure."

"Make small talk with the marshal. Try to distract him."

"Cool," Wanda said, "but what do we talk about?"

"The weather's always good. Just do that for a while for me, okay?"

Wanda smiled. "You got it, cuz."

Dwight poured a shot of tequila as a familiar-looking, short, chubby Hawaiian woman parked herself two stools down.

"Hey, aloha," she said, "how's it going?"

"Getting better." He gulped the shot. "What about you?"

"Trying to get used to this weird weather," she said. "All this sun, we aren't getting the rain like we normally do."

"So I've heard." Dwight studied her for a moment. Up close, she was cute enough, probably late thirties, no make-up except for ruby-red lipstick, wearing a Disneyland tee-shirt and calf-length jeans a couple sizes too big. "Have I seen you somewhere?"

"Everyone I know says I have a common face. But, nope, I doubt it." The woman wiped her hands on her pants. "Um, you're not from around here, yeah?"

"Good observation."

"My name's Wanda."

"Nice to meet you."

"And you are?"

"Me."

"Oh, um." She smiled and flagged down Wally and ordered a beer, the best you have, she told him. Wally filled a glass with a hazy, yellowish-colored brew from a tap and placed it on a coaster in front of her. Wanda thanked him and drank some.

"Oh dang, this is seriously good," she said. "This beer, local lady makes it with like lilikoi—you know what lilikoi is?"

Dwight said, "Not sure I do."

"The Hawaiian word for passion fruit, and dang, it's tasty." Wanda took another long gulp, at least half of the glass's contents. Then she looked at Dwight. "You wanna try?"

Dwight held up his tequila bottle. "I got all I need right here, but thanks."

Wanda said, "Well, you change your mind, try this beer. The sistah who makes it, she knows her stuff."

"Do you know her? The 'sistah' who makes the beer?"

"No, uh, nope. But she makes great stuff."

"Are you sure?"

"Well, yeah, it's great stuff, I'm sure."

"I mean, are you sure you don't know the woman." Dwight

adjusted his ass on the stool. "I'm starting to learn, because this town is only so big, everyone seems to know each other."

Wanda sipped her beer. "Next thing I know, you're gonna say we all look alike, too, huh?"

Dwight chuckled and poured another shot. As he did, another customer—a man—came through Wally's front door.

Oh for hell's sake.

Sitting alone in her booth, Noelani Lee caught a glimpse of Paul Templeton as he entered the bar. He strolled to a stool between Wanda and Dwight Broussard and sat down. The man with the brown hair, Mitchell Ratliff, drank something and watched television.

She watched Wally fill a glass with club soda and garnish it with a lemon wedge, and hand the drink to Paul Templeton. The former preacher and ex-mayor of Rancho de los Ancianos, California, sipped it, seemingly ignoring Dwight, who once again filled his shot glass to the rim.

Ears open, Wanda. Keep your ears open.

Dwight Broussard downed the shot and said to Paul Templeton, "You look like a drinking man. Want to try the best damn tequila this side of Jalisco?"

Paul said, "Not if it causes me to make a face like yours after I do."

"Oh, where are my manners?" Dwight introduced Wanda to Paul. He responded to her "aloha" and her extended hand with a curt glance and a grunt.

Dwight said to Wanda, "Tell me again about this beer?"

Wanda lifted her half-empty glass from the bar. "She calls it lilikoi wheat, so it's like this light summery beer." She looked at Paul. "Maybe you want to try it, sir?"

Paul stared straight ahead as he sipped his soda. "No, thank you."

Dwight said, "And you say a local woman makes it?"

"Uh huh," Wanda said. "I don't know her name or nothing,

but she's got it down tight."

Dwight leaned over and said to Paul, "Now if that isn't something. How many times, I mean, have you heard of a woman making beer? And in Hawaii?"

Paul said, "Never, I suppose."

"I'd like to meet her. Wouldn't you?"

Paul said nothing; he just pretended to watch TV.

Dwight said to Wanda, "He's not impressed."

"He oughta be." Wanda gulped more beer.

In her peripheral vision, Noelani watched Wanda and Dwight talk around Paul, and as the old preacher's face turned several shades of red.

At the same time, she saw Wally shake hands with the other man, and then point in her direction. He turned on his stool, looked at her for a moment, and then spun back around and continued his conversation with Wally.

Mitchell Ratliff said, "She sounded ditzy on the phone."

"Ho brah, don't you go saying it to her face," Wally said. "Besides, she's smarter'n what she lets on. Sistah's connected, too."

"How so?"

"Lived here all her life. Well, most of it. Total local girl, knows the island backwards and forwards. She's a schmooze machine." Wally leaned across the bar. "What I'm saying is, no offense intended, okay?"

"Go for it."

"You got a better chance of people taking you serious around here if you get her doing your promoting, since she's local. Most people like me—except me, and no offense—"

"None taken."

"They see a haole coming at them," Wally said, "starting da kine craft-beer company here, trying to sell them his product? They'll tell you to get the hell out of Hawaii."

Mitchell blinked at him.

"Just the way it is, man," Wally said. "And besides, like I said, if you get the sistah a job, I'll give you all the taps you want. Are you feeling me?"

Mitchell turned and studied the woman. Bad angle to get a decent look at her, but she was okay. Not much for tits, but she had exquisite legs.

"Go talk with her, man," Wally said. "Give her a chance, and maybe I'll give you a chance."

As Noelani had hoped, Mitchell Ratliff made his way across the bar to her booth. She looked up at him, assumed her Amber persona, and said, "Hi there."

Mitchell said, "Mind if I join you?"

She removed her sunglasses. "Well, it totally depends who you are and what it is you want from me. I mean, don't expect nothing on a first date, plus this actually isn't a date anyway. I hope you understand."

"Is that a 'yes'?"

"You know how guys in bars can be." She motioned toward the empty bench across the table. "Have a seat."

He did. "My name is Mitchell Ratliff. We spoke earlier today."

"Oh yeah, the beer dude. I'm Amber," she said. "Wally totally digs your honey brew. I mean I don't drink beer because it's like gross and I have allergies, but he says it's completely awesome."

"Oh, he liked it?"

"He literally said it was one of the best beers he ever drank."

"Huh. Well, there's more where that came from," Mitchell said. "So you're looking for a job."

"Seriously. It's tough out there, you know?"

Mitchell sat back in the bench. "Yeah. Totally. Well, to be clear, I'm not sure if I'm hiring now but I might be soon."

"Oh."

"What is it you're good at? You have a skill set?"

"Well, I can type like a hundred words a minute, and I used

to be a waitress—server, excuse me—and I'm pretty good at organizing stuff. Like my closet." She reached in her bag and handed him a paper, folded in quarters. "Here's my resume and references like you asked for."

He shunted the papers aside. "Your closet?"

"I arranged my tops like the rainbow, red-orange-yellow-green-blue-indigo-violet. Roy G. Biv? I remember it from junior high. Well, I don't have much violet because it literally makes me look sick. Some black and white, too, but I keep them separate from my rainbow."

Mitchell stared at her for what to Amber felt like a solid, creepy minute, until she said, "What, are you trying to do some weird psych-out on me?"

"No, I'm just trying to figure you out," he said.

She giggled. "People're always confused, but here's the deal: My father was half Korean and like one-quarter native Hawaiian and one-quarter Portuguese, and my mother's like a quarter Chinese, Filipino, Samoan, and Hawaiian. Each. Go back far enough and you find some Japanese, too."

"Fascinating, but not what I meant. I mean, the get-up—you have presentable professional clothes, I hope."

"Oh, sorry—yeah, I have a couple suits. Why, is there something wrong with what I have on?"

"Wally says you're good with people," Mitchell said. "Have you ever worked in sales before?"

"If you look at my resume you'll see, but I always say I'm selling myself. But like, but don't we all?"

"Sure. I guess," Mitchell said. "But do you have practical experience in sales? I mean, have you ever successfully marketed a product?"

"I was number one in my region with this herbal weight-loss system a few years ago and before that, I totally kicked butt with timeshares."

"And you know a lot of people on the island."

"Tons, the kind you need to get like a huge market share."

He blinked. "What kind?"

"Like buyers at restaurants and bars and literally anywhere else who would be retailing your product. You know, the whole

B-to-B thing."

Mitchell sat forward. "Go on."

"See, even before you have anything to sell, like when you're almost ready to get it to market, I'd generate buzz by leveraging traditional and non-traditional platforms—you know, social media, Twitter, all the cool stuff. Then I'd do like focus groups to gauge customer attitudes about craft beers and figure out our target demos. Then when we do hit the shelves, we literally do this awesome guerrilla campaign with like point-of-sale pieces and bumper stickers and maybe logo stickers we slap on stop signs around town, especially over by the schools. The colleges, not high schools, I mean. That would be so wrong."

"Right."

"At the same time, we position the brand as unique to Hilo and the whole leeward side—hey, have you considered changing the name to Leeward Brewing or something awesome like that?"

"Um, no."

"Anyway, after we're out there for a while I'd totally do a brand audit and benchmark market share with other brewers on the island, even though there's actually only like the one big one over in Kona and a couple brewpubs, plus all these people making it in like their garages. But you'd totally kill them."

A few moments passed. Mitchell stared at her but said nothing. Noelani assumed he was trying to determine whether all the stuff Amber said was canned marketing jargon she'd memorized for the occasion—which it was—or whether he was trying to picture her in a short skirt and ultra-high heels.

At last, he said, "You're almost perfect."

"Uh, I am?"

"With you, I don't have to do two jobs at once," he said. "I can concentrate on making quality product and you can be the, um, brains behind selling it." He took out his wallet and handed her a card. "Come by tomorrow morning, say, nine o'clock."

She accepted the card. "Oh, like, wow."

"I'll show you around the place. You'll get to meet the rest of the staff, then we'll discuss your future with the Saddle Road Ale Company." He leaned over and said, "And do me a favor, tell Wally he owes me for this. Huge."

He turned and, either forgetting or ignoring Amber's resume on the table, left the bar. On his way out, he waved to Wally.

Noelani examined the business card. It bore the same Saddle Road Ale Company logo as the tin sign Wally had under his bar, along with Mitchell Ratliff's title, Director of Marketing/Chief Operating Officer. Below his phone number and address on East Kawili Street, the company's slogan: "Handcrafted in Paradise."

She slipped the card in a pocket. Then she turned her attention back to Wanda, Paul, and Dwight.

Paul Templeton felt his jaw muscles twitch as he listened to Dwight and the Hawaiian girl named Wanda prattle on about alcoholic beverages and the weather. Having enough, he turned to her and said, "Not to sound rude or anything—"

Dwight said, "But you will."

The woman said, "Oh, hey, you two know each other?"

"We've had drinks before," Dwight said. "In fact, he bought the first round. Play your cards right and he'll do the same for you."

"If you could please excuse us," Paul said, "this gentleman and I have some things of a personal nature to discuss."

Wanda smiled. "I get it. You two just go on and do your talking. Me, I got to watch this guy on TV. He's way funny."

Paul turned to face Dwight. "What could you possibly want?"

Dwight refilled his shot glass. "Just curious to know if you're done with her yet."

Paul bent over his drink and guided the straw into his mouth. He sucked up half the club soda, and then sat upright. "You worry too much about the Jezebel."

"When you're around, hell yes, I do. But you didn't answer my question, which is a simple one requiring a simple answer."

Paul dawdled with the straw for a moment or two. Then he said, not looking at Dwight, "'Be angry and do not sin; do not let the sun go down on your anger, and give no opportunity to the devil.'"

"I remember another one," Dwight said. "'See that no one repays anyone evil for evil, but always seek to do good to one another and to everyone.'" He pounded the shot, and slammed the empty glass on the bar. "Here's one for you."

Paul buried his face in his hands.

"Did you know tequila originated in a town of the same name? You can look it up. And, by law, tequila can be produced only in the Mexican state of Jalisco, plus parts of a few others."

Paul said, "Why are you telling me this?"

"Because it's like champagne," Dwight said. "For a beverage to technically be called 'champagne,' it can only come from the part of France with the same name. The same rule applies to Cognac, though I never developed a taste for that crap." He rolled the shot glass between the palms of his hands. "I take it from your recitation of scripture, you've finished with whatever sordid business you had with Cynamin and you'll be flying home soon."

"Tonight."

"Ah, a red-eye. Bet you'll sleep well, maybe."

Paul finished his drink. "Don't worry, she's still in one piece. Now you can get a piece."

"If you want, I'd be happy to help you pack."

Paul said, "What about you? Still playing Don Quixote, tilting at black, bald windmills?"

"Don't worry about me, Sancho. I have all the time in the world."

Paul rose from his stool. "Go tell it to your daddy." He dropped a pair of five-dollar bills on the bar. "I'm glad we didn't see each other here, or anywhere else, for that matter."

"The sentiments are mutual."

Paul put a hand on Dwight's shoulder. "I'd pray for you, but some souls aren't worth the effort." He turned and strolled out of the bar, cursing the sticky floor with each step.

Noelani peered over her sunglasses at Paul Templeton's silhouette, exiting the bar. *Hope you were paying attention,*

Wanda.

A minute or so passed. Then Noelani spotted Cynamin Allgood come in. Close call.

Cynamin sat across from her. "You weren't kidding when you said you were going to show some leg tonight. But hey, if you got 'em, flaunt 'em, I always say."

Noelani whispered, "If anyone asks, my name is Amber."

Cynamin winked. "Got it, hon."

"Um, I didn't expect you to be here."

"I just started a fresh batch and had some time to kill, plus I wanted to see you in action. So, here I am."

"Well, all right, but try to be subtle." Noelani motioned toward the bar. "Don't look, but you see the marshal's here, sitting at the bar, right?"

"Mmm-hmm."

"He just met with Paul Templeton again."

"Yes, I saw the old man walk out."

"He didn't see you, I hope."

"Don't worry, I was discreet." The waitress came. Cynamin ordered a draft lilikoi wheat ale. Noelani declined a refill. When the waitress left, Cynamin said to Noelani, "I like to go out and sample my wares from time to time, just to make sure they're getting the carbonation right."

"Quality control, huh?"

Cynamin smiled. "While we're on the subject," she said, "what's new with you, Amber?"

The woman named Wanda was going on about something, well, Dwight Broussard didn't know what because he stopped paying attention to her the moment Cynamin Allgood sashayed into the tavern.

"And that's when I was like, 'Dude, you do all that crap and you expect me not to divorce your sorry ass?'" Wanda polished off her beer and signaled Wally to bring her a refill. "I'm thinking, it happened to you, you'd do the same thing, huh?"

Dwight, the tequila warming him, said, "Hey listen, the woman over there in the booth, the one with the huge sunglasses?"

"Yeah?"

"You were sitting with her when I came in. Is she a friend of yours?"

"No. She's my, uh, sister. Her name's Amber. Why?"

"I was thinking you might be nice enough to introduce us."

Wanda looked at Amber, and then at Dwight. Her eyes had gone as round as her sister's shades. "Um, well, I think she's busy talking with the black lady there."

"Oh, a friend of hers, maybe? Do you know her?"

Wanda shook her head, with maybe too much emphasis. She said, "I have no idea. I mean, I never met her and maybe, I think my sister knows her. She must know her since they're sitting there all talking story together."

"I'd just like to say hello. Pardon me—aloha, would that be okay?"

Wanda accepted the fresh draft from Wally. She gulped half of it, and then belched. Wally said, "Damn, sistah."

Wanda said to Dwight, "She's got a boyfriend. My sister does. And he's a cop."

"Wow, interesting, I happen to know some cops on this island," Dwight said. "One of them, anyway. Maybe it's the same fella."

Dwight watched Wanda grip her glass in a stranglehold. She licked her lips and looked toward her sister, Amber, and Cynamin Allgood, over in the booth.

"You know," he said, "not once in the whole time you've been sitting here, you haven't asked me where I'm from, or why I'm in Hawaii. You haven't inquired about my funny accent or why I'm wearing boots when everyone else here's in flip-flops. How come?"

"We call them slippahs." Wanda's mouth formed a crooked, thin smile. "Maybe I'm just trying to be polite and not all nosy and stuff. Besides, I think you've had way too much to drink for me to invite you over there. To the table. With my sister. And her black lady friend."

"Could be." He poured another shot. "By the way, the woman your sister is chatting with? She's the one who made your beer."

Wanda didn't respond.

"But I'd be surprised if you didn't already know that." Dwight downed the shot.

Noelani Lee explained to Cynamin Allgood about how and why she got a job at the Saddle Road Ale Company.

Cynamin said, "The email address on the keg of the nasty honey ale knockoff that was dropped here, the one Wally and I tried, was for this Mitchell Ratliff person?"

"Please understand, it doesn't prove anything," Noelani said, "and it also doesn't prove Kawika and Jervy are in on it. But I think I can start finding out a lot more when I go there tomorrow."

"When he starts copycatting my beer for sale and I don't get anything for my trouble." Cynamin slumped in the booth.

The waitress delivered her beer. Cynamin paid her. Noelani again declined a refill.

As the waitress walked away, Noelani said, "Um, yes, getting nothing for your trouble would be a bad thing." Though six figures is a far cry from nothing.

"What about the key? Did the boys fall for your trick?"

Before she and Wanda went to the bar, Noelani debated whether she should tell her client about how Jervy coldcocked her and ripped the keychain from her neck. Besides, since the GPS was still attached to Kawika's truck, she'd know whether they were up to anything. When she last checked, the truck was parked at Kawika's house on Ekaha Street, where he'd driven after work.

"I'm afraid not," she said.

Through her dark glasses, Noelani looked at Dwight Broussard, at the bar, talking to Wanda Fong. Based on Wanda's body language, Noelani knew things weren't going well.

"Cynamin," Noelani said, "I just need to confirm something."

"Sure, hon, but make it quick—the redneck marshal keeps checking us out."

Noelani said, "Are you positive Milt Nihoa shared nothing with you about what he found out?"

Cynamin reiterated that Milt gave her only vague updates about his investigation, feeding her tidbits about following unnamed people, taking pictures—he told her all of it was in a file somewhere. And, the last thing he said to her, about closing in on an unnamed bastard.

Noelani said, "I should tell you—and please don't share this with anyone—but the police told me they found no such files."

Cynamin sat forward. "How'd they get his stuff?"

"All part of their investigation, into his drowning."

"They don't think he drowned? I mean he drowned—he had to."

Had to? "They do, but they're just—they're just doing their cop thing."

Cynamin said, "The Detective Ahuna fellow, you mean, the one who came visiting me earlier today."

"Uh huh. Him."

"He seemed awful interested in my brewing equipment."

Noelani said, "Oh. Um, there's something else—the marshal over there—don't look at him, please—it turns out he hired Milt to track down Landry Jenkins."

Cynamin waited a beat. "He did?"

"There's a twenty-five-thousand-dollar reward, which the marshal also offered me."

"For a thief who's not even worth a nickel." Cynamin said, "Paul Templeton hires him to find me, the marshal hires Mr. Nihoa to find Landry Jenkins, and then he tries to do the same with you after poor Milt passes." She said, "Did you tell him you'd do it?"

Noelani said, "Not in so many words."

Cynamin turned and stared at Dwight. Noelani begged her to stop just as Wanda returned to the table, beer in hand. "Sweetie, what did you hear?"

Wanda sat beside her. "He's acting all kinds of suspicious."

"I can tell. But did you catch anything he talked about with Paul Templeton?"

"What I understand is, the Templeton buggah's flying home

tonight. He said something about he was done with you, Cynamin."

Cynamin said, "He what? Like, what did he say he did?"

"He just recited a Bible quote and made it sound like he's leaving."

Noelani said to Cynamin, "Has he bothered you since this morning?"

"I haven't seen a single hair on the old man's head in years, until I saw him walk out of here just before I came in."

"Well, I'm grateful you showed restraint."

"I don't have a quarrel with him." Cynamin sipped her beer. "Bygones are bygones."

Noelani cast a wary eye at Dwight, who wavered on his stool as he continued downing tequila shots. She felt a headache coming on, but resisted the urge to rub her temples. Instead, she retrieved her smart phone from her pocket and opened her GPS tracking app. She watched the monitor for a moment, and then looked at Cynamin.

"Miss Lee," Cynamin said, "what's wrong?"

"Yeah," Wanda said, "you look like you just seen our dead Uncle Clement."

Noelani grabbed her handbag. "We need to get out of here."

Chapter Nineteen:
The Hellfire and Brimstone

Earlier in the evening, when Jervy Salazar explained how he got his hands on the key, Kawika Hailama didn't say a word for several long moments.

They sat in lawn chairs on Kawika's front yard on Ekaha Street, drinking cheap beer and sharing pakalolo.

Breaking the silence, Jervy said, "Well?"

"You two-timing asshole," Kawika said. "You went and took the key from the new guy and didn't say nothing to me."

"Brah," Jervy said. "It ain't what you think, man."

"Sure, right. You're a douchebag." Kawika took a hit from their joint and stared into space.

Jervy waited for Kawika to mellow, which didn't take long, thanks to the dank herb.

Kawika passed the joint to Jervy. He said, "Mitch wants it tonight."

Jervy said, "Tonight? Shit, man. I mean, the debate'll be on in a few, and I don't want to miss the debate."

"Easy, brah, your girl's ginormous mammaries aren't going anywhere."

"She's not my girl. She happens to be the most qualified person for the most important job on the island." Jervy took a hit and passed the joint back to Kawika. "Show some respect," he said, holding the smoke as long as possible. "You're talking stink about the next mayor."

Kawika accepted the joint but didn't toke. Instead, he dropped his chin to his chest.

He looked like he'd fallen asleep. Jervy reached over and jostled him and told him to wake up.

Kawika looked at him and said, "Chill, brah, I'm thinking here."

"About what?"

"Here," Kawika said, returning the joint, "you need this more than I do."

***

They arrived at Cynamin's house long after dusk. To be on the safe side, Kawika drove by a couple times, to make sure Cynamin wasn't home and no one else was around. He parked in front of her neighbor's place and Jervy said, "Brah, c'mon, let's do this already."

They crept toward her front door. Jervy peered in the big picture window facing the street. Inside, the house was dark.

They snuck around the side of the house until they reached a window. Kawika, being taller, looked inside and confirmed it was Cynamin's office. The window, though, was locked. He told Jervy he was afraid breaking the glass might alert someone and said they needed to find another way in.

Jervy suggested the next room, Cynamin's master bedroom, but that window also was locked. He wondered to Kawika how hot it must be inside, what with no air conditioning and Cynamin keeping all the windows closed and locked all the time.

Kawika said he didn't care.

Then he remembered the sliding back doors.

***

Paul Templeton left Dwight Broussard at that miserable bar and walked to his tidy room at the little downtown B&B. There, he surveyed his tools and decided he'd need a couple more items to complete his mission.

Whether Cynamin Allgood would be home when he exacted his God-given vengeance mattered little to him. For what it was worth, he hoped she'd be there, maybe even in her garage making her infernal brew, so he could get in her face and unleash his own brand of hellfire and brimstone on her wayward black ass.

Hmm, hellfire and brimstone. I need to get some fire.

Even though God had provided him with a plan and had emboldened him with the resolve to see it through, Paul still wasn't quite sure whether Dwight bought his story about having finished his "business" with Cynamin. But the lawman was well on his way to a tequila-induced stupor, which meant there was no way he'd know what Paul was about to do, or even suspect him when the deed was complete. Paul knew he could get away with it. Go, do it, be done. Then he'd drop off his rental and hop on a plane, a nine o'clock non-stop to Los Angeles—no layover in Honolulu to trip him up—and then go to his comfortable home in Rancho de los Ancianos.

The town for which he once served as mayor. Before the black bitch Cynamin Allgood ignited a media firestorm that defamed his character and shot his integrity down in a ball of flames.

Oh, fire.

Even if what they wrote was true. But still, she should have kept her big mouth shut and perhaps prayed for the Lord's guidance instead.

Paul packed his bag and lugged it down to his rental. He returned to the room and retrieved two large jugs of laundry detergent, the big red marker, and the roll of duct tape. He went back to the car and tossed the items in the back seat, next to a cheap aluminum baseball bat he'd purchased at a sporting goods store earlier in the day. He went back to the lobby and formally checked out, thanked the night clerk and said he'd recommend the inn to all his friends who might visit the island in the future. He offered her a "God bless you," to which she replied with a polite though noncommittal smile and a "thank you, sir."

On his way to Cynamin's house—following the same route as in the morning, so he wouldn't get lost—he stopped at the same chain pharmacy as before and bought one of those multi-purpose lighters used for propane grills and campfires and such. They came two to a pack, which was okay, since he figured more firepower was better than not enough.

Then he thanked God from whom all blessings flow and continued on to the black Jezebel's house.

***

Standing on the lanai, Jervy Salazar said, "She leaves it unlocked?"

Kawika Hailama slid the glass doors open. "Whoa, what'd I

tell you, brah?"

Jervy pointed at a large clamshell sitting in the middle of a picnic table. Even though it smelled like cigarettes mixed with kitchen cleaner, it was pretty cool. "Think she'll miss that thing?"

"Take it when we leave," Kawika said. "Now come on, you want to see your politician girlfriend and her bodacious boobies on TV so bad, let's get this done with quick."

They passed through a bedroom—it looked like no one ever used it, it was so clean—and, guided by the glow of Kawika's flashlight app, moved down a hallway, past a bedroom, to Cynamin's office.

The door was wide open. Kawika snickered. "Almost there, brah."

They stepped inside, Jervy holding the key at the ready. Kawika scanned the room with his phone, illuminating in pale light a small desk, an upright fan, stacks of paper and books, and big, brown glass jugs. Kawika halted his survey when the light came to rest on a file cabinet. "Showtime, yeah."

Jervy stepped toward the cabinet. "Brah, how's it feel to be almost rich?"

***

When Paul Templeton arrived at Cynamin Allgood's house, he was so relieved to see the place was empty that he got down on his knees and offered a brief prayer of thanks.

Although it appeared the bitch wasn't home, some other person had parked on the street in front of the house next door. But there didn't seem to be activity there, either.

Emboldened by the neighborhood's solitude and tranquility, Paul took the detergent bottles and the baseball bat from the back seat. He left the duct tape and the red marker behind, thinking if he needed them for any reason, he had plenty of time to come back for them.

He strode across the lawn to the garage. He set the detergent and the bat down and tried lifting the rolling door, but it didn't budge. So he retrieved his load and walked around the side of the garage, where he found a door.

He turned the knob. It opened.

***

For some reason, the key wasn't working.

Kawika said, "What do you mean, it's not working?"

"Brah, I'm trying, man," Jervy said, "but the stupid thing won't unlock, is what I'm saying."

Kawika groaned. "You just got to be smarter than the lock, yeah. Give it to me."

As Jervy held the smart phone to provide light, Kawika slid the key into the cabinet's lock. But it didn't budge when he tried to turn it. "Damn, brah, what'd you do to it?"

"I didn't do nothing, okay? Thing's not working."

Kawika turned to him. "And you're sure the Augie bruddah said this is the key for this particular file cabinet, right?"

"Yeah, the one she keeps the book in. The only one she's got here."

Kawika released the key, stood back, and put his hands on his hips. "This is some unbelievable shit right here." He took a breath and tried again, being careful not to break the key. But after about thirty frustrating seconds, the cabinet remained locked.

Jervy said, "What's a bruddah have to do to steal stuff these days?"

***

Paul stepped inside the garage, his adrenaline so high and his faith in the Lord so complete he forgot to close the door behind him. He fumbled for a light switch, flipped it on, and beheld Cynamin Allgood's brewing equipment.

It was a stainless-steel monstrosity, large tank-like paraphernalia and tubes and pipes and gauges. Like some monster demon from Satan's attic. Paul examined it for a moment, trying to remember from the brief research he did on the B&B's computer how it all worked, and which thing did what in the process.

Paul inspected each piece of equipment until he found what he was looking for. The brew kettle's burner was turned on, and the lid was secured with wing nuts. He found a valve and turned off the burner. Then he loosened the nuts and looked inside at a golden-brown liquid. It smelled of honey.

How dare she.

He propped the baseball bat against a wall, and then he opened both bottles of liquid detergent.

***

Jervy slapped the side of the file cabinet. Then he kicked the bottom drawer. "What is up with this thing?"

"I hope you don't think bashing it's gonna make it open," Kawika said.

Jervy tried the key again, to no avail. He growled, put his arms around the cabinet, and began punching it, alternating his fists.

Kawika adjusted his Kangol cap and said, "Come on, man, ease up already."

"This is fucked up," Jervy said. "It has to be the sistah's key, so why the hell isn't it working?" He kicked the cabinet, twice.

Kawika shushed him. "Dude—"

"Man, I'm pretty pissed right now."

"No," Kawika said. "I mean, I think I heard something." He peered out the doorway.

Jervy whispered, "Damn, you think she's home?"

"No. I mean I don't know," Kawika said. "I think I heard noise in the garage, yeah."

"Well, shit, we need to get out of here."

"Not till we get the book."

"But dude, the lock, the key, this stupid—"

Jervy shut up when he heard a series of banging sounds coming from the garage.

"Grab the key," Kawika said. When Jervy did as instructed, Kawika told him to take off his shirt.

"Wait, what?"

"We need to wipe down prints, yeah? Like on the cop

shows," Kawika said.

"You're kidding."

"Brah, there's gotta be some basis of truth to it. Otherwise, they wouldn't put it in scripts all the time."

Jervy did as he was told and peeled off his tee and handed it to Kawika, who gave the file cabinet and office door a good wipe. When he finished, he said, "Come on, we need to see what's going on out there."

"Dude," Jervy said, "what we need to do is get out of here."

"Not if someone's messing with Cynamin's stuff."

"And there's the thing, man. It's Cynamin's stuff."

"Show some respect." Kawika turned and shoved a finger in Jervy's face. "You can run away like some scared little girl, if you want to, and besides, I know you think the sistah's lolo. But I like her. Black sistah making beer in Hawaii, it's a haole's game. What she did and what she got, she earned for herself. So if you want to be a pussy boy, say the word and I'll take care of things myself." Kawika, Jervy's shirt in hand, turned and jogged from the office, down the hallway toward the back door.

Jervy caught up with him in the backyard. "Damn, brah, all right. What're you going to do?"

"First I gotta wipe our prints off the sliding door, too," Kawika said. "Then you go around the front and I'll come up in the back, and we'll meet by the side door to the garage. Cool?"

"No," Jervy said, "it ain't cool."

***

After Paul drained both bottles of detergent into the brew kettle, he scanned the garage and noted stacks of brown paper and canvas bags tucked in a corner. Each bore a label with its contents—hops, barley, malt, roasted coffee beans. He hauled several bags to the brew kettle, one by one, and tore them open. Then he dumped each bag in the kettle. Then he resealed the lid, tightening the wing nuts as far as they could go. Then he turned the burner up full blast.

Drink this, you Godless black bitch.

As he waited for the temperature to rise, he picked up the

baseball bat and began swinging. The aluminum bat met stainless-steel with a resounding clang, a sound he repeated a few more times as he bashed the tanks into submission. Satisfied with the results, he moved on to a gauge of some sort, which shattered with the bat's first blow.

Then he spotted a full case of honey in eight-ounce glass jars. Each had a label of a smiling bee and the company name, South Kona Honey Farm.

Paul hesitated, and then remembered he didn't have a proper souvenir of his trip to Hawaii. He pocketed a couple of jars, and then bowed his head.

In him we have redemption through his blood, the forgiveness of our trespasses, according to the riches of his grace, he prayed. Besides, I know you get it. Then he proceeded to bash the remaining jars. Glass shards flew with each downward swing of the bat. He finally stopped, satisfied with his work, when the honey flowed in a slow-moving trickle on the garage's concrete floor.

Heaving and panting from the excess exertion, Paul tossed the bat aside and returned to what remained of the stack of dry ingredients and took the multi-purpose lighter from his pocket.

He was about to ignite it when, from the corner of his eye, he spotted an unmarked three-ring binder sitting atop a plain, wood stool. He picked up the book and leafed through the pages; printed on each was a list of ingredients and a slew of numbers he didn't understand, under headings for different beers—pineapple lager, macadamia nut porter, Ka'u coffee stout, lilikoi wheat ale, guava red ale, banana hefeweizen, papaya amber ale, Kona honey ale. On one page, a big X in green ink had been scrawled over the recipe for something called Poi Pounder German Lager.

He tore a random page from the book, flicked the lighter, and set the paper afire. He laughed as the page incinerated, a little ball of flame degenerating into leaves of ash.

Rarely had doing the Lord's work ever felt so good.

And it felt much better than the pain he experienced when a hard object plowed into the side of his head.

He went down, landing face-first with a thud and a groan.

Then he blacked out, which proved to be a blessing as doing so kept him from feeling the next eight blows to the back of his skull.

***

They agreed to split up, with Kawika going through the backyard and around the rear of the garage. Jervy slipped back into his tee-shirt and swung around the opposite side of the house to the front yard. He cut across the lawn and crept toward the garage door.

The banging noise inside had stopped. The next thing he heard was shattering glass.

Jervy slunk along the garage wall and edged closer to the the open side doorway; light spilled into the dark night. In the shadows he made out Kawika, coming from the other direction. When they were on opposite sides of the door, Jervy heard a thud. Then a different muffled noise, which reminded him of the time when, as a kid, he saw the comedian Gallagher on TV, smashing a watermelon with a giant sledgehammer.

He looked at Kawika. They nodded at each other.

Someone bounded from the garage just as they stepped into the doorway. The person ran into Kawika first, toppling him, and then turned right and bowled over Jervy, throwing an elbow into his throat. Jervy's head whacked the ground as he sprawled flat on his back.

Jervy wrapped a hand around his throbbing Adam's apple and struggled to sit up. As he did, Kawika pulled himself to his feet and ran toward the street. A couple of seconds later, a car roared away from the neighborhood, down Waianuenue Road toward Hilo.

Kawika came back and helped Jervy to his feet. "Brah, you okay?"

"I don't know, man—feels like my throat's broken," Jervy said. "Probably gonna have a bump on my head, too, but damn. What about you?"

"No lies, but the dude scared the living shit out of me," Kawika said. "You get a look at the buggah?"

"No, he was on us way too fast." Jervy nodded toward the open doorway. "Now I'm gonna say it and mean it—I should've stayed home and watched the debate, no matter what Mitch wants."

Kawika said, "We gotta check out what the asshole did in there."

Jervy wanted to argue, thinking any minute now, a neighbor would call the cops, who would find him in Cynamin's house and call his probation officer. The complicating kind of back-to-jail shit he didn't need in his life.

But instead he said, "Yeah, fine, just so long as we split, like, now."

They passed through the open door into the garage. It took a few seconds to sink in, but Jervy finally said, "Oh hell no."

Kawika said, "Dude, those are brains. You ever seen real brains before?"

Jervy's stomach did a somersault. "Who is this haole?"

"Half the dude's head's smashed in. How can you tell he's a haole?"

"Look what he did to Cynamin's stuff."

"That's fucked up, yeah," Kawika said, "but who did this to him?"

Jervy backed toward the doorway. "I don't know, and I don't care, so let's just get out of here like now."

"Hold on." Kawika stepped past the bludgeoned, brain-splattered body and around a bloodstained aluminum baseball bat in the middle of the floor. He pointed at an open, empty, three-ring binder, and sheets of paper lying around it. "Dude, it's her recipes."

Jervy said, "Shit. I knew it."

"What'd you know?"

"That maybe the sistah kept them in here, since this is where she does her beer voodoo."

Kawika said, "Seriously, you're telling me this now?"

"Brah, can we please get our asses gone?"

"Hold on, brah." Kawika began picking up the sheets of paper.

"Damn," Jervy said, "be careful. We ain't here for no cops

to find us standing next to some old dead dude."

"It's cool," Kawika said, bypassing the body again. "I got them all. You wanna call Mitch now and let him know?"

Jervy, his guts roiling, grabbed Kawika by the arm and pulled him outside. "Come on, let's bounce before I puke my incriminating DNA all over the place."

Chapter Twenty:
The Same Wavelength

From his stool-top vantage point at Wally's Dive Inn, between shots of Tres Idiotas tequila, Dwight Broussard kept tabs on Cynamin Allgood, the woman named Wanda, and the other one—the one in the crazy get-up, with the ridiculous legs—as they chatted in the corner booth.

They talked for a while, Cynamin throwing dirty looks at him from time to time, until the one with the legs checked something on her phone. Then all three women got up and split in a rush, Cynamin taking time to give him a behind-the-back finger on the way out.

Dwight called Wally over and said, "Those three women who just left, you know who they are?"

Wally shrugged. "The black sistah, seen her a few times. The short one? Maybe once or twice. But I got no idea who they are."

Dwight said, "What about the other one, the one with the legs?"

Wally emptied what was left of the tequila into Dwight's shot glass. "I don't know. Need another bottle?"

"Are you sure you've never seen her?"

Wally tossed the empty bottle in a recycle bin. "I didn't say never; maybe she's been here before. But I see lots of people every night, all week." He leaned on the bar with both hands. "Why, you hoping to hook up or something?"

"Some other time." Dwight stood and tossed a twenty on the bar. "I'm not sure I'll be back, but thanks for everything."

"You leaving Hilo?"

"Could be sooner, could be later." Dwight extended his hand to Wally. They shook. Then Dwight turned and staggered from the bar.

He meandered through downtown, sweat rolling off him— Hilo's humidity was crazy high, despite the lack of rain. He untucked his shirt as he approached the bed-and-breakfast on Punahoa Street. He took a deep breath and stepped inside.

A smallish woman met him at the front desk. "Aloha, how

can I help you?"

Dwight gripped the counter to balance himself. "Hi, yeah, I'm looking for a guest, a friend of mine. He's staying here."

"Oh, well, we ordinarily don't give out information about our guests."

Dwight flashed his star. "His name's Paul Templeton. He in?"

The woman's eyes popped at the badge and she placed a hand on her chest. "Well, he checked out earlier, sir."

"Did he now?"

"Yes," the woman said. "Is he, um, is he in trouble? Should I be concerned about being robbed?"

Dwight assured her Paul would do her no harm. Then he asked her whether she knew where he went.

The woman said no, he left with his bag and that was the last she saw of him.

Dwight pulled a twenty from his wallet, handed it to her, and thanked her. She refused the money but he wrapped her fingers around the bill and said, "Consider it a gift."

He stepped outside and strolled across the street to a grassy park. Leaning against a palm tree for stability, he took out his cell and sent a text to Paul Templeton:

Good-bye and good riddance.

Then he shoved the phone in his pocket and began the slow wobble back to his hotel, thinking, All right, Cynamin, I need you to give my old man one more chance.

***

Headaches were a common side effect of Noelani Lee's hyperadrenalism, and as she sat at Cynamin Allgood's dining room table, she felt another one preparing to unleash its wrath.

Most often, Noelani's headaches often resulted from putting up with stupid people doing stupid things, or when she faced unusual amounts of stress. As she watched Detective Ahuna remove a pair of surgical gloves and flip open a pocket notebook, her latest brain-crusher throbbed without mercy. She rubbed her temples and groaned.

Detective Ahuna sat down and said, "Miss Lee, are you all right?"

"I will be," she said. "I hope."

Noelani looked at Cynamin, sitting to her right, resplendent in fresh make-up. Her eyes were wide and her breathing short and erratic. Noelani patted her hand, and then she looked to her left at Wanda Fong, who sat stone-stiff—with the exception of a quivering lower lip.

"Now, Miss Allgood," Detective Ahuna said, "do you feel well enough to discuss the events of this evening?"

Cynamin responded with a single, slow nod. "Yes. Miss Lee and Wanda and I were at a bar downtown. It was Wally's Dive Inn. He can tell you we were there."

Noelani tracked her client's eyes as they darted back and forth from the detective to the scene outside her picture window—red-and-blue lights atop police cars and an ambulance bounced off the trees across the street, uniformed cops patrolled the front yard, neighbors gathered behind yellow crime-scene tape with their cell phone cameras. Something in Cynamin's demeanor registered more excitement than apprehension.

Please don't say anything about "producers" or "cameras." Noelani squeezed Cynamin's hand.

Detective Ahuna said, "You're not a drinker."

"No," Noelani said, "but we decided to get together so I could brief Miss Allgood about her case."

Detective Ahuna said, "What sort of case?"

"Cynamin—Miss Allgood—is convinced someone is trying to sabotage her beer-making business," Noelani said.

"Oh, I am beyond convinced, hon," Cynamin said. "Especially now. Did you see the unholy mess he made in my garage?"

Detective Ahuna said, "You mean the dead man with his head split open."

"My fermentation tank's got big dents in it and my brew kettle's full of detergent. My honey ale's ruined and my equipment will be impossible to replace."

Noelani spotted a real tear leave a trail down Cynamin's cheek.

Detective Ahuna took notes. "Did anything unusual happen at the bar, while you were there?"

Cynamin said, "We just sat and chatted. God's honest truth, Detective. It was just three attractive women having a combination business meeting and night on the town."

"Okay." Detective Ahuna said to Wanda, "What was your role in this meeting? My understanding is, you are not a licensed private investigator."

"I drove Noe to the bar," Wanda said. "So I was her ride." She hiccupped.

"I hope you didn't drive from there."

"Uh, nope," Wanda said.

"Any other reason for you being there?"

Wanda looked at Noelani, and then back at the detective. "Not really. Except Wally has Cynamin's beer on tap and I wanted to try it. You should, too. I mean, if it's okay for me to say such a thing to a policeman."

"I'm a detective."

"It's the lilikoi wheat," Cynamin said. She smiled as she brushed away a tear. "Crisp and refreshing with well-rounded flavor, perfect for hot days like today."

Detective Ahuna turned his attention to Noelani. "What prompted you to move your meeting from the bar to Miss Allgood's home?"

"It was getting noisy," Noelani said. "You know how bars can be."

"In the middle of the week." Detective Ahuna again jotted notes. "So you drove here separately—Miss Allgood in her car, and you and Miss Fong together in the blue one, yes?"

"Yes," Noelani said. "It's Wanda's car."

Detective Ahuna looked at Cynamin. "And when you arrived, what did you see?"

"We—the first thing I noticed was the side door for my garage was open, and the light was on," she said. "I waited for Miss Lee and we went inside, and that's when we found, we found—" Cynamin put a hand over her mouth and made a gagging sound. More tears.

Detective Ahuna waited a moment, before he said, "Miss

Fong, you're the one who called nine-one-one, is that correct?"

"Uh huh, yep," Wanda said, "when Noe and Cynamin came out of the garage. They wouldn't let me look inside. But I got a peek anyway. It was pretty gross."

Detective Ahuna asked Cynamin why the door was unlocked.

She said she must have forgotten it when she left the house, because she was running late for her meeting with Noelani and Wanda.

Then he asked whether there was any sign of a break-in in the home.

Cynamin said no.

No other doors unlocked or left open, Detective Ahuna said.

Cynamin said she double-checked them all just before she drove downtown. She said she simply forgot the side door to the garage. "I mean, I live out here in the sticks. Who's going to bother my stuff?"

Detective Ahuna said, "You and the victim had a rocky history, didn't you?"

Cynamin detailed the rivalry on American Election, and how afterward, Paul Templeton blamed her for every bad thing that befell him.

"But here's what I'm trying to understand," Detective Ahuna said. "Why would Templeton, the victim, come all the way from California simply to break into your garage and smash up your gear? And, how would he know you even lived here?"

"Anyone can find anyone these days," Noelani said. "All they have to do is some online research. I do it all the time."

Detective Ahuna maintained a poker face. "Or maybe they hire someone to do the dirty work for them?"

Noelani rubbed her temples. "Yeah, possibly."

Cynamin said, "Listen, he messed up my beer, then he trashed my system, which set me back thirty thousand dollars, thank you very much."

Noelani squeezed her hand again. It didn't stop her. Cynamin pulled her hand away. "And then he up and destroyed all my dry supplies. He's set my production back a long, long time. I don't know if I'll ever recover."

Detective Ahuna said, "Miss Allgood, does the baseball bat belong to you?"

"No. Why would I need one? I don't play baseball and neither does my Edward."

"So you have no idea where the apparent murder weapon came from."

"If I did," Cynamin said, "I wouldn't go whacking some old man's head with it, especially at my own house."

Detective Ahuna said, "Do you smoke, by chance?"

Cynamin's jaw dropped. "No. Are you serious? Smoking is a nasty, unhealthy, detestable habit."

"Would you happen to know anyone who smokes?"

Noelani said, "Why do you ask, Detective?"

"We found a butt next to the garage," Detective Ahuna said. "I'm not sure of the brand but it has a red ring printed along the edge of the filter. Perhaps if Miss Allgood knows anyone who—"

Cynamin snapped her fingers. "I knew it. I knew it. See, Miss Lee? I knew he was behind all this."

Detective Ahuna sat forward. "Who is 'he'?"

"A snake named Mitchell Ratliff," Cynamin said. "He's running this new brewery in town." She looked at Noelani. "What did I tell you, hon?"

Noelani said, "How do you know he smokes?"

"I, um, because I've met him a couple times, and he's always lighting up. I told him, 'I do not and will not tolerate your stinky cigarettes anywhere near my house, and especially not near my brewery.'" Cynamin said to Detective Ahuna, "It's important to keep the brewing environment as sanitary as possible."

"Correct me if I'm wrong, but what you're telling me," Detective Ahuna said, "is this Mitchell Ratliff person has been here, to your home. Which means, he would know about your stuff in the garage."

A uniformed officer came through the open front door. Noelani saw he was carrying an old, flip-style cell phone in his gloved hands. He whispered to Detective Ahuna, opened the phone, and showed the detective something on its screen. Detective Ahuna told the officer to bag the phone.

He said, "Miss Allgood, is your husband home yet, from wherever it is he went?"

She said, "No. He should be home in the next couple of days at the earliest."

"He's, where, exactly?"

"Flying back from Honolulu. Well, from Guam, via Honolulu."

"When he arrives," the detective said, "let him know I need to ask him a few questions." He handed Cynamin a card. "Have him call me as soon as possible."

Cynamin said, "Do I need a lawyer?"

Detective Ahuna closed his notebook. "If you think so, you have that right. Please excuse me." He and the uniformed cop stepped outside.

Noelani turned to face Cynamin, who again dabbed at fake tears, staining a white paper napkin with chunks of blue eyeshadow and black mascara.

"When these guys leave," Noelani said, motioning toward the cops swarming the house, "you and I need to talk."

Cynamin, between theatrical sobs, said, "Fine, okay."

Detective Ahuna returned a minute or so later and reassumed his seat. He then continued the interrogation. He questioned all three women, asking for specific information— what time they left their homes, when they arrived at the bar, what they drank or ate there, what time they left the bar, whether they recognized anyone else there aside from the bartender. How long did it take them to drive back to the house, did they touch anything after they found the body, did any of the neighbors call them or tell them they had seen anything. He then repeated his questions about whether there were any signs of a break-in in the house, was anything missing, or did it appear anything had been moved.

Wanda, admitting she had a couple of beers in quick succession at Wally's, was a bit hazy on times. But Noelani and Cynamin made it clear, the three of them couldn't have been anywhere near the house when someone bashed in Paul

Templeton's head.

Detective Ahuna said to Cynamin, "Now you said it looked like the recipes are missing from the binder. Is that correct?"

"Not just looked like it," she said. "They are gone. Someone stole them. It had to be Mitchell. You need to interview him."

"I will," he said. "Can you tell if anything else is missing?"

She paused, then said, "My lucky towel. It's just an old purple dishtowel, but I use it when I get sweaty while I'm working."

"And you say, it's lucky."

"Whenever I have it with me, the beer I make turns out perfect," she said. "The one time I didn't, which was the last time I had it in the laundry, was when I experimented with the poi ale."

Detective Ahuna scrunched his nose. "Beer made with poi?"

Wanda giggled. "Can't un-think that one, huh, can you?"

"It'll take awhile." He closed his notebook and thanked the women for their time. As he rose, he motioned for Noelani to follow him outside.

Standing on the porch, Noelani watched EMTs load a body bag containing Paul Templeton's remains into an ambulance.

Detective Ahuna said, "I imagine you know what I'm going to say next."

"If it's about how a man working for Cynamin Allgood ends up dead on a beach, and another man from her past who turns up dead in her garage," Noelani said, "then yes, I have a feeling I know what's next."

"Close," Detective Ahuna said. "What I mean is, it seems you ladies all have your story down pat."

"We should," Noelani said. "Because it's true."

"I also suspect you and I are on the same wavelength."

"You mean," Noelani said, "regarding a potentially common human denominator."

"Was he at the bar?"

"When we left, he was still nursing a bottle of tequila."

"And this Mitchell Ratliff character? Familiar with him?"

Noelani told him he'd been at the bar, too, and departed within minutes after Paul Templeton. "But I see no reason why he'd kill him. I'd be surprised if they knew each other."

"Would he be motivated to trash Miss Allgood's brewery?"

Noelani recalled the offer sheet and shrugged.

Detective Ahuna stuck his hands in his pockets. "What I don't get is, why'd the killer leave the bat behind. Maybe it's a statement of some kind?"

"Weirder still," Noelani said, "is what would motivate him to take Cynamin's purple towel instead."

Detective Ahuna nodded, and then said, "Come here a second."

Noelani followed him to a silver sedan. Detective Ahuna opened the passenger door and picked up a sealed, nine-by-twelve envelope from the passenger seat. He handed it to her. "Here's a little something you may find interesting. Perhaps even useful."

She said, "Any hints?"

Detective Ahuna said, "Remember when I said I couldn't tell you about what we didn't find on Milt Nihoa's computer or in his files, about the work he was doing for Miss Allgood?"

"I do, hypothetically."

"Well, Mr. Nihoa—and again, I'm not free to share this with you, so it would be pure speculation on my part—managed to rake in some serious bucks over the past year."

Noelani said, "He did? How? Who was he blackmailing?"

"Knowing your aversion to sleep, I'm sure this will keep you entertained at least until sunrise."

Noelani said, "Does this mean you need help with the Milt thing?"

"Don't confuse my generosity as a sign of weakness, much less an invitation." He shut the car door. "The uniforms will be done and out of your hair before long. Just give them room to work, don't go anywhere near the garage, and don't touch anything."

"I understand. We'll behave, honest."

"Oh, I will need to see all of you downtown again, just to review."

"And for now?"

"For now, I'm going to say 'hi' to Wally," Detective Ahuna said. "Then I'm going to rouse a big, hungry, drunk dog from his slumber."

Later, when the cops finished doing their duties, Noelani went back inside. She found Cynamin and Wanda at the dining room table.

Cynamin said, "Miss Lee, can I get you something to drink?"

"No, but perhaps you can explain why you didn't tell me Mitchell Ratliff has been to your home."

Cynamin looked at Wanda, and then at Noelani. "Guess I didn't think it mattered."

Noelani hung her head. "Well, it does, especially since I'm working on the assumption he and Jervy and Kawika are working together against you."

"Well, he—" Cynamin stopped herself. "He, uh, we've gotten close over the last few months." Cynamin sat back, took a deep breath, and exhaled, slow. "Anyway, I'm still wondering how something this awful could happen to a good person like me."

"Cynamin, all due respect," Wanda said, "but the bad thing happened tonight? See, it happened to someone who didn't like you much."

"And blamed you for everything that went wrong in his life," Noelani said. "With the rivalry and bad blood you had on the show, you can see why the police are interested in you— never mind the fact he died in your garage."

"I'm sorry he's dead, I truly am," Cynamin said. "Lord knows, I don't wish this sort of thing on anyone. But the other stuff? He had it all coming."

"I'm pretty sure Detective Ahuna doesn't see things the same way." Noelani thought for a moment, debating whether this was the right time to play an ace she had up her sleeve. But her client's blasé attitude about the night's events, other than her pain at losing thousands of dollars' worth of brewing equipment—and the missing contents of a three-ring binder—

forced her hand.

She said, "When were you going to tell me Mitchell Ratliff was trying to buy you out?"

"You know about his offers." Cynamin said. She looked at Wanda, who smiled and shrugged.

Noelani said, "Am I wasting my time? Are you going to sign the deal?"

Cynamin said no. "I can't bring myself to do it, hon, tempting as it is. And besides, he probably has my recipes now."

"If it was him who took them."

"Don't forget," Wanda said, "those two bruddahs were here, same time, all like trying to break open your file cabinet."

"The GPS doesn't lie," Noelani said. "But why didn't you lock the book in the file cabinet?"

"I needed it because I just started a batch of honey ale, like I told you," Cynamin said. "I guess I forgot to put it away when I left. Though it doesn't matter now."

Noelani sat at the table. She rested her chin in her hands and closed her eyes.

Cynamin said, "Miss Lee? Are you okay?"

Noelani's mind went into overdrive. If one happened before the other, it would mean someone killed Templeton and another person—or persons—stole the recipes. But what if the same person who stole the recipes killed Templeton? Who would have reason to do both?

She opened her eyes.

"Noe," Wanda said, "what're you thinking?"

"Cynamin, I need you to get on Twitter and Facebook," Noelani said, "and tell the world you're making your honey beer and it'll be ready soon."

"Hon," Cynamin said, "you're asking me to do something impossible. In case you didn't notice, my equipment is damaged and my honey is ruined."

Wanda held up a hand. "Hang on, Miss Allgood—I think I might know where Noe's going with this." She looked at her cousin. "At least I think you are, huh?"

"Yes," Noelani said. "But I won't know for sure until I start my new job tomorrow."

Chapter Twenty-one:
The Early Overnights

Kawika Hailama apologized to Mitchell Ratliff for disturbing him in the middle of the night. "But we wouldn't be here if it wasn't a serious emergency, yeah."

Mitchell, in green boxers and a blue tank top, said, "Yeah. Sure. It better be one damn huge emergency. Where's Jervy?"

"In the truck."

"Oh I get it—he gets to sleep and I don't."

"Bruddah ain't sleeping," Kawika said. "He's in a real bad way, considering what happened tonight."

"Which was?"

"Mitch, see, there was a problem." Kawika then relayed the events at Cynamin's house, from the moment he and Jervy arrived and broke in, to the moment some dude ran them over and when they looked in the garage and found a bloody corpse.

Mitchell said, "Wait a minute. Who was this guy?"

"Some haole," Kawika said. "Well, some dead haole, but I got no idea who he is. Was."

"No, not him. I mean, the guy who plowed over you guys."

Kawika shrugged. "Can't say, man. It was dark and he was coming from out of the light. Why's it so important?"

"Because he saw you, and he probably thinks you can ID him if the cops ever figure out you were there. And you know the saying about shit rolling downhill."

"Let me guess, you're the one standing at the bottom, huh?" Kawika grinned. "Trust me, no way no one's gonna know we were at the sistah's house."

"You better be right. What made you decide to pull off this little caper tonight?"

Kawika pulled sheets of paper from his pocket. "We got them."

Mitchell yawned at the papers. "Here's the thing, Kawika— you're telling me someone went apeshit on her gear and even went so far as to mash all her honey, right?"

"That's what you can call the gist of it, yeah."

"And these are her recipes."

"What you've been wanting, here in my hand."

"So then, why did she tweet about how she just started making her honey ale?"

Kawika halted for a beat, and then said, "Sistah did what?"

"Posted it on Facebook, too. She says she's got a bunch of orders all over the island." Mitchell scratched his nuts. "Now either you're blowing sunshine up my butt, or she's lying to the known universe."

"I saw what I saw and Jervy did, too. Her shit's all busted up; there's no way she'll be making beer anytime soon, yeah."

"Then this can only mean," Mitchell said, reaching for the papers, "you won't mind handing those over."

Kawika pulled them away. "Dude, not so fast."

Mitchell, his empty hand outstretched, said, "Come on. Don't jerk me around, Kawika. If what you're saying is true, about her not being able to make product, then you should have no problem handing them over. Remember, we had a deal."

"Oh yeah, we do. But now me and Jervy got these things like you wanted, it's time for us to collect our bonuses."

"Your bonuses." Mitchell laughed. "What bonuses? You mean covering your rent and paying off your car loan wasn't enough? You're getting too greedy for your own good."

"Dude," Kawika said, "after the shit me and Jervy saw? Gave us chicken skin and made Jervy all woozy and sick. Which means we got it coming, yeah."

Mitchell leaned back against the front door. He took a deep breath and exhaled, slow. "Well, there's nothing I can do tonight. It's not like I have a company checkbook under my pillow."

"Tomorrow works, then, yeah," Kawika said. "We bring them bumbye, you pay us, and life's good."

"But I can't count on you to be there first thing in the morning," Mitchell said, "since you sort of have a real job and getting out of bed isn't exactly something you do with ease."

Kawika smirked. "Tell me, then, you're gonna start making the beer tomorrow, aren't you, now we got the sistah's recipes?"

Mitchell nodded.

"Which ones you gonna start with?"

"If she's making the honey ale, then I'll need that one. Plus she's got the passion fruit stuff out there now." He rubbed his cheek. "Seeing as we have capacity for two at a time, I think we'll go with them."

"What, you're gonna make those she's already got going?"

"I hired a new girl whose job is to sell the hell out of our product," Mitchell said. "She's got connections, and with our production capacity, there's no way Cynamin can keep up. Especially since she doesn't have these anymore."

Kawika said, "You really think you can make her brew better than she can, even though me and you both know what happens when you try doing it, yeah."

Mitchell gave him stink eye. "Hand them over and say good night."

Kawika leafed through the pages. "Here's your honey brew"—he handed a sheet to Mitchell—"and let's see, well, there's no lilikoi in here."

"What, seriously? Did you lose it?" Mitchell motioned toward the recipes. "All right. What about the macadamia nut porter?"

Kawika again rifled through the pages, stopped, and handed one to Mitchell. "Mac nuts in beer. Some crazy shit right there." He looked at Mitchell. "Should get you started, brah. You get the rest when me and Jervy get the bonuses."

Mitchell nodded toward the papers. "What's the one with the big X on it?"

Kawika pulled the sheet of paper out. "Whoa, shit, poi? See, I told you, she's twisted in the brain. Nice lady and all, but poi beer? That's nuts, yeah."

"Give me that one."

Kawika handed it over. "Dude, please tell me you're not gonna make it."

"No. I have other plans." Mitchell folded the sheet in half. "Come by when you're off the other job, with the rest of them. Then you guys'll get your fricking bonuses."

Sitting in her car in front of a neighboring house, Noelani Lee heard snippets of the conversation emanating from Mitchell

Ratliff's front porch.

She turned her attention to Kawika's truck. Someone sat slumped over in the passenger seat.

She got out of her car, closing but not latching the door, and tiptoed in a crouch toward the truck. Peering over the hood, she watched Mitchell yawn yet again while Kawika talked about his eventful evening. Then, cursing herself for not changing from her Amber disguise, she got on her back and scooched under the truck.

Even as the gravel nicked at her legs, Noelani marveled at the truck's ground clearance as she found her GPS transponder. It was where she'd planted it, directly under the extended cab's passenger door. But as she reached for it, the door flew open and a stream of vomit splashed in the driveway, next to her hand. Over Jervy's moans, she heard Kawika call to him, asking whether he was okay. Jervy replied with a grunt. She also heard Mitchell say something about cleaning up that mess. The next voice she heard was Jervy's, offering up a "sorry, man" just as he slammed the door shut.

Supine under the truck, Noelani held her breath—since childhood, the smell of puke made her want to throw up, too. When Mitchell and Kawika resumed their conversation, she removed the GPS transponder and slid out into the open, under the driver's side, let herself breathe again, and retraced her steps to her car. She slipped behind the wheel and gave the door a tentative pull shut.

A few seconds later, Mitchell went inside his house and Kawika got in the truck. He backed out of the driveway at the same time as the front porch light went dark.

Noelani waited a beat, and then again slipped out of her Sentra. In her bare feet, she followed the driveway to Mitchell's carport. Inside, a Jeep Wrangler and a light-colored coupe with a Saddle Road Ale Company decal on the rear window reflected the moonlight. She got on her knees and attached the transponder to the Jeep's chassis, under the driver's door. Then she trotted back to her car and drove home.

***

Each click of Detective Ahuna's pen, combined with the incessant, vitamin-draining glow of overhead fluorescent lights, sent the tequila-induced thump in Dwight Broussard's brain into fiendish overdrive.

"Please," Dwight said, "must you do that?"

They sat in the interrogation room at police headquarters, a uniformed cop—one of two who had roused Dwight from his hotel room—standing outside the door.

"Sorry," Detective Ahuna said. "Force of habit."

"Like dragging people out of bed at oh-dark-thirty in the morning." Dwight rubbed his eyes with the heels of his palms. "I sure hope you don't treat all your tourists this way."

"Ordinarily, no. Only when bad things happen to other visitors to my island."

Dwight peeled his eyes open. "What are you talking about?"

"How well do you know a gentleman named Paul Templeton?"

Dwight worked up saliva, hoping to cut through the cotton. "I guess that depends on what you already know."

"Humor me," Detective Ahuna said. "Be a straight shooter."

Dwight grinned. "Did he do it?"

"Do what?"

"Fuck with Cynamin. They hated each other, in case you aren't aware."

"I'm aware of their shared disdain. But what makes you think he was going to—how did you put it?—fuck with her?"

"I ran into him the other day, by accident. We know each other from San Diego. Big city, small town, in a lot of ways. He suggested he was going to get back at her for all the reality TV crap, but I didn't think much about it. An old coot like him?" Dwight leaned forward and lowered his voice. "So what did he manage to do, uproot her garden?"

"You and he are simply casual acquaintances?"

"Detective, if you're asking me about him, then you know he's on your island. Well, he was until last night."

Detective Ahuna said, "What do you mean, 'was' here?"

"By now he's on a plane, headed home. That's what he told me at the bar, the proprietor of which I am sure you've already spoken to."

"I have. Did Templeton tell you what, if anything, he was going to do to Miss Allgood or her property?"

"He didn't tell me anything."

"How did he know she's in Hilo?"

Dwight shrugged. "There's a million ways to find people. You do it all the time. Part of the job."

"What's strange to me," Detective Ahuna said, "is how all these coincidences are piling up."

"How do you mean?"

"Well, you're here trying to find Landry Jenkins, and Paul Templeton's here at the same time, seeking revenge against Miss Allgood for one transgression or another."

Dwight held up the palms of his hands. "Since he figured out where she was, maybe it proves Templeton's a better bloodhound than I am."

"You told me you're a big, hungry dog."

"A tahyo, yeah, but I've got some hound in me, too."

Detective Ahuna tossed a plastic evidence bag on the table.

Dwight blinked at its contents: a flip-style cell phone. He looked at Detective Ahuna. "Okay."

"Marshal—"

"Deputy US marshal."

"This is Mr. Templeton's phone. We found it next to his body."

"His—" Dwight felt a tightness in his chest. "Wait, what?"

"Miss Allgood found Mr. Templeton's body at her home this evening." Detective Ahuna noted the time on a wall clock. "Sorry. Late last night."

Dwight wanted to speak but couldn't, his throat muscles being uncooperative.

"It looks as if someone bashed his head open with an aluminum baseball bat."

Dwight swallowed. "Oh, shit."

"Now, before you infer anything," Detective Ahuna said, "the bartender also assured me Miss Allgood spent some time in his tavern last night, too. He's positive she was there at the same time as you and Mr. Templeton, meeting with some friends of hers. He—the victim—left before either of you did. Long before you, to be technical, which alibis you out."

Dwight stared at the phone in the plastic bag, his mind tossing theories around as the cobwebs started to clear.

Detective Ahuna said, "What I'm wondering is, if you can explain how a text from you wound up on Mr. Templeton's phone? A text reading, 'Good-bye and good riddance'? And what does it mean? It sounds awfully personal for someone who's just an acquaintance." He clicked his pen, five times in quick succession.

Dwight reached for a glass of water, stopped, and looked at Detective Ahuna.

"Something wrong, Marshal?"

***

An impatient Master Po greeted Noelani Lee when she returned home.

"Oh, yeah," she said to the cat, "food. Although you could live off your fat for a month. No offense."

She poured kibble into his bowl, and then went to her bedroom. She changed from her Amber attire into an oversized white tee-shirt and a pair of gray cotton gym shorts. In the bathroom, she wiped away layers of theatrical make-up, and then returned to the kitchen, where she made a cup of green tea. Then she sat at her table and opened the envelope Detective Ahuna gave her.

Inside was a thick stack of papers, printouts of a bank account summary. She read them, more than a year's worth of Milt Nihoa's spending habits—occasional debit transactions at grocery stores and sporadic deposits she assumed were from clients, most of which preceded purchases at local liquor retailers. There also were utility, car, and rent payments, and a handful of transactions with some of the same Internet-based private investigator supply companies Noelani used.

Amid the deposits and withdrawals, Noelani found that

every other week for four months, a bank in St. Louis, Missouri, had wired fifteen hundred dollars into Milt's checking account. The last such deposit occurred just a couple of days before he floated onto the beach. Going back a year, Noelani discovered, Milt also had made monthly cash deposits of five hundred dollars each, preceded by a single cash deposit of a thousand dollars.

She set the paperwork aside and, from the envelope, removed several black-and-white copies of photos she assumed were digital images the cops pulled from Milt's computer. The first two showed the exterior of a building, taken from different angles. On the next sheet, a horizontal shot of a loading dock and a vertical photo of an exterior doorway for the same building; empty pallets sat stacked on one side, and a bucket, with small white objects scattered around it, stood on the other.

On another sheet were two pictures Noelani assumed were interiors of the same building. In one, large metal cylinders—overgrown versions of the same beer-making apparatus in Cynamin Allgood's garage—sat in two rows. The picture below it was of yet another door with a sign reading NO ADMITTANCE, and below it, a third picture, a cropped close-up of a deadbolt on the same door.

She flipped the last sheet over and found, copied on its back, a crude diagram. It was a floor plan, with spaces marked "office," "reception desk," "keg storage," "bottling area," "rest rooms," and "dry storage." One entrance was marked "main" and another, "back door."

Inside the squiggly lines representing walls—Noelani had no doubt, Milt must've been plastered when he drew it—was a space marked with an X. Like a big target.

Noelani flipped the diagram over and again pored over the pictures of the interior door and its deadbolt. Then she referred back to the diagram.

Master Po jumped onto the chair next to her and purred.

Noelani looked at the cat and said, "You know what? The fool was onto something." She scratched behind his ears. "Yeah. I can't believe it, either."

Her cell buzzed. "Hi Wanda."

"Hey, Noe, I wake you up?"

"You know better. What's going on?"

"Well," Wanda said, "I just got off Cynamin's Facebook and Twitter pages. And, uh, I figured I better call you. See, like you asked her to, she's promoting her honey beer she says she's making."

"Good."

"But then she posted something, about how she's gonna confess her sins to her husband and how scared she is about what might happen."

Noelani sat up. "She did what?"

Chapter Twenty-two:
The Truman Show Delusion

A little before seven in the morning on Thursday, someone knocked on Noelani Lee's front door. She pulled herself up from the sofa, where she'd dozed off for a few hours, and shuffled to the door.

She opened it to find a black man in dark gray pants and a blue shirt. He was bald and had a mustache. And he wore wire-rimmed glasses.

"I'm terribly sorry to bother you at this hour," he said, "but are you by chance Noelani Lee?"

Bad things happen when I sleep, and they only get worse when I wake up. "Yes, I am. And you are?"

"I'm Edward Vaughn," he said. "I believe you know my wife, Cynamin Allgood." He peered inside the house. "Would you have some time to talk?"

She invited him in and asked him to take a seat. "I would offer you some coffee but I don't keep any on hand."

"No, please," Edward said, "it's okay."

"Green tea?"

"No, thank you. I'm fine." He sat back on the sofa, relaxed, looking at her with a blank face.

She sat in a chair opposite him and said, "You must have had a long flight."

He stared at her, his eyes perplexed.

"I mean," she said, "you flew all the way back from Guam, didn't you?"

After a moment, he leaned forward and said, "You have something on your lip."

Noelani touched around her mouth with her fingertips. She stopped when she felt a slight mustache, which had begun sprouting under her nose. "Oh, um, I have hair issues. It's a long story."

He sat back and crossed his legs. "Yes, Guam to Honolulu to here," Edward said. "I left Guam about four thirty in the afternoon local time and had a layover in Nagoya, of all places, before changing planes in Honolulu. It's a haul, but the trip was worth it from a professional perspective."

"Good contacts?"

"Some of the best so far."

"Has your wife told you about everything that has happened since you've been away?"

"In her own way," Edward said. "She mentioned she hired you about her beer thing. The funny thing is, I thought she was imagining it all."

"Really? What do you mean?"

"Clarisse has what I'd charitably call a wild imagination. She doesn't lie, don't get me wrong. It's just she sometimes thinks things are happening when they really aren't."

"She embellishes things."

"Apparently you've seen her in action."

"Well," Noelani said, "in this case, I think she's not making stuff up." She provided a condensed recap of her investigation of Cynamin's beer situation, culminating with Milt Nihoa's apparent murder—leaving out the part about the buyout offer from Mitchell Ratliff and the Saddle Road Ale Company.

"Clarisse said she'd hired him to check this out," Edward said. "Poor man. Who'd do such a thing?"

Noelani weighed her words before she said, "Um, some other things have happened lately which you should be aware of before you go home."

Noelani then got Edward up to speed on Paul Templeton and his demise in Cynamin's garage.

Edward sat back. He said nothing for several long moments, just lightly tapped the fingertips of his left hand on his leg. "You're saying someone killed him? At my—at our home?"

Noelani nodded and yawned.

"But what on earth was he doing there? That despicable man lives in San Diego."

"I take it there was no love lost with him."

"For starters," Edward said, "he ran my wife's reputation through the mud, all to win some TV-generated election. Then once he was in office, he displayed his hypocritical morals with the stripper and the abortion. So, yes, I didn't like the man."

"I guess I can't blame you." Noelani then outlined her

encounters with Deputy US Marshal Dwight Broussard and his search for the elusive Landry Jenkins. She also said the marshal was convinced Edward and Landry were the same person.

Edward grinned. Then he chuckled. "You know, she's told me that before, about his wild ideas. All he'd have to do is some of his fancy research to find out I am real. What the hell."

"Even though nobody, it seems, has ever seen you in person?"

"I am a writer and a researcher and I'm away from home more than I am there," he said. "And when I am home, I'm usually parked in front of a computer for hours on end. It's what I do. I'm not what you could call a 'public face.'"

"Not like Cynamin."

"Some people are made for the limelight, and some of us are destined to be supporting actors."

Funny way of putting it. "What led you to move to Hawaii? It's, uh, a big leap, coming from the mainland."

Edward said, "Well, it was all Clarisse's idea."

"Oh, it was?"

"You see, she spent a week or so on the island about a year and a half ago—her sister, Chantelle, from Baltimore came with her," Edward said. "I was on the road, in one of those square states—Wyoming or Colorado, I don't recall which one. Well, she called me from a beach and asked me if I'd consider leaving San Diego and moving to Hilo."

"So, you agreed to it."

"You've met her. There's no middle ground." He smiled. "She seemed taken by the town and, plus, I'd been thinking about pursuing my current project for some time. I figured this would be a good staging point for my research trips all over the Pacific Rim. So, we moved into our little house about a year ago."

"It's a nice house, by the way," Noelani said, "but it seems small for someone as famous and, I'd assume, as well-off as Cynamin."

Edward looked at her over his glasses and sniffed. "Her thinking was, why not live like the locals? Anyway, she'd had enough of standing out from the crowd. She wanted a simpler life, and then she got back into brewing beer. Which is fine. It keeps her occupied while I'm away."

"So, does your writing help subsidize Cynamin's brewing stuff?"

"No, no, Clarisse paid for it all on her own," Edward said. He took off his glasses and rubbed his eyes. "Clarisse made a lot of money off the show. Yeah, I know, it was silly but it gave her boutique some cred, so much so she made a killing when she sold it."

"You keep calling her Clarisse, instead of Cynamin."

Edward slipped the glasses back on. "She'll always be Clarisse to me, since we met in high school back in Baltimore. After we got married, she got this acting bug. Well, she always had it; she was in school plays and did some local small theater. Then one day she said she wanted to move to LA to make it big in movies. I was cool with it, being between jobs then. She started calling herself Cynamin Allgood because it would get her noticed."

"Apparently it worked for reality TV."

"But not Hollywood. Not for lack of trying, you understand, but Clarisse just couldn't get an acting job, even in commercials."

Noelani said, "She must still be angry with Landry Jenkins, about the Ponzi scheme, the money laundering, him vanishing the way he did."

"I never mention him around her," Edward said. "Thanks to him, and what happened on the show, we lost all semblance of a normal life in San Diego. People hounded her, especially when word got out about the mayor and then this whole thing with Landry ripping her and all these other people off."

"What did you think?"

"He needs to be brought to justice and pay his debt to society. Don't you agree?"

Noelani then described how she determined Dwight had been working for Paul Templeton to find Cynamin. "To give him his due, the marshal kept him at arm's length. But Templeton slipped through a crack when he went to Cynamin's—to your house last night."

Edward leaned forward and clasped his hands. "The marshal? He tracked Clarisse for Templeton?"

"Probably figured he was coming here anyway and he knew you were here, so why not pocket some change while he was at it."

"So indirectly, the marshal's the reason Templeton was murdered. What a son of a bitch, setting Clarisse up like that." He waited a beat, and then said, "The police don't think Clarisse did it, do they?"

"They questioned her, but she and I and my cousin were all together downtown when it happened."

Edward nodded and sat back. "How is she holding up?"

"Not well, the last time I saw her, but she refused to get a hotel room or even come stay with me. But then, I guess finding a body in your garage makes you do irrational things." Noelani smiled. "Sort of like pretending you're still a reality TV star."

Edward grinned. "There's a condition called the Truman Show delusion. You know the movie, The Truman Show?"

"Sure, the one where Jim Carrey's the guy who lives in a made-up town but he's convinced it's real."

"Since American Election," Edward said, "well, not right away, but shortly after we moved here, Clarisse started doing odd things when we'd go out in public. She'd bark at a cashier for no good reason or spout non sequiturs when we'd go out for dinner. I asked her what she was doing and she would say things like, 'It's what the people at home expect from me' or 'it's what the director wants.'"

He said, "I've tried to convince her there are no cameras, and she's good with it for a while. But then she calls me when I'm on the road and starts going on about story lines and having to do multiple takes and re-shoots."

Noelani said, "So, then, you must've assumed this delusional thing made her think someone was trying to sabotage her brewery."

"Until you told me you think it's real."

Noelani rubbed her eyes. "Do you have any reason to believe Landry Jenkins is on the island?"

"No," Edward said, "and I'm certain Clarisse wouldn't

know, either. She said she doesn't and I believe her." He checked his watch. "Miss Lee, my apologies but I need to get home now. I'm awfully tired and I still have to organize the notes from my trip."

They both rose. Noelani escorted Edward to the front door. "Give Cynamin my best and let her know I'll try to be in touch later today. I have work to do so she probably won't be able to reach me."

"Sure, absolutely."

"Plus I'll have a different phone with me, so she may not recognize the number. But just tell her, I'll update her when I can."

Edward opened the door. "You know, everything you've shared with me—all this business with the marshal nosing around and Templeton—it's a lot to take in."

"I'm sure it is. I'm sorry."

"Well, whatever it is you're going to do, good luck with it."

Noelani said, "Can I offer a suggestion?"

"Sure."

"When you get home, tell Cynamin the camera crews are respecting her privacy for the next couple of days and they'll be staying away."

"She'll insist they should be there because her emotions will make for good TV."

"They would," Noelani said. If they were real.

***

Edward Vaughn pulled into the driveway and first thing he saw was his garage sealed off with crime-scene tape. He killed the engine and, leaving his suitcase in the car, went to the front door.

Cynamin Allgood, tears rolling down her face, greeted him there. Without a word, she wrapped her arms around him and squeezed. Edward returned the greeting, holding her closer than he ever had before.

"Oh baby," he said. "Oh my precious Clarisse."

Through sobs, her face buried in his chest, she said,

"Sweetheart, I am so sorry."

"It's not your fault, my baby. You did nothing wrong."

Gripping his arms, she pushed away and looked in his face. "But I did, hon. I did do something terrible."

Edward held her by the shoulders. "No, I just met with the lady detective. She told me you're in the clear, there's no way you could have done it."

Cynamin rubbed her eyes with her right hand and took him by the forearm with her left. "But I did."

"Clarisse, what are you—"

"I need to show you."

She led him into the house, through the living room, past the kitchen and her office, to their bedroom. Standing at the threshold, she looked around the room, and then at Edward. Then she dropped her chin and sobbed.

"Clarisse," he said, putting a hand on her shoulder, "what is going on? Baby, are you all right?"

"No, baby," she said. "Don't you see? Look at this room." She wiped her hands on her jeans. "See this bed? See the pillows? See the sheets all messed up?"

"You hate making the bed."

"But I'm not the only one's been sleeping in it."

Edward closed his eyes. "Oh, Clarisse."

"While you've been gone," she said, "I've been seeing another man."

"Oh, now, don't say these things again," he said. "We've talked about this how many times before. It's just not true and you know it."

"But it is," she said. "And if this doesn't prove it to you, then I know something else will."

She led him down the hall and through the guest bedroom, through the sliding glass doors, and onto the lanai. He followed her gaze to the clamshell ashtray on the picnic table. In it were about a half-dozen butts.

"I'll be damned," Edward said. He reached and removed one of the butts, crushed and mashed. He turned around and said, "So you mean, he's here after all?"

But Cynamin was gone. He called for her but she did not

respond. He went back inside but as he reached the living room, he heard her car start. He stepped outside and watched her drive out of sight.

He closed his eyes and shook his head. "Oh, Clarisse. When will you ever learn?"

Chapter Twenty-three:
The Chase

Noelani Lee's cell rang as she stepped out of the shower.

She answered it and heard Detective Ahuna say, "Good morning, Miss Lee, did I reach you at a bad time?"

"No, I'm just getting ready for work." She wrapped herself in a towel and stepped into her bedroom. She put the phone on speaker and set it atop her dresser. "How can I help you?" she said, as she opened her closet.

"Have you seen our friend, the Cajun deputy, this morning?"

She took a gray pants suit from the closet. "Sorry, no, but didn't you question him last night?'

"Way early this morning, before sunrise," he said. "I just got a call from a gentleman who identified himself as Dwight Broussard's supervisor."

Noelani stopped what she was doing. "Oh?"

Detective Ahuna said, "He said a woman named Cynamin Allgood called him and read him the riot act about Dwight Broussard harassing her over Landry Jenkins."

Noelani looked at the phone as she slipped on a pair of panties. "It sounds like something she'd do."

"He told me," Detective Ahuna said, "after he endured Miss Allgood's wrath and she hung up in a huff, that he has no documentation of Broussard being in Hawaii on any official business related to her or Landry Jenkins."

Noelani put on a bra. "They don't?"

"Broussard told everyone he was going on vacation, deep-sea fishing in Cabo with his father. He even bought two round-trip tickets. So the supervisor said he sent a deputy to Broussard's house, and guess who was returning from a walk at the same time?"

Noelani picked up the phone, took it off speaker, and said, "What did Broussard's father say?"

"Nothing. They backed off him for the time being. But the supervisor told me they're going to question him unless they hear from Broussard today."

"Did this supervisor say what he wants you to do?"

"If I have any contact with Broussard, I'm supposed to encourage him to call in."

"And if I see or hear from him first?"

"Then you call me and I'll take it from there."

Noelani sat on the bed. "Do you think that's a good idea?"

"Do you think it isn't?"

"No, but I mean if he's here on legitimate business, should we get in his way?"

A couple of beats passed, and then Detective Ahuna said, "If he's here on legitimate business, then why did he lie about fishing in Mexico, and involve his dad, no less?"

"Maybe," she said, "he's got a lead on Jenkins and he didn't want to blow it. He says he's good at his job."

Another beat, then: "There's something you're not telling me, huh?"

"Detective, you know what I know. Besides, I'm working for Cynamin. It would be a conflict of interest for me to help Dwight, too."

"Now you're on a first-name basis." She heard him sigh. "How are things going with your case? Find anything new?"

Noelani smiled. "Unofficially, maybe."

"Good for you."

"Today I think I might learn more on my own."

Detective Ahuna said, "Well, best of luck. But if you run into our favorite deputy, do me a favor and let him know I need to speak with him two hours ago."

"Sure, yes, I will."

***

Dwight Broussard, too tired to give a shit, hauled his ass out of bed, put on a white V-neck undershirt and jeans—commando-style—and a pair of rubber shower shoes. He clipped the Glock and the star to his waistband and covered them both with his untucked shirt. Accustomed to routine, he also slipped his handcuffs in a pocket. Then he took the elevator to the ground level, went to the hotel's café and bought a to-go coffee—black, three sugars—and stepped outside into the morning light.

He'd only gotten maybe two or three hours of fitful sleep, thanks to Detective Ahuna. The cop grilled him about the late Paul Templeton. A persistent one, the detective; he latched on to the text Dwight sent Paul and refused to let go. Dwight sloughed it off, saying he was drunk when he hit Send and besides, he had no idea Templeton planned to visit Cynamin's place. How could he, since he barely knew Templeton?

The detective backed off, and then asked Dwight whether he smoked.

Dwight said, No, why?

Because in addition to the victim's cell phone, the detective said, we found a butt on the ground outside of the garage.

Dwight said, Did it have a red band on it?

When the detective told him yes, Dwight presented his theory:

Landry Jenkins used to smoke the same brand, back when he was Cynamin's benefactor, when he was running his Ponzi scheme. Dwight said Landry probably came by Cynamin's house—maybe to catch up on old times, get some nookie, whatever—found Templeton in the garage instead, bludgeoned him, and dropped the butt by accident before he split.

It had to have been him, Dwight said. No one I know who's close to Cynamin smokes that particular brand. He's here; she knows it. I find him and we wrap up a lot of shit, Detective.

The detective said, Are you positive? You sure?

I will find his ass, Dwight said, and I will do it today.

A uniform drove him back to the hotel. Now, as he stood outside the hotel's lobby, sipping crappy coffee and feeling the morning air fill with humidity, he ran a hand over his stubbly face. He turned to enter the hotel when—

A car drove past, late model sedan, dark blue. Something inside Dwight said, Take a look.

So he did.

"You are shitting me. You are shitting me."

Can you believe this? All this time spent chasing my own dick, and he's at the same hotel as me.

Dwight tossed the coffee in a trashcan, pulled the SUV keys from his pocket, and dashed into the parking lot.

Dwight caught up to the car—a Mazda—waiting out a signal at Kilauea Avenue and Kawili Street. When the light turned green, a car between Dwight and the Mazda hung a right. Dwight dropped back a dozen feet or so and allowed a motorcycle to cut in front of him.

He followed the Mazda and its two-wheeled buffer southwest on Kawili and past a collection of buildings; brass letters on a black lava-rock wall formed the words UNIVERSITY OF HAWAI'I AT HILO.

The motorcycle turned in to the school's parking lot. He drove on, behind the sedan, past the campus, where the street swung due south. In a few seconds, both he and the driver of the Mazda stopped at another light.

Dwight saw houses ahead. The light turned green. The Mazda went straight through the intersection, and as he followed, Dwight noticed the street signs had changed from Kawili Street to Iwalani Street.

Moments later, the Mazda signaled, slowed, and turned in to a driveway.

It was Noelani Lee's house.

Dwight rolled on another hundred yards, and then did a U-turn and backed the SUV into the neighboring driveway. A jungle's worth of trees and shrubs and flowers hid the house from the street. As he killed the engine, he hoped he wouldn't have to tell yet another fat, tatted Polynesian male to go fuck himself, but then he doubted they could see him anyway without first hacking a path with a machete.

Along the property line, palm trees and lush, exotic plants obstructed his view, except for a gap, which provided a line of sight to Noelani's front door. He rolled down the passenger window in time to see her in the doorway, shaking hands with the Mazda's driver—a bald black man in a blue shirt and gray pants.

Dwight waited. As the minutes passed, Dwight wondered why she wasn't calling him, what with a twenty-five-grand reward hanging in the balance. The more he thought, the more he narrowed it down to one of two possibilities:

Cynamin told Jenkins to get help from Noelani in devising some sort of escape plan. Dwight hoped that wasn't the situation. He had no desire or heart to slap cuffs on Noelani. He was straight as an arrow.

Besides being smart-hot, in her own peculiar way.

Then he remembered Detective Ahuna's warning, how she sometimes bent rules.

The second option:

Jenkins was preparing to turn himself in. Then Noelani would call and ask, When and where and how do I get my reward?

The time passed. Dwight focused on Noelani's front door, until it opened and the bald black man stepped outside. He and Noelani exchanged pleasantries and as the man returned to his Mazda, Dwight had the unnerving feeling that Noelani looked him in the eye as she shut the door.

Dwight started the SUV the same time as the Mazda went into reverse. Then he crept from the residential jungle and followed the sedan, to a street called Kilauea Avenue. Dwight had tailed suspects hundreds of times, but he wondered why Jenkins didn't make him; for a guy on the lam, no doubt looking over his shoulder every waking minute for several years, he never once peered in the rearview except to check traffic.

Approaching downtown, the Mazda's turn signal flicked on and the car made a right and entered a bank parking lot. Well, this is more like it. Dwight wondered whether Jenkins planned on withdrawing some of the millions he stole when he was running his scheme—maybe even some of Owen Broussard's long-gone life savings—in preparation to run again.

Then again, he might make a handsome deposit, the windfall from some new scam. Old habits die hard, after all.

Dwight parked in a corner of the lot and watched Jenkins approach an ATM. He inserted his debit card and punched in his PIN and withdrew some cash. He stuffed it in his wallet and reclaimed the card.

That's when Dwight got his first good look at him—the

same bald head, but the mustache not as bushy and prominent as it was in the old pictures, and his eyes hidden behind aviator-style sunglasses. He got in the sedan and back on Kilauea Avenue, heading northwest.

Dwight followed, not exactly sure where he was; but the path Jenkins took meant he could only have one destination in mind.

Confident, Dwight broke off the chase for a brief stop at a convenience store. A large coffee and a shrink-wrapped raspberry Danish later, he again put the rented SUV on a heading for Cynamin Allgood's house.

***

Rowena met the new girl waiting outside the Saddle Road Ale Company.

"Hello," she said. "You must be Amber."

"Totally in the flesh."

Though there wasn't much flesh on display. Amber wore a conservative gray pants suit with a long-sleeved white blouse buttoned to the neck, black shoes with chunky heels, and a matching fake-leather bag over her left shoulder. Rowena contrasted it with her own jeans, flip-flops, and red tee-shirt, emblazoned with the words, **STEP ASIDE, COFFEE, THIS IS A JOB FOR ALCOHOL.**

"Mitchell said you'd be here around nine." Rowena spotted Mitchell's Jeep parked in its marked space. "Did you knock?"

"Um, no. I figured no one else would be here yet."

Rowena tried the doorknob but it was locked. She produced a key from her pocket. "He must've come in the back way. Come on in."

"Go ahead," Amber said. "I think I left something in my car."

Rowena entered the building and closed the door behind her. She turned on the lights and dropped her purse on the desk in the small reception area, and then wandered inside the brewery. She found Mitchell, hands on his hips, staring at the equipment. Something he did a lot.

"Sir," she said, "did you know the new girl was waiting outside?"

A couple of seconds passed before Mitchell said, "Rowena, have you ever done something and wondered later if it was, maybe not the right thing to do, but what you probably should've done in the first place?"

"I, um, sir, I don't understand."

When he turned to face her, she saw stubble sprouting from his cheeks and chin. And he reeked of peaches.

She said, "Sir, are you all right? You look like crap, if you don't mind me saying."

"You said she's here?"

Rowena heard the front door open and the new girl, Amber, call out a hello. "Yes, she was waiting at the door."

"All right. Fine. Bring her to my office."

Rowena met Amber in reception and escorted her into the brewery. The new girl uttered "wow" as Rowena led her past the silent brewing apparatus to Mitchell's office.

Rowena pulled Amber aside. "Just so you know, he's acting awful strange today."

"Oh? I mean I like wouldn't totally know what 'strange' is for Mr. Ratliff, since we literally just met last night."

"To begin with, he usually shaves and he doesn't normally stink. Plus he's acting like his head's on another planet."

"Maybe he has a lot stressing him," Amber said. "I mean, you guys are getting ready to crank out beer, right?"

Rowena rapped on the open door. "Sir, this is Amber."

"Come in, please." Mitchell sat behind his desk, facing an open laptop. He pressed a button on the keyboard; a printer on a stand behind him began spitting out a document. He nodded toward a pair of empty chairs facing him. "Both of you ladies, please, have a seat."

The women sat. Amber looked around and said, "Seriously, I have never been in an office this neat."

Mitchell blinked at her. "Is that so?"

"I mean, like, look at all the orderly stacks of stuff on your desk, and things on the shelves? Like everything has a place and it's all in it."

Mitchell said. "In this business, you learn how critical it is for everything to be organized and above all, sanitary. The floor out there?"

Amber said, "You can eat off it?"

"What? Sheesh, no. Who eats off floors?" Mitchell poured coffee from a bullet-shaped Thermos into a Saddle Road Ale Company mug. "I'd offer you some but my ass is dragging through the mud this morning. No offense, Rowena."

Rowena said, "None taken, sir."

"I'm way more into tea myself," Amber said. She crossed her legs.

Rowena thought the new girl's pose made her look even more professional. Still, she mirrored her, though her faded, frayed jeans canceled out any hope she had for keeping up appearances.

"What I mean," Mitchell said, "is our floor squeaks when you look at it, it's so clean. Any germs or bacteria or crap gets into our beer, and someone drinks it and gets the squirts because we didn't take time to make sure we're being as sanitary as possible? Well, we're out of business faster than you can say 'class-action suit.'"

Amber said, "Okay, well, I'll make sure to wash my hands like every five minutes or something."

"Excellent. Now, Miss Amber—what is your last name?"

"Oh, it's Porter."

Mitchell smirked. "Amber Porter? Please."

Amber said, "Um, what do you mean?"

Rowena said, "Your first and last names are both beer terms."

Amber hesitated for a moment, and then she laughed, one loud, ear-piercing cackle. "Okay, now that's funny. Maybe I'm totally destined to work in this industry, you think?"

"There's that," Mitchell said, "and the fact Wally Yoshiro will only sell my product if I hire you. Which I've done."

"Yeah, but you know Wally's totally awesome, too." Amber leaned forward, an elbow on her leg. "So, are you actually making beer now?"

"Working on it." He turned and grabbed the papers from

the printer, and then rifled through them. He pulled one from the stack and set it aside. Then he spun his chair around and handed the rest to Rowena. "Give these to Donald."

Rowena leafed through the pages. "Oh, wow, this is real, yeah?"

"As real as it gets." His cell rang. Mitchell took the phone from his pocket and examined the display. "Hey, I gotta take this. Rowena, give Amber here the five-dollar tour." When the women rose, he said, "Tell Donald I'll talk to him in a few. And shut the door behind you. Please and thank you."

Rowena did as instructed. She said to Amber, "Not to make any excuses, but his bosses on the mainland are leaning on him awful hard."

"What bosses?"

"In St. Louis. Mitchell didn't tell you?" When Amber said no, Rowena explained that Saddle Road Ale Company was a subsidiary of Schneckenkorn, a gigantic beer company that had invested a ton of money into the Hilo brewery. She said they wanted product on shelves in two weeks, or else Mitchell would have to seek employment elsewhere.

"Whoa, I'd be nervous if I was him, too," Amber said. She looked around and said, "So you mean, all this stuff, they shipped it here and you haven't started using it yet?"

Rowena pointed to a door marked **NO ADMITTANCE**. "He's made some test batches in there before, but"—she held up the papers Mitchell had given her—"it looks like we're going to get started for real after all." She smiled. "Knowing Mitch, he was up all night coming up with these. Probably explains why he's a mess this morning."

"Yeah, I bet." Amber said, "So the test room, is that why there's the padlock on it, so no one can get in and see what he's making?"

"He just put that on a few days ago," Rowena said. "Mitchell said he broke his key in the deadbolt, but he wants to keep it secure."

"Cool. So who's Donald?"

"He's my husband. Follow me, I'll introduce you."

Rowena led Amber toward an area in the brewery where

metal shelves overflowed with brown paper bags. Several pallets filled with larger canvas bags sat on the floor, and beside them stood a bald, bearded man with a clipboard.

Amber smiled. "Oh, he's kind of cute. You're totally lucky, girl."

"Yeah," Rowena said. "He's my boo."

Amber said, "What's that thing on his neck?"

Just as Rowena was about to introduce her husband to the new girl, Mitchell burst from his office. "Rowena, Donald, I have to split for a few. You, too, new girl."

Rowena said, "Oh, I don't remember you had a meeting on your sched—"

"Last-minute thing," Mitchell said. "Donald?"

"Yeah, boss?"

"Rowena's got everything you need. And say hello to Amber. She's new."

Donald nodded. Amber said, "Hi."

Mitchell looked at his watch. "I'll be back in an hour. For now, Rowena'll fill you in on the deets. Gotta split." He double-timed it across the brewery and out the front door.

Amber looked at Rowena and said, "Something got him moving, huh?"

"Sometimes, it's hard to figure the man out," Rowena said. "Once in a while, he has these spur-of-the-moment meetings he never tells me anything about."

Donald sidled up beside her. "So what's he got?"

Rowena handed him the papers. Donald leafed through them. "Well, I'll be damned. Looks like this is no drill, babe. The honey ale and the mac nut porter." He looked at her. "He come up with these himself?"

"I guess he got inspired." Rowena said, "We have everything we need, huh?"

"Sure do. Got it all."

"Um," Amber said, "I'm sorry, but I have to pee real bad. There a ladies' room here?"

"Sure," Rowena said, "right over there where the forklift's parked."

"Thanks." Amber trotted to the restroom.

Rowena turned to Donald and said, "Weird sistah, don't you think?"

"Hey, if she can sell the stuff," Donald said, "then maybe she'll be all right." He kissed her on the cheek. "Gotta get to work, baby."

Noelani Lee locked the restroom door and then studied a GPS signal on her smart phone's screen. The little animated car departed the Saddle Road Ale Company and headed west on Kawili Street; at Manono Street, it turned right, and then hung a left on Lanikaula Street.

The cell buzzed. "Wanda, you have him?"

"Yep," Wanda Fong said. "Like you told me to, I'm staying a little bit behind."

"Good. And you're comfortable with the camera, right?"

"Nothing I can't handle, cuz."

"Fantastic. Text me when things start happening, okay?"

"Shoots, no worries."

"Oh, and one more thing?"

"What's up, Noe?"

"As soon as you get a chance, I need you to look something up for me."

***

Mitchell Ratliff parked his Jeep in the Rainbow Falls parking lot and wandered to the overlook. As advertised, the morning sun created a prism of colors at the base of the falls. *Gotta be a sign of good things ahead.*

A minute or so later, a small blue car pulled into the lot. A chubby woman with a camera emerged from the car and waddled up beside him. "Eh, howzit," she said. "Nice day, huh?"

"Sure, if you say so."

"I mean I dig on all the sunshine. Makes having a day off big time cool." She aimed the camera at the falls and squeezed off a shot. "My cousin, though, she's into the rain."

Mitchell said nothing.

"I tell her, rain's okay, as long as it's not falling on my day off. Know what I mean?" She took another picture. "You come out here a lot?"

"Usually," Mitchell said, "when I want to get away from people."

She sat on the overlook's stone wall. "Yeah, me too. I think more locals, they should check this place out, don't you think?"

In his peripheral vision, Mitchell saw another car park next to his Jeep. Cynamin Allgood stepped out from behind the wheel.

"Seriously," the chubby woman said, "locals should learn to appreciate—"

"Nice meeting you," Mitchell said.

"Huh? Oh, yeah, you too."

"Have fun with your picture-taking." He turned and walked toward Cynamin, who stood waiting beside her car.

"Mitchell, hon," Cynamin said, with a weak smile, "no offense, but you look like hell warmed over."

"I had a long night." He looked her up and down—she was almost pitiful in dirty jeans, black rubber flip-flops, and a teal Fisherman's Wharf souvenir tee-shirt. "So, you called me. You changed your mind?"

She bowed her head. "My husband's home."

Mitchell shrugged. "Okay, and this has what to do with what?"

Cynamin looked at him, eyes pleading. "It means we have to stop seeing each other."

Mitchell put his hands on his hips and shook his head. "Jesus. I mean, Cynamin, get it through your head; we are not having an affair."

"I told him," she said. She stepped forward and put her hands on his chest. "He knows now. And it means we have to choose, either end it or else run off together. For the rest of our lives."

Mitchell took her by the wrists and then released her as he stepped backwards. "Listen to me, okay? We are not 'seeing' each other. We never have, except in a professional sense, and never will. Okay? This"—he waved a finger between them—

"never happened."

"Mitchell, hon, I know you're confused. I understand. I've always had that effect on men for as long as I can remember." She looked at her feet, avoiding eye contact. "I showed him the cigarettes you smoked."

Mitchell rubbed his face with both hands. "Cynamin?" He took a cigarette from his shirt pocket. "It's electronic, see? Okay? I've been trying to quit for like six or seven years. No ash, no smoke, just fruit smells."

"But Mitchell—"

"Wait. Stop." He put the cigarette between his teeth, and then handed her a folded piece of paper.

She opened it. Her eyes widened and she began trembling.

"I was hoping the reason you called me was you came to your senses and signed the deal," Mitchell said. "But based on your tweets and Facebook posts, it appears that's not the case."

Cynamin looked at him, eyes welling.

"Honest, I didn't want it to come to this," he said, "but you know I was on a deadline. So. Well. Here you go. We start production today."

"Oh Mitchell," she said, "how could you do this to me after all we've meant for each other?"

Mitchell ran a hand through his hair. "This is proof I'm about to make Saddle Road the premier beer in Hawaii. Now, you can go on making your honey ale and whatever else for your bartender friends, but now we're about to start production and you'll be on the outside looking in." He dropped the cigarette in his pocket. "Good-bye, Cynamin. Have fun with your hobby."

Mitchell got in his Jeep and, as he drove out of the parking lot, watched as Cynamin slumped against the side of her car.

***

From her vantage point at the overlook, Wanda Fong fumbled with Noelani Lee's fancy camera, trying to get decent pics of Cynamin and the guy with the brown hair. Then the man handed Cynamin a sheet of paper and drove away and Cynamin looked like she was sobbing, the way her shoulders bobbed up and down. Then, without warning, Cynamin stood up straight and, with a giant smile all over her face, yelled, "CUT!"

Wanda hid behind the big tree at the overlook and looked around, but there was no one else anywhere in the park.

She decided to go talk to Cynamin, but as she started across the lot, Cynamin climbed in her car and typed something on her smart phone. Then she buckled up, started the car, and left.

Wanda trotted out to the street but Cynamin was long gone. As she turned and walked back to her car, her phone made a dinging sound—signaling a new tweet. She stopped and read it.

Oh, dang.

Chapter Twenty-four:
The Nice Day for a Ride

Dwight Broussard parked in front of Cynamin Allgood's house. He racked the Glock's slide and did a quick visual inspection:

Crime-scene tape sealed the garage. The dark sedan he'd followed from the hotel sat in the driveway, windows rolled down. But Cynamin's car was gone.

Front screen door closed, but the inside door open. So was the front window. Jenkins, no doubt, trying to get some sort of cross-ventilation going in the morning heat.

Sounds: the distinctive musical cooing of birds, what the front-desk clerk at the hotel told him were zebra doves. Heard them everywhere. From down the street, the echo of someone hammering metal, the steady beat riding a breeze from the west.

He got out and raced across the yard to the front door. He peered inside but saw nothing or nobody.

A sweat droplet rolled into his right eye. He wiped it with his left hand.

He shouted, "Landry Jenkins? Federal agent."

No response.

"Landry Jenkins, I am Deputy United States Marshal Dwight Broussard. Please come out with your hands in the—"

Inside, a toilet flushed.

Give me a break—the man's taking a dump.

Dwight huffed. Screw it. He held the Glock close to his right leg and opened the screen door with his left hand.

He stepped inside and drew his weapon. He swept the living room and the kitchen and stepped toward the hallway— and locked eyes with a male African-American, bald, mustache, glasses.

The man said, "Who the hell—"

"Landry Jenkins," Dwight said, "stop right where you are and put your hands where I can see them."

The man raised his arms. Dwight studied him. Well, he's had some work done. His nose was narrower, his mustache trimmed close to his lip, and he even had a smattering of freckles on his cheeks.

And something was off with his voice. Damn, did he even get his vocal cords fixed?

The man said, "Hey, look, I'm not—who are you?"

Dwight flashed his star. "Federal agent. You're under arrest."

"Wait, what?"

Dwight motioned toward the sofa with his Glock. "Have a seat."

The man blinked several times before he walked sideways into the living room, arms above his head. Dwight shoved him to the sofa with his left hand, keeping the Glock trained on him with his right.

Dwight watched the man's eyes widen as he said, "You're the one my Clarisse told me about."

"Yes I am." He opted not to correct him. "So what name are you using these days, Landry?"

The man squinted. "What are you talking about? My name is Edward Vaughn." The man lowered his arms. He raised them again when Dwight took a step toward him, the gun pointed between his eyes.

"Listen," the man said, "you've got the wrong person. I am not Landry Jenkins."

"Yeah, and I bet you aren't Brian Junkins or La'Voris Stanley anymore, either," Dwight said, "or whatever the hell *nom de plume* you used when you fucked my daddy out of his life's savings."

"What the hell are you talking about?"

Dwight said, "Let's start with conspiracy and wire fraud, then we'll work our way up to mail fraud, money laundering, and income tax evasion." He scanned the living room. "See, I'd have figured you'd used some of the millions you pilfered to buy yourself a real house."

"This is ridiculous. You're making a huge mistake."

"Not as huge as the one you made."

"You can't arrest me for things I have not done."

Dwight smirked. "What makes you think I'm going to arrest you?"

***

Donald pointed his chin at the ladies' room. "Think she fell in?"

Rowena crossed her arms over her chest. "Maybe. With this one, I'm starting to think anything's possible."

"Where'd he find her, anyway?"

"She says she's friends with Wally Yoshiro, but I've known Wally a hella long time and I don't remember hearing him talk about her."

They heard a flush. The restroom door opened. Amber Porter emerged and said, "Gotta go, talk to you later," on her cell. She crossed the squeaky-clean brewery floor and approached Donald and Rowena. "Sorry, my best BFF called and it was sort of urgent."

"No worries," Rowena said. "Listen, I need to get back to the phones." She looked at Donald. "Can you finish showing her around?"

Donald said, "Yeah, okay." Rowena excused herself and Donald led Amber to an open area in the brewery.

"Back there's where we keep the kegs," he said. "Next to it's the bottling area. Once we get started, we're gonna sell the six-packs at stores and such. The kegs are for bars and restaurants." He grinned. "You got your work cut out for you."

"Hey, like, I am ready," she said.

Donald led her to the section with the pallets and the bags. "In here's where we keep the yeast and the malt and the hops and the barley," he said. "If we don't have this stuff, we don't make the beer."

"This is so cool," Amber said. "So how long have you been here?"

"Few months, give or take."

"Ah, cool. How many people work here?"

"Me and Ro, some other guys Mitch knows, and Mitch, of course. He's the micromanager-type, always working here late, doing lots of the stuff by himself." Donald said, "He sometimes says he trusts himself to get things done more than other people.

Then he usually apologizes to me." He laughed.

"Ever work with a dude named Fred?"

Donald said, "Yeah, Hawaiian guy, for a little while anyway. He didn't last long, not like there's a lot to do around here. Why, you know him?"

"Yeah, he said something about this place like a couple times," Amber said. "But between you and me? He's actually kind of a jerk."

Donald chuckled. "Heard that."

"How about you? Have you always been a beer maker?"

"Nah. I was what you could call 'between jobs' when Ro said Mitch was looking for help. Hired me on the spot."

"I think it's all kind of fascinating," Amber said. "My friend, Wally? He knows a lot about beer."

"Uh huh."

"Well, mostly about drinking it instead of making it, if you know what I mean." Amber brushed hair from her face. "He says there's this woman in town, she makes great beer. Maybe you heard of her?"

"A woman? Could be." Donald said, "She have a name?"

"No, he never mentioned it," Amber said. "All he said was she's black."

Donald's stomach sank at the same time his head went light. He leaned against a pallet of canvas bags for balance.

"Gosh, I am sorry." Amber put a hand on his arm. "Was I supposed to say African American instead?"

"I think I need a smoke," Donald said.

He set the recipes aside and went out the back door. Amber followed him. He squinted in the harsh morning sun as they stepped out onto a loading dock. He extracted a cig from a pack he took from his shirt pocket. He offered one to Amber but she declined. Then he lit the cigarette and took in a giant drag and stared at the ground.

"This must be the designated smoke-break place," Amber said. "I mean look at all these butts out here. I don't myself; it smells bad and totally makes my hair reek."

Donald blew smoke out his nose and looked at her.

Amber said, "You know what's ironic? I don't mean, like,

the definition of 'irony,' but like what's ironic about me getting this job?"

"No," Donald said, "tell me."

She leaned closer and whispered, "Don't tell anyone, but I'm not into alcohol."

Donald drew more smoke into his lungs. He closed his eyes as he exhaled.

Amber said, "Have you heard of her, the bla—African American lady? I mean, being in the business, I bet you have, yeah?"

"Naw, man," Donald said. "Did he say where she lives?"

"Who, Wally?"

"Who else?"

"I think it's like somewhere here in Hilo."

Donald dropped the cigarette and smashed it with his left heel. He took a step toward Amber and grabbed both of her arms and pinned her against the back door.

"Hey, get your hands off me," she said. "I'll scream—I swear to God I will."

Donald said, "She send you?"

"Um, what? Who?"

"She sent you to find me, didn't she?"

Amber's eyes looked as if they were about to pop out of her head. "Who?"

"You know damn well who. The woman you say makes the beer. How'd you know to find me here?'

"I didn't, like, honest. All I did was apply for a job, well, my friend—"

"Like the last guy, all of a sudden just shows up and starts with the questions, all the goddamn time. Maybe let her name slip. In passing."

"Hey, look, I literally have no idea who she is, okay?" She struggled against his grip. "Wally talks about her, is all, and he says maybe Mr. Ratliff knows her, too."

Donald released her but stood close enough, she couldn't run away. "What'd you just say?"

Amber rubbed her upper arms. "Well, he, uh, he tells me there aren't like many people around here making their own beer, so I assumed Mr. Ratliff knows this lady since it's what he does, too. You know, small world, right?"

Donald felt his teeth grinding. "Goddamn. Goddamn."

Amber waited a beat, and then said, "Listen, I am completely sorry if I said something wrong."

Donald studied her face. "I just remembered," he said. "Mitch wanted me to go get some things." He took a set of keys from his jeans pocket. "Do me a favor, tell Ro I'm running an errand. Can you do that for me?"

"Yeah, I will," Amber said. She rubbed her upper arms.

"And one more thing?"

"Sure, whatever you want."

"This whole conversation? Treat it like it never happened." Donald jumped down from the loading dock and walked to his sedan, parked a few feet away. He got in and started the engine.

When he was gone, Noelani Lee bent over and picked up the remains of Donald's cigarette. She held it up and studied it. Maybe he changed brands. Then she dropped the butt in her handbag.

She opened the back door and went inside, past the giant brew kettles to the reception area. Rowena sat at her computer, writing an email. "Oh, hey," she said. "Donald show you around the place?"

"Well, kinda," Noelani again became Amber, "before he started looking like he was totally going to projectile vomit and said something about running an errand for Mr. Ratliff."

Rowena stopped typing and turned to face her. "He did what?"

"Yeah, he was on a smoke break and he literally got this weird look. He told me to tell you he had this errand to run for Mr. Ratliff and he like got in his car and bounced."

"Hmm. Mitch didn't tell me about any errands or anything."

"Could be he forgot," Amber said. "So, like, do I actually get an office around here?"

"Huh? Oh, um, probably not," Rowena said.

"So what am I supposed to do now? I literally have nothing to do."

Rowena turned her attention back to the computer. "I need to catch up on some stuff. How about you go wait in Mitch's office till he gets back?"

"You sure Mr. Ratliff won't mind?"

"Yeah, he'll probably tell you what he wants you to do when he gets back." She finished typing the email and hit Send, and then picked up her phone. "Just be sure you don't mess up his desk."

"Oh. So you think it's okay if I look at the stuff he gave Donald?"

"What, the recipes?" Rowena shrugged. "Guess it can't hurt anything. You need to know what you're selling, huh?"

"Yep," Amber said. "It would totally help."

***

Dwight said, "Why don't you just tell the truth? It'll make both our lives a whole lot easier in the long haul."

He'd allowed the man on the sofa to lower his arms and rest his hands flat on his legs. "Clarisse told me all about you," he said, "and how you asked all these questions about Landry Jenkins, back in San Diego."

"You, in other words."

"I admire your tenacity, but I don't understand what makes you think I am him when it is abundantly clear to all who know me I am not."

"Huh. From what I understand, no one knows you because you're damn near invisible," Dwight said. "Well, you were, until now. See, I got this figured out long ago, you being the same man as her alleged husband."

"There's nothing alleged about it. See the ring on my finger?"

"You claim to go around interviewing people and doing research for books but, based on a cursory search on Amazon, they never seem to get published."

"They're written for academics, not the general public." He

hesitated, and then said, "Besides, it's not my fault university presses reject them. They're outstanding books."

"Now I'd assume you'd leave a trail wherever you go, credit card receipts and whatnot, maybe even charges on hotel mini-bars," Dwight said. "Which are a complete rip-off, so if you avoid those, more power to you. But there's no activity to speak of, no path to follow. How does this happen, over and over and over again?"

"I've had benefactors," the man said, "who have underwritten much of my research. And I prefer using cash and traveler's checks."

"Cash? Man, get with it; this is the twenty-first century." Dwight adjusted his grip on the Glock. "To set your mind at ease," he said, "I'm letting her slide. No charges against her. She's a good woman who simply got caught up with a dishonest heel of a man. Which would be you. Of course, she thinks she's doing it for ratings, but I digress."

The man stared at Dwight for a moment, and then said, "I wonder if your bosses know what kind of mess you're making. With a good enough lawyer, I'll walk away before you can say 'who dat.'"

Dwight had to laugh. "Yeah, good one there." He waved the gun at the front door. "Come on, it's a nice day. Let's go for a ride."

***

Noelani Lee heard Rowena on the phone, talking with someone about coming in to work, because Mr. Ratliff was going to get things started this evening and it might be an all-nighter.

Sitting in Mitchell's office, she conducted a quick search of his immaculate desk, inside and out, for anything that might connect him with Cynamin Allgood and her beers—other than the recipes, which she snatched from the dry storage area after Donald left and while Rowena wasn't looking. But she found nothing, and the computer was off-limits, as Mitch had logged off before he left to meet Cynamin at Rainbow Falls.

Wanda texted what she had seen there, her message ending with call me.

Wanda answered on the first ring. "Hey Noe, you all right?"

"Fine but I can't talk long," Noelani said. "So what did you see?"

"Cynamin met with some white dude who gave her a sheet of paper."

"Did you see what was on it?"

"No, I was too far away. But anyway, they talked for a little while until the dude got in his Jeep and split. Then things got weird."

"How?"

"Well, Cynamin was crying, or I think she was, before she yelled 'cut' like the movie people do," Wanda said. "She left, too, but before she did, she sent a tweet that said, 'This is the end of my marriage, and it's killing me.'"

Noelani examined the mashed butt she'd lifted outside of the brewery. "Sweetie, hang tight. I'll call you back as soon as I can, okay?"

"Sure thing, cuz." Wanda hung up.

Rowena, a FedEx envelope in hand, appeared at the office door. "Amber, you okay in here?"

Noelani, back in character: "Yeah, sure. I mean, I was totally going to use the computer to write down some ideas I have, but Mitchell logged out and I literally do not have a password."

"Ideas? For what?"

"You know. Marketing things."

"Well, he's picky about who uses computers around here. It's pretty much just me and him." Rowena said, "If you have a laptop or a tablet at home, you should go get it."

"Cool, I will."

"Anyway, he just called and said his meeting's done, so he's on his way back. He asked me to go send this"—she held up the envelope—"overnight to St. Louis, so can you just hang till he gets here?"

"Definitely. I promise I won't touch anything, too."

Rowena thanked her, turned, and left. When Noelani heard

the front door close, she picked up her bag and stepped into the empty brewery. Figuring she had less than fifteen minutes left before Mitchell Ratliff returned, she turned her attention to the padlocked door. Recalling Rowena's explanation about Mitchell breaking a key, she got down on her knees and inspected the deadbolt. A piece of metal stuck out of the lock by maybe an eighth of an inch. She searched her bag and found a pair of tweezers, which she used to extract the metal fragment from the deadbolt. She was surprised to find it looked nothing like the mortal remains of a key; instead, it was thin and gray, shaped like a hook, and bore a striking resemblance to similar objects she sometimes used on the job.

Noelani slipped the object back into the lock. Then she dropped to all fours and peered under the door. The lights inside the room were turned off, but the brewery's bright fluorescents provided enough illumination to help her spot a shiny object, on the floor several inches inside the doorway.

She got to her knees, reached into her bag, and took out a small leather case. She unzipped it and removed a couple of tools, one shaped like an L and the other a long metal piece with a hook on the end. Checking the front door and seeing no one outside, she stood and picked the padlock. Within seconds, the shaft popped open.

Noelani lifted the lock from the hook and, looking over her shoulder, opened the door. "Oh, wow."

Two medium-sized metal barrels lay on the floor, in front of a four-wheeled cart that rested on its side; a third barrel, about half full of a brownish-red liquid, sat upright. Shards of glass and plastic hoses lay in a puddle of the same substance, which gave off a sickly-sweet smell.

It reminded her of coconuts.

Careful not to step in the liquid or touch any of the room's contents, Noelani bent over and examined the shiny thing on the floor; she recognized it as a torsion wrench, identical to the L-shaped tool she just used to pick the padlock and another half-dozen she had at home.

About then her phone buzzed. She checked the caller ID and answered. "Hey, Wanda, what's going on?"

"Cuz," Wanda Fong said, "this a bad time? Can you talk?"

Something about her voice was off, like she was breathing hard. "Not a lot." Noelani got back on her feet and cast a wary eye toward the brewery's entrance. "What's wrong?"

"Cynamin's freaking out and so am I."

"Are you two okay?"

"Yeah, we're fine," Wanda said. "See, I followed her home, but when we got here her husband's car's in the driveway and the front door's unlocked, but he's gone."

"Gone?"

"Like, not here, Noe."

A headache started taking root. Noelani rubbed her forehead.

"Cuz," Wanda said, "Cynamin told me she's big time worried because she told him she had an affair and now she's thinking he's maybe run off and killed himself or something. What should I do?"

"Sweetie," Noelani said, "Cynamin is not having an affair. She just thinks she is."

"Um, huh?"

Noelani heard a vehicle pull into the parking lot. She jumped from the room and replaced the padlock on the hook. "I'll be there as soon as I can, okay? Oh, and did you find the information I asked you to look up?"

"I was just getting ready to text it to you now."

Noelani heard a car door slam shut. "Awesome. I need to go but just try to keep her calm." Noelani disconnected the call and clipped the phone to her waist as she raced to the reception area. Just as she sat at Rowena's desk, Mitchell Ratliff came through the front door.

"Oh, hey, new girl," he said,. "Where's Rowena?"

Noelani again became Amber. "She had this thing you wanted her to like FedEx somewhere."

"Ah, right. Good." He looked into the empty brewery. "And, um, where's Donald? Another smoke break?"

"He said you wanted him to get stuff." She felt her phone buzz: an incoming text.

Mitchell stared at her. "Really. Hmm. I did?"

Amber shrugged. "It's what he said, anyway. Oh, Rowena told me I should go home and get my laptop? Since I don't have a computer to work on and, well, I actually have like tons of ideas and I want to write them down before I forget them."

Mitchell shrugged. "All right. Go get it maybe we can talk marketing later. Take the rest of the day, what the hell, but I want a detailed marketing plan on my desk tomorrow morning. I need to get to work now."

"Ah, cool, okay." She collected her handbag and left the building.

Outside, Noelani opened the text from Wanda. She read it, climbed in her car, and dialed Detective Ahuna.

"Hello, Miss Lee," he said. "Talk to the deputy yet?"

"Not yet, but can you meet me at Cynamin Allgood's house in twenty minutes?"

***

Mitchell Ratliff watched Amber drive away and wondered, *What the hell's she talking about?*

No way would he ever let Donald and Rowena leave the brewery unattended and in the hands of a brand-new employee, by herself. Especially today, when he was about to start production, at long last.

Speaking of which, he needed to let the bosses at the home office know he had what he needed. *Gentlemen, get ready for the big rollout because we're about to conquer Hawaii,* is what he planned on telling them. *You finally happy now, assholes?* is what he would think but not tell them.

Mitchell crossed the immaculate brewery floor to his test room, the off-limits small-batch brewery he installed himself long before the home office shipped over the large-capacity equipment. It was his secret lab, where he could experiment and use local bars as guinea pigs to see how people accepted them. Of course, his attempt to mimic Cyanmin's honey ale crapped out. But now he had her recipes, all of them, which made the little room unnecessary except as storage.

He fished a key from his pocket and stuck it in the lock, and saw the shackle was already open.

Mitchell froze. No one else had a key. No one else was allowed in. Donald and Rowena, and even Jervy and Kawika, all understood this.

But someone else didn't.

Chapter Twenty-five:
The Unfinished Errands

Kawika Hailama's boss with the parks and recreation department, a short bruddah named Abe, said, "Shoots, brah, it's Thursday. Almost Friday, yeah? Go down Lincoln Park, clean up da crap, take da long lunch break bumbye. Pau hana ain't till two thirty, but you know, don't go stressing."

Kawika liked Abe because he assigned easy jobs that offered ample time to loaf. And, he was Kawika's brother-in-law's second cousin.

"Oh yeah, no worries," Kawika said, picturing the case of beer in his fridge and the big bag of pakalolo in his sock drawer.

"Another hot one today," Abe said. "We can't risk you getting no heatstroke. You stay hydrated and in da shade, when you need to. You drop dead, man, your old lady'll rip off my ala-alas, eh."

"Just protect yourself, like this." Kawika covered his crotch with both hands. "Trust me. It's all I got to say."

Kawika drove a county pickup to the park, on Kinoole Street. When he got there, he made it look good—Abe had reminded him the newspaper office was next door and you never knew when those nosy buggahs were looking for some poor public employee to fuck with. He walked the grassy park's perimeter and picked up pieces of trash no matter how small, plus a few piles of dog poop he almost stepped in, even though a sign said animals were prohibited in the park. He also snagged a couple empty beer bottles, brought into the park despite another sign that warned, **NO DRINKING OF ALCOHOLIC BEVERAGES ON PREMISES.**

Finished with the patrol, he sidestepped a homeless guy snoring in the pavilion and emptied out the trash, did the same in both restrooms, and then wandered to a bench in the shade of a tree. He sat down and guzzled water and watched keiki on the playground equipment, their moms and tutus making sure they didn't hurt themselves when they came down the sliding boards and hit the playground's rubber surface.

They didn't. Instead, the kids kind of bounced off it and

laughed.

He relaxed there close to fifteen minutes. Then to make things look good, he decided he'd go across the street to the tennis courts and make sure the trash cans there weren't too full. But as he hoisted himself up, his cell rang. "Yeah, who's this?"

"Hey. Augie."

Kawika waited for a moment, and then said, "Oh yeah, Augie. Howzit?"

"Where you at?"

"I'm working, why?"

"Where's the other bruddah? Jervy?"

"Probably at home sleeping. Why? What's up?"

"She wants us today."

Kawika's heart might've skipped a beat or two. "Uh, well, what is it she wants?"

"Sistah's got more crap she wants us to get. For her beer, I think."

"All right," Kawika said. "Where do we meet?"

"Her place."

Kawika downed a big gulp of water to wash away the lump in his throat.

Augie said, "Brah, you there?"

"Yeah, uh huh." Kawika scanned the playground; what he was looking for, he didn't know. But all he saw were kids and families and the sleeping homeless dude. "You heard what happened at her place, yeah?"

"What?"

"Seriously? On the news. Some old haole got killed out there."

"Geez, brah, she do it?"

"Her? No way. Sistah's da crazy kine but she's got morals. Look, since it happened, there's no way I'm going to her place. Creeps the shit out of me, thinking about the old man getting his head bashed in the way he did with that baseball bat. Jervy's worse, yeah."

After a beat, Augie said, "She says it's important. Plus there's serious cash in it this time."

Kawika had a payment due on his truck and his wife needed

a new pair of nice shoes for her job. "How much?"

"Didn't say, except said it would be worth our time."

"When's she want us?"

"ASAP, brah. You can ditch?"

Kawika again surveyed the park, almost pristine thanks to him. But he still needed to get the trash cans at the tennis courts. He had to do it for Abe. "Give me twenty, then I'll get Jervy and be there bumbye, yeah?"

***

Rowena was on her way to the FedEx office out by the airport, when her cell rang. "Oh, hey, boo."

"Ro, what're you doing?"

"Overnighting something for Mitchell. Where are you? The new girl said you ran off on some errand. Are you all right?"

Donald said nothing for a few moments.

"Boo?"

"Ro," he said, "when you're done, come to the apartment."

His voice was edgy, cracking. "But Boo," she said, "Mitchell's expecting us. We've got lots to do."

"Ro, forget all that," Donald said. "Just come home and whatever you do, do not call him or anyone else. Please?"

Rowena had never heard him plea, never heard him get this way, like he was going to cry or have a nervous breakdown. It unsettled her.

"Sure," she said, "I'll be there fast as I can."

***

Dwight Broussard said, "I love a nice, leisurely drive, don't you?"

The bald man in the passenger seat, who did not resist when Dwight led him from Cynamin Allgood's living room to the SUV, said, "It really doesn't count when a white man with a gun doesn't tell me where we're going."

After they left Cynamin's house, Dwight drove toward downtown Hilo with no particular destination in mind.

Although, his short-term goal was to keep driving, all day and all the way around the island, if necessary, to squeeze as much information as he could out of the man he was convinced was Landry Jenkins. A rolling interrogation, something he'd done countless times with suspects and captured fugitives.

Except this time, Dwight had only one subject in mind: his father's stolen retirement.

He also hadn't figured out what to do with the man once he had finished, although he knew of only two viable options: The right thing, which would be to arrest him and haul him back to San Diego; or the other right thing, which would be to fulfill Pop's wishes.

"A white man with a badge and a gun," Dwight said.

The man stared hard at Dwight. "You will regret this, once my lawyer is through with you. You'll end up using a toothbrush to shovel dog turds in some K9 cop's kennel."

"I remember one time," Dwight said, "Pop tells Mom we're going for a ride, says we're going to visit my aunt and uncle in Houston." He said, "Well, it doesn't take Mom long to figure out we're driving away from Houston. Now, Mom always was a good sport but she got pissed because Pop wouldn't say where it is we were headed. He tells her it's a surprise. Eventually, we end up in Memphis and the next thing she knows, we're standing at the gates of Graceland." He looked at the man and said, "Mom adored the King. You should've seen the smile on her face. From then on, Pop could do no wrong."

"Nice story," the man said, "but how does it apply to our situation?"

"Simple. Our road trip, and it'll be short, considering we're on an island, will end with me smiling, just like my mother did that day in Memphis."

The man said, "Whatever it is you're planning is doomed to fail."

Dwight said, "You hungry? It's early for lunch, but all I've had all day was a stale Danish and coffee someone filtered through a gym sock."

"What you're asking me is, what do I want for my last meal."

"Hey, you said it, not me."

Dwight's cell buzzed. He checked the incoming number, didn't recognize it, but answered. "Dwight Broussard."

"Well, hello there."

Dwight froze at the man's voice. "Who's this?"

"It's your old friend from San Diego. What, you don't recognize me?"

Dwight remembered the voice from hundreds of wiretaps. "If you are who you say you are," he said, "then you should know I don't have many friends in San Diego."

"True, except for the co-workers, but they don't count. Never do, in my experience." After a pause, the man on the phone said, "Oh, I almost forgot, there's the father. How's the old man doing these days? Retirement treating him okay?"

Dwight saw a directional sign with the words **VOLCANO 25** and an arrow pointing to his right. Beside it was a gas station. He pulled in and parked but kept the engine running. "What would you know about Pop?"

"You two still eat at the Mexican seafood joint? I seen you there a bunch of times. The one with the kick-ass shrimp burritos. What'd they call it, La Almeja Barbuda? What's that mean, anyway?"

"The Bearded Clam."

The man on the phone said, "Next time you talk to him, tell him I'm sorry, the investment didn't pan out. But I did good by it."

Dwight said, "Whoever you are, I don't like being fucked with."

"What do you mean, 'whoever you are'? Nah, man, I know you're here on the island looking for me. The lady at the soul food joint, the barber—they all told me about the redneck in the Saints hat and the 'gator-skin boots come around asking for me."

After a moment, the man on the phone said, "Then there's the farm system, the Hawaiian guy and the chick."

Dwight stared and the man in the passenger seat exchanged harsh glares. "I don't know what it is you're talking about."

"The one with the legs? If I wasn't married—did I tell you

I'm married?" The man on the phone said, "Cynamin might've dropped the dime on you, too. In passing."

Dwight waited a beat. "So are you calling just to give me a ration of shit, or is there a purpose behind this conversation?"

"Could be I'm done running."

Dwight waited a moment. Huh. He must have run out of money. "So you're turning yourself in. Is this what I'm supposed to believe?" He looked at the bald man in the passenger seat, his eyes now filling with question marks.

"It would make your job easier, now, wouldn't it, if I did?"

"There's a lot of people who want you dead."

"Including you and your daddy, I'm thinking. About as dead as the old preacher in Cynamin's garage, too. Shame about him."

"Not really."

"Uh huh."

"As you may know, depending how long you've been here, the land mass of this island encompasses more than four thousand square miles," Dwight said. "Its population density, according to the 2010 census, is about forty-six persons per square mile. Which means there's a lot of unoccupied dry space surrounded by a big, wet ocean. Now, if you are indeed who you say you are—"

"Did I say who I was?"

"—then you will have to be more specific about where we can meet. And when."

Several moments of silence, interrupted only by the SUV's engine and its air conditioner on high, ended when the man on the phone said, "Driving right now. Running errands for the boss."

Dwight laughed. The man in the passenger seat arched his eyebrows. "You have a job? I mean, a real, salary-paying, income tax-generating job?"

"Proves I'm now a law-abiding citizen."

"No doubt."

"Understand, I need to explain things to the wife and the boss before me and you can close the books."

"Well, all right. If you don't mind me saying so, as

diversions go, this one's awful damn lame."

"Diversion? Yeah, whatever," the man on the phone said. "I'll text the time and the place to you in a few." He hung up.

After a moment, the man in the passenger seat said, "That was him, wasn't it?"

"Him, being, who?"

"I showed you my driver's license. I even showed you my neck, and you still think I'm Landry Jenkins even though the man just called you while I'm sitting right here beside you."

Dwight said, "I'd like to see the volcano. Have you been there?"

His cell rang again. "Dwight Broussard."

"Oh, hey, Deputy US Marshal Broussard—it's me, Noelani Lee."

Dwight looked at the man in the passenger seat, who had his eyes locked on the phone. "Hello, Miss Lee," Dwight said. "How are you this morning? Find any more bodies since last night?"

"Not so far," she said, "but I do know where you can find a live one."

***

In his official county pickup, Kawika Hailama picked Jervy Salazar up at the apartment Jervy shared with two other guys.

Halfway to Cynamin Allgood's house, Jervy said, "This gonna take long? I need to be at work by one."

"Dude, that's the fifth time you asked me, and for the fifth time, I'm telling you, I don't know," Kawika said.

Jervy looked out the window. "I'm serious, brah. I can't be there. Place scares the hell out of me."

"Yeah, well, if she makes it quick, we can split fast. And she better because me driving around town in this truck on personal matters? It's not cool if I get caught."

"Think she's figured it out yet?"

"Probably not. She can't get in the garage, I'm thinking."

Jervy said, "You talk to Mitch today?"

"Sent him a text but he didn't answer it."

Jervy nodded. "Think he'll come through?"

"He said he would," Kawika said. "I just need to go see him when I'm pau."

Several minutes later, they parked in front of Cynamin's house. Kawika turned to Jervy and said, "You want to stay in the truck?"

"Nah, man." Jervy opened his door. "Let's just do it and get it over with."

Kawika knocked on the screen door, looked inside and heard Cynamin say, "Come in." He and Jervy stepped inside and found her in the kitchen, washing dishes in the sink. Two chicks sat at the dining room table; one was fat but kind of cute, and the other one was okay-looking and wore a gray business suit. The fat one was drinking coffee, and the other one had a hand wrapped around a glass of water. At the head of the table sat a closed laptop, a bunch of notebooks, and some folders.

"Hey, guys," Cynamin said. "I am so glad you could drop by."

"Yeah, no worries," Kawika said. "I just got to get back to work."

"I understand," Cynamin said. "Oh, silly me." She motioned toward the fat chick. "This is my friend Wanda. Wanda, this is Kawika and Jervy. They work for me."

"Eh, howzit," the chubby chick said.

"And," Cynamin said, "this is Amber. Did I tell you, she's Augie's sister?"

Kawika said, "Oh, yeah? Augie never mentioned he has a sister, yeah."

"Especially one who's good-looking," Jervy said, grinning.

Amber rolled her eyes. "Whatever."

Kawika said to Amber, "Where's your brother?"

"I think he's like on his way," Amber said. "Should be here soon."

"So," Jervy said to Cynamin, "you don't seem too bent out of shape for some guy getting killed in your garage."

Kawika could see right through his brave front, so he compounded it. "Yeah, me? I'd be afraid to hang here anymore."

Cynamin dried her hands on a dishtowel and stepped into

the dining room. "Well, hon, you just have to move on after things like this happen. And that means, for me, to start making beer, which is why I need you today."

Kawika adjusted his Kangol cap and licked his lips. "Can't be gone long," he said. "My boss is a total hard ass, you know?"

Someone knocked on the door. Cynamin said, "Could be him now," as she crossed the living room to the door.

She opened it and an older dude, maybe in his fifties, in a red short-sleeved shirt and tan pants, came in. He looked at Jervy and Kawika and pulled his shirttail aside.

Kawika shivered when he saw the badge clipped to the man's belt. And when two uniformed police officers followed him in, his stomach roiled.

Kawika tossed a quick glance at Jervy, whose eyes darted from Kawika to the man in the red shirt to Cynamin to the cops.

"I'm Detective Ahuna," the man said. He approached Kawika. "I don't believe we've met. You must be Kawika Hailama, am I right?"

"Uh, yeah, that's me."

Detective Ahuna turned to face Jervy. "And Jervy Salazar. You know I know who you are?"

"Um, no?"

"Your probation officer is my wife's nephew. Small world, huh?"

Kawika tried to steel himself as he studied Jervy's reaction, which wasn't good.

"See, it's like this," Jervy said. "I can't get in trouble. I can't, man."

Detective Ahuna looked at Cynamin, and then at Amber. "Nobody said you were in trouble. Why would you think you're in trouble?"

"See, um—"

Kawika interrupted him. "Officer, we didn't kill the man, the old man, out there in Cynamin's garage."

"Yeah, the one we heard about on the radio," Jervy said. "The one got his head bashed in with da kine baseball bat, right?"

"Okay, but now I wonder, how did you know he was

beaten to death with a bat?" Detective Ahuna said, "We never released that information to the press."

Kawika couldn't speak. Neither could Jervy.

Detective Ahuna instructed them to have a seat on the sofa. The uniformed cops shadowed them, and the detective sat in a chair facing them. The Amber chick got up from the table and stood beside the detective.

Detective Ahuna opened a notebook and clicked a pen. "You were here last night, weren't you?"

Kawika looked at Amber, and then at the detective. "Um, no?"

"But you were," Amber said. "You came looking for Cynamin's recipe book."

Her voice had changed. Kawika looked at the detective, who blinked and waited for an answer. Instead, he turned toward Jervy and said, "Brah, what'd you tell Augie?"

Detective Ahuna said, "Who is Augie?"

Jervy propped his elbows on his knees and covered his face with his hands. "Oh man, I'm so fucking screwed."

Kawika took off his cap and ran a hand through his hair. "Listen, we didn't kill no one. All we did was—"

"Brah," Jervy said, "shut up, man."

"What you did," Amber said, "was break into Cynamin's house when she was out last night, trying to find her recipe book. You had a key that you believed worked for her file cabinet—the one you took from Augie."

"Who are you, lady?" Kawika hesitated for a moment, then said, "Augie tell you all of this?"

"All I want to know is," Detective Ahuna said, "what did you see and hear last night, and what did you do?"

"We didn't kill the man," Jervy said. He closed his eyes. "I am so screwed."

Detective Ahuna said to Kawika, "You can make things a lot easier for us all if you simply tell your side of the story."

Cynamin and the fat chick stood at the edge of the living room. Cynamin said, "Boys, please tell the truth."

Kawika looked at Cynamin, and then at Jervy, who again covered his face with his hands. Now he was whimpering.

Detective Ahuna said, "Tell me what happened last night."

So Kawika told his story, about being in the house, about how they got the key from Augie and tried to steal the recipe book but couldn't find it in Cynamin's office, where they figured she kept it. He said when they were trying to get the cabinet open, they heard loud noises in the garage, so they went to check it out and when they got there, somebody ran over them and got into a car and drove away. Then they looked inside the garage and found the old man with his brains beat out.

Detective Ahuna said to Jervy, "Is this how it happened?"

Jervy uncovered his face, looked at the detective, and nodded.

"Did you go inside the garage," Detective Ahuna said, "and steal anything? Like a purple towel, for example?"

Kawika squinted. "A towel? No way, not a towel."

"I don't remember seeing a towel," Jervy said.

"But," Amber said, "you did steal Cynamin's recipes." She held up a piece of paper. Kawika recognized the big X covered the whole page. "After this mystery person ran out of the garage, you went in and took them, including this one. Am I right?"

"For Cynamin's beers," Wanda said. "Sistah makes the best beer on the island and you were working for her and you stole her recipes for someone, which is uncool."

Kawika fell back in the sofa. "Oh man."

"The ones Mitchell Ratliff has now at his brewery," Amber said. "The ones he's planning to make for his bosses in St. Louis."

Jervy said, "So totally fucking screwed."

Detective Ahuna asked whether they got a good look at whoever it was who ran out of the garage—white, black, Hawaiian, maybe even Samoan or Asian or even Hispanic.

Both Kawika and Jervy said no, it was dark and the man ran out too fast.

"Did you see what he was driving?"

"No, man," Kawika said. "I tried catching up but the bruddah got in a car and drove away. Just a dark car, is all I saw."

Detective Ahuna said, "Why didn't you call nine-one-one?"

"We freaked," Kawika said. "Old haole gets beat to death and we're in the same house—we didn't stick around for no welcoming committee."

Jervy looked at Amber and said, "Seriously, who are you chicks? Is this all one set-up?"

"I work for Miss Allgood," Amber said. "You don't need to know anything else."

"You're real name's not Amber, huh?" Jervy said. "You ain't Augie's sister."

"If there is an Augie," Kawika said. "I knew there was something about that bruddah I didn't like."

"Damn," Jervy said, "I am way too screwed."

"Gentlemen," Detective Ahuna said, "these officers will take you downtown now."

Noelani Lee followed Detective Ahuna outside, as the uniforms stuffed Kawika and Jervy into a patrol car. She said, "They didn't do it, you know."

Detective Ahuna scratched the top of his head and blinked at the bright sunshine. "You ever wonder if it'll rain again?"

Noelani looked up at the blue sky. "It's not so much I wonder if it will as it is I hope it does."

"This weird weather. I'm beginning to think there's something to this whole global warming thing." Detective Ahuna said, "I'd like to think they don't have it in them. Besides, the only prints on the bat were Templeton's. And the only other ones in the garage belong to Miss Allgood."

"They came for her recipe book, nothing more," Noelani said.

Detective Ahuna said, "You were tracking them, weren't you?"

"A GPS on Kawika's truck. Oh, and the key they had? It doesn't open Cynamin's file cabinet."

"Ah, a fake key."

"No, it's real." She smiled. "It's just not for her cabinet."

Detective Ahuna blinked at her. "So this key, whatever it opens—how'd they get their hands on it in the first place?"

"The part about Jervy taking it from Augie is a true story." Noelani's recollection incited a dull throb in her chest. "As soon as we knew they were here, we left Wally's, but they were gone and Templeton was, well, dead."

Detective Ahuna clicked his pen. "Hear from our bayou buddy yet today?"

"He hasn't called me, no."

"You know what I think? I think he thinks Landry Jenkins popped Templeton."

Noelani looked down at her feet. "What makes you so certain?"

"He thinks Miss Allgood and Jenkins are still friends— lovers—which means he also thinks Jenkins is watching out for her and may have whacked Templeton to protect her."

"What he said was, he thinks Jenkins is her husband."

"I know. Interesting theory."

"If, ah, this is—do you think he's onto something?"

"Anything's possible." The way he said it, his voice, the look in his eyes, the thin smile on his face: he had something in reserve. She hoped she wasn't giving anything away, either.

Noelani gazed over Cynamin's front yard, the grass turning brown from lack of rain. "Do you mind if I go in and talk to her?"

"Knock yourself out. She's your client," Detective Ahuna said. "I'll call you later."

Noelani went back inside. Cynamin and Wanda sat in the living room, chatting.

"Miss Lee," Cynamin said, "how awful for those boys. I mean, I was right all along, right?"

"Yes, apparently you were."

"Noe," Wanda said, "if they didn't kill the old preacher, do you think they killed Milt Nihoa?"

"I doubt it." Noelani sat beside Cynamin on the sofa. "Can I ask why you sent a tweet saying you cheated on your husband?"

"Well, because I have," her matter-of-fact tone tinged with regret, "and I feel so bad about it, too. It's probably why he's not home. Though it's weird—his car's here and he left his computer and all his research notes."

Noelani said, "No, you are not having an affair with Landry Jenkins."

Wanda gasped and slapped a hand over her mouth. "No way."

Cynamin huffed. "Yes, I am. The cigarette butt the detective found? It's Landry's favorite brand. He's smoked them as long as I've known him."

Noelani took a plastic baggie from her handbag. "See this butt? I found it at Mitchell's brewery." She tossed it on the coffee table. "Do you know who smokes these?"

"Hon," Cynamin said, picking up the baggie, "could you speak up, please? I don't think the sound tech—"

A new headache. Noelani tried not to explode. "There is no TV crew, Cynamin. Nobody's following you with cameras and you do not have a new show. You haven't been in one since American Election went off the air."

"Well, see," Cynamin said, as she examined the butt, "Mitch smokes too, except he claims it's one of those electronic cig—"

"This is one of Landry Jenkins's cigarettes," Noelani said. "I watched him smoke it this morning. His wife said he started on this brand a couple years ago, which you wouldn't have known because he switched after he left San Diego and before you found out he lives here."

Cynamin dropped the baggie, her hands shaking. She closed her eyes and tried to calm herself. "You mean, he really is here?"

Noelani relayed her conversation that morning with Edward Vaughn—about Cynamin's vacation on the Big Island, and her subsequent and sudden desire to move to Hilo.

"He thought you came up with the idea out of nowhere," Noelani said.

"No, see, Edward didn't tell me he met you."

"But you had an ulterior motive that you didn't share with him. Didn't you?"

A solitary tear rolled down Cynamin's left cheek. This one looked real. She said, "I found out when Mr. Nihoa contacted me."

Wanda whistled and said, "Wow, for reals?"

"One day he emailed me—I think he got my address from my dress shop website—and said he'd spotted a man in Hilo who favored Landry." Cynamin said, "I wanted to see for myself, and since Edward was on the road researching his Western book, my sister and I came over on vacation. I met with Mr. Nihoa. I told him about Landry's birthmark and he said he'd seen this man but he couldn't get close enough to be sure it was Landry. But Mr. Nihoa said he'd help me if I paid him a retainer and five hundred a month after, and he promised not to tell anyone else."

Noelani waited a moment, and then said, "Then, later, he got wind of the feds and their reward. He would collect a lot more money from them if he turned Landry in to Dwight Broussard, on top of what you already paid him."

Cynamin rubbed her forehead. "He said nothing for a long time, until last weekend, when he left the voicemail. But, how do you know he was working for the marshal? Did he tell you?"

"Yes, and so did Milt, in a way. He sent me a copy of the wanted poster before he died. And the key that Jervy and Kawika thought opened your file cabinet."

"But Noe," Wanda said, "you still haven't explained why the buggah Milt mailed you the key, too, huh? And if it's not for Cynamin's cabinet, what's it for?"

Noelani had wondered about that from the moment she opened the envelope. She chalked it up to Milt being a drunken, classless jerk. But she also knew he was insecure and, when he was drunk, a raging paranoid. "Well, I may never know for certain."

She said to Cynamin, "So, what plan did Milt feed you, in the event he did find Landry Jenkins and didn't take him to the marshal?"

Cynamin said Milt told her they would offer Jenkins a deal: repay Cynamin the money he laundered through her, in exchange for letting him flee or be handed over to the government. Then she and Milt would split the reward.

"Trust me, he would never share a big payday like that with you. Which explains why he never kept you updated." Noelani said, "So, what did your husband know about all of this?"

"Nothing. It was my secret with Mr. Nihoa."

Noelani said, "Like the offers you received from Mitchell Ratliff, to sell your business to him. When you hired me, I'll be honest, I didn't believe anyone was out to shut you down." She said, "I assumed it was your imagination, maybe just another of your phony reality-show story lines. Like you concocted the whole Milt Nihoa thing to cover the fact you actually hired him to find Landry Jenkins."

Cynamin smiled. "It's a good one, you have to admit."

"But it was only when Jervy decked me and took the key when I started thinking, well, maybe there's something to it. Maybe Milt was looking into it for you, but Milt being who he was, didn't exactly go after it with enthusiasm." Noelani picked a piece of lint from her pants. "Yes, those mokes stole your recipes and now Ratliff is going to use them, starting today."

"Oh, geez, Noe," Wanda said, "you've gotta stop him. We can't let no one take credit for what Cynamin does."

"You're absolutely right," Noelani said. "I plan on doing just that." She looked at Cynamin. "I also plan on convincing your husband you were not having an affair."

"He may never come home," Cynamin said, "after what I did."

"Oh, he will, once I find him," Noelani said. She felt another headache taking shape. "I need to get back to the brewery."

Chapter Twenty-six:
The One Take

Rowena's heart ached as Donald prowled their sixth-floor condo on Aupuni Street, rubbing his hands, panting, sweating.

She said, "Boo, honey, why don't you tell me what's wrong?"

He looked out the window, pulling the curtain aside just enough to check out the parking lot below. "I'm...I don't..." He stopped and looked at her, and she saw the panic. Again.

He'd been like this before. They'd be out driving and he'd take a strange, long route home, instead of main streets which would be fifteen or twenty minutes quicker. She'd say, Why are you making a right here instead of a left? And Donald would say, Change of scenery; besides, who's in a hurry?

Then there were the times Donald would close the blinds on beautiful sunny days, and she'd ask why, and he'd tell her bright light sometimes bothers his eyes.

They celebrated their anniversary at home, didn't go out much at all, period. If he needed or wanted anything from the store, she'd pick it up, and if she was late or didn't call, he'd panic and when she got home he'd hug her like he'd never let her go and she swore one time, he cried like a baby.

These things scared the bejesus out of her. Then he'd apologize and within minutes he'd be doing his Eddie Murphy imitation—he had a good one, too—and they would laugh and things would be as normal as they ever were with Donald.

Rowena wanted him to see a psychiatrist. She also was sure Donald bought a gun. But she never saw it and decided it was best to not look for it, much less ask him if he did.

Then there was the most recent spell, a month ago, after a weasel named Fred came to the brewery. This Fred started talking up Mitchell Ratliff, trying to get a job, asking all kinds of questions about what kinds of beers he was planning to make, what stuff he was going to put in them, where he'd get it, all of that. But the whole time he kept looking funny at Donald. Then when Mitchell introduced them, Fred started asking Donald strange questions, about people he knew, where he lived before

Hilo, and off-the-wall stuff about women who make beer and if he'd ever known any. And this Fred, he kept staring at Donald's neck, to the point Donald began wearing his work shirt buttoned all the way up, even on the hottest days.

This went on for a couple of weeks, until late last week, the last time Rowena saw Fred at the brewery. She didn't think much of it until Monday, when Mitchell announced Fred went to work somewhere else and wouldn't be coming back. Then Mitchell said he accidentally broke a key in the deadbolt on the door to his small-batch room and that he spent Sunday putting the hook and padlock on it.

Hearing this, Donald entered a state of absolute calm. It lasted all week.

Until now.

Rowena said, "Honey, what happened at work? Did Mitchell say something to you?"

"No, it wasn't him." He tried to smile. "Look, sorry. I heard a backfire, some truck when I was on the road today. Made me snap."

"Oh, when you were out running your errand for Mitchell?"

"The new girl said this?"

Rowena nodded.

"Yeah. Mitch, uh, he wanted me to check on, to see if something was in stock at this store."

She approached him and put her arms around his waist. "Are you sure?"

"What do you mean, am I sure?" She felt him relax as he smiled, big and bright. "Ro, I'd know what I was doing, huh?"

She patted his butt with both hands. "Yeah, you would. Are you okay to go back to work now? Mitchell's counting on you. We have a lot of work to do today."

"The new recipes. Yeah, he seems in a hurry to get cranking."

"Uh huh. He's not even bothering to make a test batch first. Must be the 'home office' is on his case real hard again."

"Wouldn't surprise me none." He bent over and kissed her. "Want to drive together?"

When they arrived at the brewery, they found Mitchell

Ratliff lifting bags of barley from a pallet. "Oh. Hey. Glad you two could get back." He looked at Donald and said, "Let's do this."

Donald nodded and said, "All right by me."

***

Outside, in her car, Noelani Lee watched the couple enter the building. She called Dwight Broussard.

"He's here."

After a beat, Dwight said, "Give me the address again. And stay put."

When he hung up, Dwight looked at the bald man in his passenger seat. "Ready to go for a ride?"

"We already are, aren't we? Even though you never said where to."

"Yeah, well, I think you'll like where we're going."

Noelani Lee disconnected the call. Then she dialed Detective Ahuna.

"Miss Lee," he said, "long time no talk."

"I'll make this quick."

"Okay."

"I know who killed Paul Templeton."

***

Rowena looked up as Amber Porter came through the front door, carrying a laptop case. "Hey, Amber."

"Aloha, Rowena. Sorry it took me so long."

"No worries," Rowena said. "Me and Donald just got back."

"Oh, cool." Amber peered into the brewery. "Is Mitchell here, too?"

"Donald and him are working now. Listen, I don't think Mitchell will be upset if you use his office again, just so long as you keep it arranged the way he has it, okay?"

"Totally. Hey, I have some awesome ideas. I just can't wait to write them down."

Rowena could almost feel the eagerness rolling off the new girl. "Glad you're excited. Um, listen, I need to call a couple guys Mitchell wanted to come in and help."

"Oh, yeah, okay."

"But they aren't answering my call or texts, the lazy mokes."

Amber said, "Who are they? Maybe I know them?"

"Friends of Mitchell's," Rowena said. "I think he said their names are Jervy and Kawika."

***

Cynamin Allgood delivered a plate of manapua—steamed dumplings filled with Chinese-style barbecued pork—to Wanda Fong, seated at the picnic table on her backyard lanai.

Wanda said, "Oh man, those smell awesome."

"I'm glad you think so." Cynamin sat down and said, "Since we need to pass the time until she calls."

"Well, I'm sure Noe, she just wants us out of her way," Wanda said. She picked up a manapua, blew on it, waited a moment, and then took a bite. "She gets that way sometimes," she said, her mouth full, "when she's working. I sometimes help her but usually, I don't mess with what she's up to." She washed down her food with a slug of guava juice.

"I just wish I knew what was going on."

"You ask me, I bet she's gonna nail the Mitchell dude for stealing your stuff. Well, for getting those two buggahs to steal your stuff for him."

Cynamin dawdled with her empty juice glass. "I hope she finds my Edward, too."

"You really told him you were having an affair, huh?"

Cynamin nodded. "I was positive he didn't want to see me again, so I left to take care of something in town. When I got back, he was gone."

She looked at Wanda, who responded with a nervous grin. "Even though," Wanda said, finishing the snack and taking another manapua from the plate, "Noelani knew you weren't."

"Hon, it's hard to explain. I guess I knew I wasn't on television anymore, but once you've had a taste of the fame that comes with it? It's tough to let go."

"But you have a good life here, yeah? Nice house, quiet neighborhood—you even make fantastic beer, the best I ever had." Wanda tore the manapua in half. "I'd trade my crappy apartment for all this any day. Plus you got a great husband."

"Well, I hope I still do."

Wanda said, "My divorce is getting final, so I guess I'm just jealous," and then ate the manapua.

Cynamin watched her for a moment, and then said, "Hey, can I get you anything else? More juice?"

"Hate to be a bad guest, but, sure."

"No problem. I'll be right back."

Cynamin got up and went inside. She went down the hallway, past the master bedroom and her office, to the kitchen. Without breaking stride, she picked up her car keys from the countertop and kept going out the front door.

In the car, she opened the glove box. The gun was still there.

"Well, we only have one take," she said. "So let's make it a good one."

***

Behind the building on Kawili Street, Dwight Broussard parked the SUV just beyond the loading dock. He turned off the engine. "Give me your hand."

The man in the passenger seat said, "Really? Don't you think this has gone far enough?"

Dwight grabbed the man's left wrist and cuffed him to the steering wheel. "Don't go anywhere." Then he climbed out of the SUV, drew his Glock, and crept toward the back door.

Amber strolled across the brewery to the dry storage area, where Mitchell Ratliff and Donald tore open brown paper bags. "Mr. Ratliff? See, I brought my laptop so I'm like all totally ready to—"

"Uh, new girl," Mitchell said, "we're busy here."

"Well, sorry, but I just wanted to let you know I—"

"Okay, so, feel free to use my desk and do whatever I hired you for." He yelled to the reception area, "Rowena? You get a hold of those two bozos?"

Rowena called back, "No, they aren't answering phones or anything,"

"Keep trying. We need them here on the double." Mitchell looked at Amber. "Why are you still standing there? Go, use my office but don't touch anything."

Amber said, "Yeah, cool, okay."

Halfway there, she stopped and looked back at Mitchell and Donald, who kept working and didn't pay attention to her. Then she looked at Rowena, who had her back turned and was on the phone. Then she took a few steps to her right, toward the room with the padlock on the door.

Dwight Broussard climbed up the loading dock and approached a closed door. He heard two men talking, inside the building, snippets of a conversation about hops and yeast and who knows what.

He pressed an ear against the door. One voice did most of the talking, sounded like a white guy. The other one? The voice reminded him of Landry Jenkins.

He heard him say, "Mitch, give me a second. I need to hit the shitter."

I'll be damned.

Holding the Glock in his right hand, he gripped the doorknob with his left. He flashed on his father and how this was finally going to end: maybe not getting his money back but sure as hell evening up the score.

Then he opened the door."

Chapter Twenty-seven:
The High Potential for Drama

Noelani Lee froze when she saw the padlock's open shaft. Oh no, I forgot to—

A voice behind her growled, "Who the hell are you?"

She spun around and melted as Donald's dark eyes bore in on her. And even though he was only an inch or two taller, she felt tiny next to him as he leaned in close.

He grabbed her hair and pulled. The next thing she saw was her reddish-brown wig, in his hand. "Jesus," he said, "what the fuck?"

Noelani felt something press into her stomach. She looked down and saw a handgun.

"I'm going to ask you one more time," he said, "who the hell are you and who sent you to find me?"

"Um, I, I'm just Amber, the new girl."

Donald reached around her and lifted the lock from the hook and opened the door. "Shut up and get in."

They stepped inside and he shut the door behind them. He held the gun on her with one hand and tossed her the wig with the other. He looked around the space. "Did you do this? How'd you do this since Mr. Clean doesn't let anyone else in here?"

Noelani gripped the wig in her left hand as she leaned against a countertop laden with jars of honey. "Well, no. You see, it's like this because Mitch killed a man in here."

"Don't mess with me." Donald looked at her sideways. "You still haven't told me who you are. Who you really are."

She said, "Do you remember Fred, drunk guy that worked here with you for a while? I think you or Rowena mentioned him."

"The Hawaiian dude. He got on the nerves."

"Yeah, mine, too."

"How'd you know him?"

"His real name was Milt Nihoa and he was a private investigator."

Donald took a step toward her. Noelani pressed her back against the counter, her mind racing through options to get herself out of this situation, her original plans now blown way off course.

"Uh huh," he said. "I guess this makes you one of them, too. Like you're in the club or buddies or something."

"Believe me, Mr. Jenkins, Milt and I were not exactly pals." She bit her lower lip. Noe, you idiot, why did you say that?

He stopped and squinted. "Who—listen, my name's Donald. Donald Cropper. Did you forget already?" He pushed himself against her, the gun's muzzle shoved up against her chin. "I said, my name is Donald Cropper." His breath smelled like mint mouthwash. "There is no such person as Landry Jenkins."

Noelani swallowed. "Did I—what did I call you?"

Donald waved the gun at her. "If you're telling the truth, then tell me who the private detective was working for."

Noelani's head felt as if it were going to implode. "Well, see, this is where things get complicated."

"Make it quick. I don't have all day. Mitch thinks I'm on the toilet."

Outside the small room, in the brewery, a woman screamed. Then another woman called out something that sounded like, "Where the hell is he?" Then from another part of the building there was a crashing sound and a man yelled, "Federal agent! Nobody move."

Big as she pleased, Cynamin Allgood marched into the Saddle Road brewery brandishing a gun, which she pointed at a woman sitting at the reception desk. "Where is he?"

The woman screamed and fell out of her rolling chair.

Cynamin bypassed her and continued into the brewery. She shouted, "Where the hell is he?" and saw Mitchell Ratliff, emptying bags of malt barley into a bucket. With long strides, she made her way toward him. When he saw her gun, he dropped a bag; it broke and scattered grain all over his perfect floor.

"Holy Jesus, Cynamin," he said. "What the hell are you doing?"

About then, the back door flew open and slammed against

the wall. Dwight Broussard, Glock raised, burst in. "Federal agent! Nobody move."

Cynamin made eye contact with him. He drew on her and said, "Cynamin, drop it."

She aimed the gun at Mitchell, then Dwight, and then again at Mitchell. "Not until you tell me why you're here."

"Cynamin," Dwight said, "you ought to know it's a bad idea to aim a toy gun at a lawman."

Mitchell, his arms in the air, said, "A cop?" He looked at Cynamin. "Did you call the cops over your silly recipes?"

"I'm not a cop," Dwight said. He showed Mitchell his star. "I'm with the US Marshals Service and I have no quarrel with you."

"And this is not a toy," Cynamin said, aiming at Mitchell. "The producers wanted me to get a gun because of the high potential for drama.."

Dwight said, "It has an orange trigger and a leopard-print decal on the grip. My neighbor's daughter has one just like it."

"So? Doesn't make it any less real."

"She just turned ten."

Cynamin looked down the sight at Mitchell. "You want me to show you exactly how real it is?"

Dwight said, "Just put the thing down."

Mitchell dropped to his knees and sheltered his head with his arms. "No, please, Cynamin. Please, can we make a deal? Huh?"

Cynamin said, "It's not you I'm worried about."

Dwight looked at Mitchell, and then at Cynamin. "You two know each other?"

"Yeah we do," Cynamin said. "This son of a bitch stole my beer recipes and plans on putting me out of business."

"If you'd just signed the papers," Mitchell said through his arms, "we could have made you a wealthy woman."

"I already have more than enough money, you twerp," Cynamin said. "But anyway, we both know why I'm here."

Mitchell, cowering, looked up at her. "Why?"

Dwight, still drawn on her, said, "It's not for the beer, I'm thinking."

Cynamin smiled at Dwight. "Now you're getting somewhere, hon."

"Enough with the fairy tales." Landry Jenkins thrust the gun at Noelani Lee. "Start telling me the truth, dammit."

Noelani said, "No, it's true. Cynamin hired him to find you because she's still, um, mad at you. About the money laundering."

"You mean the investments."

She shrugged. "Mitchell killed him, even though he was unaware his bosses in St. Louis hired Milt to steal Cynamin's recipes, since she kept blowing off Mitchell's offers. But when Milt, as Fred, showed up asking Mitchell about his plans for this place, Mitchell must have assumed he was working for Cynamin, when in reality she hired him to track you down."

Landry shook his head. "Sounds crazy, lady, if it's the way it went down."

Noelani looked toward the door, and then said, "Milt made more from the folks in St. Louis than he did from Cynamin. Plus, when the marshal waved a wad of cash in front of him, a reward for finding you, he tanked the job for Cynamin because where was the incentive?" Noelani shrugged. "I told you it was complicated."

"More like convoluted, but damn." Landry rubbed his chin. "Man, that's some messed-up shit, if what you're saying's true."

A moment passed, and then Noelani said, "The beard works, but did you ever think of growing your hair out? If you didn't want anyone to find you?"

"I can't. I'm naturally bald."

"Ah. Well, um, just so you know, there's really no way you're going to get out of here, with the marshal out there."

"You think he'll kill me."

"He strikes me as a determined individual. He calls himself 'mad dog,' or something like that."

Landry's free hand balled into a fist. He looked at the door, and then scowled at Noelani. Sweat rolled down his face.

"I'm pretty certain he didn't come this far to arrest you,"

she said. "You ripped off his father, didn't you?"

Landry grabbed her arm and pulled her away from the counter. "Enough with all the talk, lady. Come on. Let's go."

Just then, from the brewery, they heard a scream and a gunshot.

Landry, panic registered in his eyes, shoved Noelani to the floor and called Rowena's name as he rushed out the door.

Chapter Twenty-eight:
The Belgian Lace

Noelani Lee allowed her mind to clear for a moment before she said, "That's when I got back on my feet and ran out after him, into the brewery."

Detective Ahuna, seated across the table in the police department's austere interrogation room early Thursday evening, said, "And you claim you heard the shot just before then?"

"Yes."

"So when you got out there, what did you see?"

"I saw the marshal kick Jenkins's gun away and then bend over him, holding his Glock against Jenkins's face. It was all pretty chaotic, what with people screaming and Jenkins moaning and holding his shoulder and bleeding. Is he all right?"

"He's going to make it. Lucky for him the marshal missed anything vital, but the slug went straight into bone. So he won't be lifting anything heavy for some time."

"Well, anyway, about then Rowena was crying and begging the marshal not to kill him."

Detective Ahuna said, "And what did the marshal do when you came out of the room?"

"He drew on me and told me to freeze. I think it took a second for him to realize who I was. I mean, there I am in a gray suit, holding a wig, and all this craziness was happening."

"And what was Miss Allgood doing during all of this?"

"She was on the floor, crawling to get Jenkins's gun. But the marshal warned her not to, just to leave it alone or else he'd shoot her, too."

"Those were his exact words?"

"It was more like, 'Cynamin, one more inch and it'll go down as self-defense.' So she started calling both him and Jenkins names and said she should be the one to put Jenkins out of his misery since he duped her, too. Then the marshal said, 'You're not the only one with a dog in this fight.'"

"Did you say anything at this point?"

"I told the marshal the police were on their way. This was before I knew Rowena had called you."

"How did he react?"

"He said he was going to haul Jenkins out of there and finish what he came to do. Of course, this set Rowena off some more. She may be little, but, wow—when she yells, she can peel paint off the walls. And that's when you and your officers arrived."

Detective Ahuna drank coffee from a white ceramic mug decorated with pictures of the Flintstones. "When this was happening, did you know your cousin was there?"

"I knew Wanda was coming since I'd texted her."

"Miss Fong," Detective Ahuna said, "said she came through the front door and passed the reception area at the same time Mrs. Cropper ran into the brewery. I'm guessing the marshal just saw someone coming at him, so he discharged his weapon in that direction. He hit a wall a couple inches behind your cousin."

"Holy smokes. No wonder you found Wanda hiding under Rowena's desk."

Detective Ahuna clicked his pen a couple of times. "Now, tell me, for the record, what were you doing at the brewery in the first place?"

Noelani watched his lips form an almost imperceptible smile. "I received solid leads from reliable sources, related to my work for Miss Allgood. It turns out Mitchell Ratliff had some of Cynamin's beer recipes, the ones Kawika Hailama and Jervy Salazar apparently stole from her garage last night. You found more on them, right?"

"What I mean specifically is," Detective Ahuna said, "what were you doing in the room with the padlock on it?"

"Oh, Jenkins forced me in there. He was suspicious of me, well, this woman named Amber Porter, thinking I—she was sent to find him, either by the marshal or Cynamin."

"Were you? Trying to find him for either of them?"

Noelani shrugged. "I just happened to be in the right place at the right time."

Detective Ahuna smirked. "Kind of a coincidence, you being there for Miss Allgood and you just happen to find out who killed Milt Nihoa and where."

"If you ask the medical examiner, I'm sure they'll find traces of coconut in the beer they drained from Milt's lungs."

"I plan on it."

"No one else anywhere in Hilo or on the island was making it, including Cynamin," Noelani said. "But Mitchell obviously tried a test batch in his little kitchen, or whatever you call it."

Detective Ahuna straightened his expression. "How did you know Milt Nihoa drowned in beer?"

She smiled. "Again, I have impeccable sources."

Detective Ahuna nodded but said nothing.

"You saw the brewery. The place is cleaner than most hospitals," Noelani said. "But this room Jenkins pushed me in was thrashed, which is unlike Mitchell. My theory is, he showed up last Saturday night and caught Milt snooping around or trying to break in."

"We've confirmed it was a broken lock pick in the deadbolt, and we are in the process of comparing it to a kit we found in Mr. Nihoa's car."

Noelani said, "Mitchell went in to work for one reason or another and found Milt had picked the lock and opened the door, so they started fighting and I guess Mitchell got the upper hand. He must have drowned Milt in the beer, then dumped him in or near the bay. When he went back to the brewery, he realized he couldn't lock the door, so he installed the padlock and made up a story for Rowena and Landry about a broken key."

Detective Ahuna said, "But how did Mr. Nihoa's car wind up at Rainbow Falls, if he'd driven to the brewery?"

"Mitchell must have driven it there to make it look like Milt abandoned it when he committed suicide by jumping in the river, which he figured would explain how Milt wound up in the bay." Noelani said, "The park is Mitchell's favorite off-site meeting spot, so it was probably the first place he'd go."

"Yes, but he'd have to return to the brewery to get his Jeep."

"Since everything happened suddenly, and if his clothes were trashed and soaked with beer, he probably walked back. It's a long hike, but he couldn't risk calling a cab at that hour, and I doubt he'd ask anyone to come pick him up."

"All because he assumed Mr. Nihoa was actually spying for Miss Allgood."

"Well, she was banking on a two-for-one from Milt—prove Mitchell was ripping her off, and find Jenkins."

"And at the same time, Mr. Nihoa was bird-dogging Jenkins for the marshal."

"With a potentially more lucrative payday," Noelani said. "It's all circumstantial, but the prosecutor's done more with less, thanks to you boys in blue." She winked.

Detective Ahuna drained his Flintstones mug and set it aside. "Now, about Paul Templeton—how do you figure Edward Vaughn killed him?"

"Easy," Noelani said. "Because of his flight from Guam." She said Edward told her his plane departed Guam at about four thirty in the afternoon local time and had lengthy layovers in both Japan and Honolulu before it arrived in Hilo.

"When he came to my house this morning, close to seven, he told me he had just landed," she said. "But the only flights he could possibly have taken from Honolulu to Hilo, which connected with his plane from Guam, would have landed last night at either twenty after six or eight o'clock."

"So he overnighted in Honolulu and flew in this morning on a different airline."

"The four thirty flight from Guam, via Nagoya, lands in Honolulu at about ten in the morning. I think he was eager to get home because Cynamin left him messages about all the stuff happening here. I doubt he'd spend a full day on Oahu and change airlines when he's this close to home. Besides, he's racking up miles with one airline, flying all over the Pacific."

Noelani asked him whether he had reviewed footage from the airport security cameras.

Detective Ahuna said no.

Noelani said, "Check and see if he arrived on the eight o'clock plane last night. I'd rule out the earlier flight since I was with Cynamin at her house then and he didn't show."

Detective Ahuna said, "But why would he kill Templeton?"

"He gets home hoping to surprise Cynamin but instead he catches her old TV nemesis—a man he detested just as much as she did—in the garage." Noelani said, "He freaks when he sees what's going on, or maybe just seeing Templeton there. So he grabs the bat Templeton just used to bash her equipment, uses her lucky towel to avoid leaving prints, and thumps Templeton in the head."

Detective Ahuna said, "So what did he do with the towel?"

"I don't know. Maybe he took it with him when he ran away. You might want to see if he booked a hotel room, and if he did, if the towel's in a Dumpster."

"Well then, how does he go from killing Templeton to being handcuffed in the marshal's rental?"

"The marshal spots him this morning somewhere, and since he was certain Edward and Jenkins were the same guy, he follows him home and snatches him when Cynamin's meeting Mitchell at the falls."

"Intending to kill him."

"He'll deny it, just like he'll deny Templeton paid him to find Cynamin. Unless you happen to find cash covered with Templeton's prints in the marshal's hotel room."

Detective Ahuna clicked his pen, twice. "The marshal told us Jenkins called him, claiming he wanted to turn himself in. But Jenkins says flat-out he made no such call." He leaned forward and said, "Before we finish here, would you mind telling me what you know about this phone call?"

"I'm not sure I follow."

"When I first met you," he said, "and you mentioned your hyperadrenalism, I did some research just to learn more about it."

"Okay."

"One of the side effects is, people with this condition can lower their voices. So it's conceivable for a woman with hyperadrenalism, for example, to be able to imitate a man. Speak in a masculine voice, in other words."

Noelani bit her lower lip. "Detective, you have enough experience to know, when you're confronted with conflicting stories, the truth is somewhere in between." She smiled. "That's just reality."

Noelani accepted Detective Ahuna's offer to walk her and Wanda to her car. She slid in behind the wheel and said, "Since we're off the record?"

"Okay."

"Why did you send me copies of Milt's files?"

Detective Ahuna said, "When we found them, I assumed it had more to do with this whole beer-stealing caper than it did with a homicide. I figured they'd be more useful to you. Why?"

"It's okay to admit you sometimes need help from people like me."

Wanda said, "People like you? Noe, he's a bruddah, too."

Noelani smiled. "I'll explain later."

"Nah, don't bother," Detective Ahuna said to Wanda. "It's not worth your time."

Noelani started the car. "Give your father my best."

"And same to your mother." He said good-bye and walked back inside the station.

Wanda looked up at the darkening sky, filled with threatening gray clouds, as Noelani backed out of her parking space. "Dang, it's going to pour, huh?"

"About time, too," Noelani said.

"So, what do you think happens now with the marshal?" Wanda leaned over and said, "Admit it, cuz. He's handsome."

Noelani waited for traffic to clear before she turned on to Kapiolani Street. "Since you were such a big help to me as usual, how about you let me buy you a drink or several?"

"I remember you told me once how much you like San Diego."

"It's a nice place to visit."

"Uh huh."

"How about your favorite beer?"

Wanda giggled. "All right, you're on. But I wish you'd have one with me."

Then the skies opened up and sheets of rain pelted the Nissan. Noelani rolled down her window and extended an arm outside as they drove toward downtown Hilo.

"Sweetie," she said, "this is all the liquid refreshment I'll ever need."

Now for a sneak preview
of the next Noelani Lee adventure,

The Pahala Twist

by

Tom Bradley Jr.

Chapter One:
The Trespasser

With an earsplitting "crack," the papaya exploded.

Seeds and pulp pelted a man as his hand grabbed at empty air where the ripe fruit used to be. When a second shot clipped a small branch from the tree, he threw his considerable girth face-first into the mud.

A voice from somewhere in the rain: "*Watufaka?*"

The man, who people back in the day used to call Waha Nui—it meant "big mouth," because it was like he could never shut up—peered at the thick koa forest behind him and considered making a run for its protective cover.

But he changed his mind when a third round hit a rock, awful damn close. Tiny pieces of ancient volcanic shrapnel stung his forehead.

The man once known as Waha Nui thought, This is nuts. Bruddah's trying to cap me over a stinking papaya. "Hey, c'mon, man. Swear I won't take none. Just let me go and we're all good. Okay?"

Mud splattered the top of his head when a fourth shot thwacked the ground a foot or so in front of him.

"No," the voice said. "It's not okay."

He felt the smartphone in his pocket, sandwiched between the ground and his meaty thigh, and wanted so bad to call for help but he remembered there were no bars on this part of the island. Besides, there was no one he could call anyway.

Because there's nobody I can trust.

His face pressed to the ground, he concentrated on sounds around him. He hoped to recognize footsteps, maybe going the opposite direction. But all he heard was rain falling, birds singing, and his heart thumping.

A minute went by and nothing happened. Whoever was out there clammed up. Thinking the other dude maybe got bored and split, Waha Nui pushed himself to his knees.

Above him stood an older man, tall—about six-foot even— with long, stringy gray hair. He wore frayed cammo cargo shorts, calf-high tabi boots, and a tee shirt with the words DEFEND

HAWAI'I printed around a picture of a machine gun.

Waha Nui winced. Damn, looks like someone chewed on his ear.

The man pointed a beat-up rifle at Waha Nui's forehead. Waha Nui closed his eyes and shielded his head with his arms. "If you're gonna kill me, then get it over with, man."

"Huh," the man said. "Brah, what the hell're you doing here?"

Chapter Two:
The Nuts

The man said, "You want to taste my nuts?"

The woman said, "Sure, if you have any."

"Of course I do. I've been working on them for a while."

The man—Ray Barnaby—steered his wheelchair down a dark hallway and led the woman to a padlocked storage room. He unlocked it, flipped a light switch, and led her inside.

The woman—Penelope Laikupu-Dowd—scanned shelves filled with stainless-steel canisters, each labeled. "Is this your secret stash zone or something?"

"My sanctum sanctorum. Top-secret stuff I'm experimenting with," he said. "Here"—he plucked a canister from a shelf and handed it to her—"you have the honor, Your Honor, of being the first to sample this exclusive new flavor."

She read the label—Tahitian Vanilla Bean—and unscrewed the lid. "Wow, they smell fantastic."

"Try one. Try two or three, for full effect."

She obliged and, one at a time, popped flavored macadamia nuts in her mouth. Ray thought she was going to drool as she chewed, slow. "Oh my goodness."

"Huh? What do you think?"

"These are crazy delicious."

"The formula needs some refinement, but we've put a lot of work into them already. I think we're almost there."

"Ray, I think they're wonderful just as they are." She handed him the canister.

"Not from extract. I used genuine vanilla beans"—he replaced the lid—"imported from Tahiti"—and placed the canister back on the shelf. "It's expensive, but if things go the way I think they will—the way they're supposed to—it'll be worth it."

"Oh, yes. Definitely."

"I'm also thinking about introducing a wasabi flavor, or even ginger. Maybe something even more exotic for the discriminating one-percenter palate. Lilikoi is a possibility. Did I ever give you the full tour?"

They exited the storeroom—Ray turned off the lights and locked the door behind them—and proceeded down the hall to the guts of his macadamia nut empire. Quiet and deserted on a Sunday, the only day of the week when the plant went dark, the hall was lit only by sunlight through windows set high on one wall.

Ray showed her where his employees roasted the nuts and where they added flavorings and another area where they smothered nuts in rich, dark chocolate—"eighty-five percent cacao, the good stuff, the only chocolate I use, and quite expensive"—and another section where workers packaged the nuts for shipment throughout Hawaii and around the world.

Penelope surveyed the operation, not huge in comparison to Ray's bigger, better-known, more commercial competitors. But nonetheless, impressive for a town the size of Pahala.

Ray said, "How's Kyle?"

"He's doing great, thank you for asking."

"Glad to hear it. What's he up to today?"

"Watching football, I think. I told him I had errands to run so—"

"I'm just glad you came all the way out here to talk shop, today, when we have the place to ourselves."

"Well, I am curious to find out what else it is you need."

"Penelope, we've been friends for how long?"

"A long time."

Ray put a hand over his heart. "Your friendship means the world to me. But you know what else means the world to me is this business. I'm term-limited, which means I'll have even more time to crank out gourmet mac nuts in the near future. And I have no plans to leave Pahala."

"I don't blame you. It's so peaceful."

"My son Kirby says I should move to the mainland, once I'm out of office. To be closer to him and his family. But you know the mainland."

Penelope nodded.

"He lives in Phoenix—Tempe. Same thing. You ever been?"

"Kyle's from Tucson, so I've passed through a few times."

"Then you know, we got it so much better here. Way better, quality of life-wise. They have smog. Good thing about seeing him—I was there a couple months ago—was Florence and I stopped in Vegas for a couple nights on the way home."

"Did you see any shows? Kyle and I saw Bette Midler once."

Ray blinked at Penelope's ample chest, its impressiveness accentuated by the blue peasant blouse tucked into her jeans. "I lost four-hundred bucks at the slots. Like I said, I'm not going anywhere, and I plan on keeping all this"—he spread his arms—"as long as I still have functioning brain cells. But Penelope, you know firsthand what happens to businesses if they don't grow."

"They stagnate."

"Or die. Which is why, if and when this thing gets approved, you know I'll need to expand, or risk biting the dust."

"Well, that would be good. Growing, I mean. You know how committed I am to revitalizing the island's economy, especially here. Ka'u could use a boost."

"True. But about that fly in the ointment."

Penelope sighed and nodded.

Ray said, "You saw all those yard signs coming up here, yeah? 'Malama Punalu'u.' He goes to the beach and sits under a tree and comes up with a slogan, and now everyone's on his bandwagon. With money, which most of them can't even afford. Thinking he can stop it."

"Ray, I'm doing all I can to educate people about why this project is so vitally important. Truthfully, I think most people down here get it."

"And you're doing a great job. But the thing is, the economy's bouncing back, and now more and more people are thinking there's no need for a project of this magnitude. These people I represent, friends and neighbors—they're pressuring me to vote against it. Do you, uh, do you remember one of the first things I taught you when you came on the council?"

She smiled and bent over and patted his forearm. "You taught me a lot of things when I first came on the council."

Ray caught a quick peek of her cleavage before she stood up. "The very first lesson was, 'Don't always vote the way your constituents want you to, because they're idiots.' Remember?"

"Yes, I do."

"Well, those people with the signs in their yards? They're idiots. They're short-sighted. Which is why you have to stay firm with your convictions about this thing. And which is why, if you want to count on my vote, I'm going to need some, ah, support, from you."

Penelope looked down at her feet. "What kind of support?"

Ray rubbed his chin. "I haven't sorted it all out yet. But one thing to keep in mind, as I said, my business will need some upgrades, if I'm going to add more workers and machinery to keep up with demand."

Penelope looked at him and nodded. "Okay."

"Only if you girls can get more of his money."

In the silence, he heard her gulp. Ray said, "How are your owls with all of this?"

"Um, well, I'm not sure. But they know what's going on."

"Then they should know you're doing what's best. When it's all said and done, they'll understand and you'll still be in their good graces." Ray beamed. "Now, how about some nuts for the road?"

Chapter Three:
The Two-Minute Warning

Kekoa Gabriel was lean and sinewy and handsome and cocky, which he expressed with a star quarterback's devil-may-care swagger even though he hadn't thrown a pass in almost ten years.

So he wasn't surprised when, late on a Sunday morning, as he helped a lady load bags of fertilizer into her truck outside the hardware store in the Keeau Shopping Center, this one hot older sistah approached him. Extra-dark sunglasses hid her eyes, and she wore her long, black hair in a ponytail. He figured she was going on forty. But still, part of him hoped she was a cougar; she had sweet legs for a woman her age, and he bet they'd feel good wrapped around his neck.

She pointed at him and tried to talk but nothing came out. Like she was star-struck or something. Which happened to Kekoa a lot.

Kekoa flashed a smarmy grin. "Can I help you?"

"Dude," she said, "you look familiar to me."

Now through a full-blown smile, he said, "Why's that?"

She snapped her fingers. "Yeah, you're him, you're the one kid played quarterback for Hilo High and almost won state all by hisself. What's your name?"

"Kekoa Gabriel. You seen me play, yeah?"

"Shoots, I saw you put a serious beat-down on Waiakea. What, you ran for like three touchdowns and threw two more?"

Kekoa puffed his chest. "Actually, three of each."

"Hey, seriously, I got a cousin needs your autograph," the woman said. "She thinks you're one of the best ever." The woman rummaged through a bag slung over her shoulder and pulled out some papers. "This is all I got to write on. Here, I know I have a pen somewhere."

She handed him the papers. Out of curiosity, and because the woman took forever trying to find something to write with, Kekoa gave the papers a casual skim.

His smile melted.

"Oh look," the woman said, "found a pen."

He said, "Hey, what is this?"

The woman took off her shades. Her brown eyes locked on his. "Kekoa Gabriel, you've been served."

"What? Served?" He felt a weird tightness in his throat. "Lady, what're you talking about, served?"

"Listen, I'm usually the first to admit I don't know much about sports, but failure to pay back child support?" She leaned in. "Did you just get intercepted, or does this count as a sack?"

Licensed private investigator Noelani B. Lee left the fuming and cussing Kekoa Gabriel behind and strolled across the parking lot to her white Nissan Sentra. She got in and removed her wig, allowing her shorter, shaggy haircut to breathe. She started the car and left the shopping center and turned north on Highway 11 toward Hilo.

Fifteen minutes later, she arrived at the firm of Sato and Cato, housed in a cream-colored, two-story building at the corner of Kapiolani and Ponohawai. Curt Sato, senior partner, met her in reception and thanked her for tracking down Kekoa Gabriel. Then he handed her a check.

She gave him the once-over—golf shirt, pressed jeans, leather slippahs. "Curt, thanks, but I didn't mean for you to come in on a Sunday. Shouldn't you be at home watching football?"

"I'm more of a rugby guy," he said. "By the way, did I mention we have a new partner? He just happens to be in today, too."

"No, you didn't," she said, anxious to get out of there because, one, she had an aversion to lawyers, and two, she needed to hit an ATM and deposit the check. "Hey, if you ever need—"

"Hang on, let me introduce you." His eyes twinkled.

"Okay. But I can't stay long. I have a hungry cat at home."

Noelani followed Curt to an office where a man sat at his desk, his back turned to the door, typing on his computer. "Hey," Curt said, getting his attention, "someone's here to see you."

The man turned to face them. Noelani's jaw dropped. "Oh my God."

"Hello, Noe." The new partner rose from his chair.

"I'll let you two get acquaint—I mean, reacquainted." Curt chuckled. "Noe, see you around." He strolled back down the hall.

Noelani's breathing came short. "Franklin Ku," she said.

"Noe, how are you?"

Her right hand balled into a fist, crushing the check. "You know how long it's been?"

"I know."

"You dumped me. Thirteen years ago."

"It's nice to see you, too." Franklin invited her in. "Have a seat."

She licked her lips. "I'm not staying."

"Only for a minute or two. What do you say? Huh?"

He flashed his pearly whites. She said, "Two minutes, then I'm out of here."

Franklin motioned to a chair in front of his desk. She sat and folded her arms over her flat chest. "So, what? Australia wasn't what you expected?"

Franklin reassumed his seat behind the desk. "They talk funny down there."

"Let me guess—she waltzed her way into another man's arms." All those years ago, after he proposed and she said yes a couple weeks later, he ran off with an Aussie ballroom dancer, a blonde with legs as long as Noelani's memory.

"More like a pasodoble, but, yeah." Franklin shrugged. "Same result."

Noelani said, "So, you're expecting me to forgive you? Because I'm pretty sure my personal statute of limitations hasn't expired."

"No, um, no, the thought never—"

"If all you want to do is catch up on old times, then you may as well—"

"Noe," he said, "I need your help. And I have nowhere else to turn."

His eyes changed. Pleading. Noelani rubbed her temple, a

headache gaining steam.

Franklin said, "Curt can't say enough good things about you and your work."

"Thank you. I like Curt. Now, tell me what it is you want so I can say no."

"A friend of mine has gone off the radar and I need you to find him."

"Well, call the cops."

"But he's not officially, legally missing."

Noelani shrugged.

"Noe, please."

"And if I don't?"

"Well," Franklin said, "there's a good chance he could end up dead."

About the Author

Tom Bradley Jr. is a former print reporter and current public relations professional who is a late bloomer in the world of fiction, self-publishing the first novel in his Noelani Lee mystery series in 2013.

After serving as a Journalist in the US Navy, Tom wrote for community and daily newspapers in San Diego County and later launched a career in public relations in Las Vegas and San Antonio. He has won numerous awards for both his news and PR writing.

A native Pennsylvanian, Tom holds a BA in Communications from National University in San Diego, and an MA in Strategic Communication and Leadership from Seton Hall University in South Orange, NJ. When he's not writing, Tom can most often be found reading, watching far too many foreign crime dramas on TV, and shopping for unusual craft beers.

He resides in suburban Las Vegas with his wife, Donna; a Bengal cat named Malia; and a basset hound who sometimes answers to Lola. *The Hilo Hustle* is the second novel in his Noelani Lee mystery series.

www.ingramcontent.com/pod-product-compliance
Lightning Source LLC
Chambersburg PA
CBHW071306140726
47996CB00005B/1646